Limerick County Library

WITHDRAWN FROM STOCK

n Chontae Luimni
OUNTY LIBR

WITHDRAWN FROM STOCK

KU-190-374

A Fatal Reunion

a&b

A Fatal Reunion

PENELOPE EVANS

LIMERICK oo46446o6
COUNTY LIBRARY

First published in Great Britain in 2005 by
Allison & Busby Limited
Bon Marche Centre
241-251 Ferndale Road
London SW9 8BJ
http://www.allisonandbusby.com

Copyright © 2005 by PENELOPE EVANS

The moral right of the author has been asserted.

This book is sold subject to the conditions that it shall not,
by way of trade or otherwise, be lent, resold, hired out or
otherwise circulated without the publisher's prior
written consent in any form of binding or cover other than
that in which it is published and without a similar condition
being imposed upon the subsequent
purchaser.

This is a work of fiction. Names, characters, places and incidents
either are products of the author's imagination or are used fictitiously.
Any resemblance to actual persons, living or dead,
events or locales, is entirely coincidental.

A catalogue record for this book is available from
the British Library.

10 9 8 7 6 5 4 3 2 1

ISBN 0 7490 8333 6
ISBN 0 7490 8362 X (trade pbk)

Printed and bound in Wales by
Creative Print & Design, Ebbw Vale

PENELOPE EVANS was born in Wales and grew up in Scotland. She attended the University of St. Andrews before becoming a criminal lawyer in London. Her first two novels, *The Lost Girl* and *Freezing*, were published to much critical acclaim. She currently lives in Buckinghamshire where she combines writing fiction with journalism.

To my daughters Katharine and Alice.

PART ONE

The Patersfield Advertiser, 3rd September

HEADLESS CORPSE DISCOVERED OUTSIDE PATERSFIELD

Council workmen have discovered an incomplete skeleton in long grass on the A40 roundabout on the outskirts of Patersfield. The corpse, whose sex has still to be established, is believed to have lain uncovered for up to three months in a spot ten yards from a busy road. Police expect that inquiries will be severely hampered by the body's advanced state of decomposition. Pathologists are blaming animals for the absence of a head and clothes.

Speaking off the record, a spokesperson for Bucks Constabulary has doubted the existence of foul play. Patersfield is a favourite stopping off point for tramps journeying between London and Oxford, an issue that has concerned the town council for some years. A member of the Treasurer's Committee who asks not to be named observed to our reporter, 'Now it's not only their litter they're leaving behind.'

The matter is to be discussed at the next Council meeting, on Thursday 18th September.

The ADVERTISER asks: how can a corpse lie undiscovered for so long, so close to the centre of Patersfield? Is the car cutting us off from our environment? After the hike in last year's Council tax, why is no one bothering to cut the grass on our roundabouts? Phone the ADVERTISER to have your say. Then turn to page 4 for our free competition to win a Mercedes S class...

I saw her the very first day I came to the university.

Her parents were outside the hall of residence, hauling her cases out of the boot of a small car. She had her back to them – and me. She was looking down at the university spread out below us. Old Scots stone – Victorian spires spiking the sky, mellowed quads. And beyond it all, the sea, with the dry twinkle of waves that are never warm, this far north. Not quite Oxford, as my father had been careful to mention. But old enough for her, for Carlie. Old and cold enough after her semi-detached home wherever. St Leonards – old after her modern house and her modern comprehensive with its light and air and one size fits all. Carlie always was impressed by age.

As she stood with her back to me, I thought she was old as well. A little old lady in a cloche hat and shaggy fur coat, too hot, surely, for a warm September day. Button up boots. Then suddenly she turned and I saw her face, and she wasn't old, she was young. As young as me.

Her face was pale, yet heated at the same time. Beneath the rim of the cloche hat, her eyes were liquid with excitement, alive to everything they saw. Suddenly I had the desire for her to see me too, include me in the reason for the glow, part of the excitement. Unconsciously I put down my single suitcase and stood, waiting for her to notice me…

…And she looked straight through me. She was turning to find her parents. They also had put down the cases to watch her, waiting quietly for just this, for her eyes to come back to them. And even then, the first time I saw her, I knew what was happening in Carlie's world. A minute after arriving and she was torn, swaying between her future and her past. I saw the excitement darken to something deeper. I saw her tilt, as if falling towards them, a short man and his short wife. And I saw them through Carlie's eyes. The best people in the world.

People who loved her, whom she was about to leave behind.

I picked up my suitcase and moved on up the steps to hall. I'd been in the same between-place myself, where the past and future separate and split right there in front of you. But it had happened when I was six, when it was time to go away to school. And all I remember is that I was torn in one direction only. Not wanting to be anywhere except home. My parents had put me on the train with other, older, boys and waved me off, my mother cuddling the puppy that everyone had told me was going to be mine, and never would be now, not really. It snuggled down in her arms and ignored me as I went. That was what she was good at, my mother: animals.

That particular dog died just before I came away to the university. It was the only time I ever saw my mother cry.

From the door of the hall, I glanced back towards the small group with the mountain of cases. They were going to have to make a second, and a third trip to carry it all. This girl must have brought every moveable scrap of her existence with her.

I found my room. A window that looked out over a golf course and in the distance a thin line of sand dunes. The sea was not far away. I liked that. Ground floor, though; I knew what that meant from school. People coming in late from the pub, after the doors were locked. They'd be knocking on the glass at all hours, trailing in mud and worse, too drunk even to say thanks.

It had breeze block walls that would sweat when winter came. A flaw in modern design. Something else to provoke the dry comment from my father. He had expected me to go to his old college, where old meant old. Where corridors and streets would be full of people I had known; old friends of his, or the children of friends. The next logical step. My father had read Greats before reading for the law. Now he said it would be harder, afterwards when I followed him to the Bar, not taking up my place in Oxford. People would think that I hadn't made the grade.

I put my alarm clock beside the bed, and the Liddell and Scott (Greek into English) on the desk. Lewis and Short (Latin into English) up on the shelf. Greek and Latin texts lined up next to it. And that was it. I had arrived.

Outside in the corridor, I heard the firedoor swing open, the creaking magnified by a breeze block echo. Voices and footsteps and cases banging against the walls. The door next to mine opened and the noise continued through the wall beside my bed. There was going to be a problem with sound-proofing. Every time someone stepped into the corridor I would know it.

Not that it was other people's noise that would bother me. Twelve years amongst other boys, you learn to blank it out. It was my own sounds that would be the trouble. A single scrape of my chair, and whoever had moved in next door would know he's not alone. It would be like school again. Friendly types who get bored – or lonesome – don't care who they talk to.

I picked my copy of Catullus off the shelf. It fell open at the poem to his faithless mistress. *Odi et amo.* I hate and I love. *Flaming Catullus* the Victorians called him, disapprovingly, before continuing to snuffle their way through his scenes of tumescence and fellatio and spunk. And love. Above all, Catullus writes about love. And hate. *Odi et amo.*

I was nineteen years old. And maybe this was already what I expected love to be: an amalgam of loving and hating. A paradox, an oxymoron – everything the Greeks had already given a name to. I was ready for it. I thought that was what love was.

But now came a banging on the door. It had started straight away, the sociableness. I tossed the book aside and considered ignoring the knock, then hauled myself out of the chair. Standing at the door was the short man I'd seen beside the car, the father of the girl with the excited eyes. He looked me up and down, not trying to hide his dismay.

'Can I help you?'

'You're a lad!' he exclaimed.

I nodded.

'Just visiting then? Helping a sister move in?' His voice was hopeful.

'This is my room.'

He stared at me a while longer, then sighed. 'Right you are. Sorry, son. See, I thought you'd be a girl. Mixed hall but with different wings. Girls on one side. Boys on the other, d'you follow?' I watched him resign himself to the new situation, and summon up a smile. He lowered his voice. 'No harm in telling you why I'm here, though. It's our girl, Carlie. She's going to be next door to you. Mind, we've had trouble with her, sitting there the past half hour saying no one's going to want to speak to her, getting herself into a right state. First time away from home, y'see. I thought, if I came and knocked next door, that would be a start for her, break the ice. You don't mind, do you?' A pause, then the smile faded. 'Ah well, maybe you're busy. Mum and Dad still with you, I'll bet. Caught you at the wrong moment.' He was giving up on me. Another moment and he'd be back in the room again, breaking the news about the chap next door, who just stared at him and never said a word.

'No,' I said. 'No parents. That is, they're at home. They don't...we don't need to... Done it all before, if you see what I... So, not busy, not busy at all. I'm...I'm just here. Alone.'

My rush of words had caught him by surprise, almost making him take a step back. Then his eyes softened. And look, he's seen right through me. A nice man, that's what he is. A lovely man. 'There lad,' he says gently. 'I get your drift. You settle yourself in. And when you're ready, go knock on our Carlie. She'll like that. Go and see Carlie.' He jerked his head towards the door he had come from. Dazed, I nodded.

Back in my chair I picked up the Catullus again. But I couldn't concentrate. She was here, the girl with the future bright in her cheeks, right next door to me. 'Go and see her,' he said.

Go and see her. Easy enough to say. Long after the parents had gone, I was still trying to psych myself up to do just that. Go and see her. But this wasn't the way, sitting in my chair, not moving. At this rate I was going to end up never even speaking to her.

Then just before midnight, there came a knock. Made me catch my breath.

I opened the door. For a moment we stared at each other.

'Hello,' she said finally. Her voice was light, tentative. 'I'm Carlie.'

Another pause as she waited. Finally, she prompted me. 'And you?'

And I felt my eyes go wild. Because with Carlie standing in front of me, I had forgotten, I truly had forgotten my own name. 'Guy,' I said at last. 'I'm Guy Latimer.'

I said that. That was me talking. Where did I find the words?

She stood in the centre of my room, looking round. She had on a sort of crocheted shift thing, over some kind of old silk thing. And even I knew this isn't what girls usually wear, not even the unfashionable ones. Certainly not the girls I'd known at home in the country, with their body warmers and hacking jackets. But she wasn't dowdy. She was wearing bright red lipstick that made her skin seem very white, almost translucent. Curly dark hair cut close to her head.

'Your father was here earlier,' I said.

She rolled her eyes. 'That was terrible, knocking on you like that! God, why do parents always think they have to interfere?'

I thought briefly of my parents, tried to imagine the same problem.

'Well they can't now, can they?' I offered finally. 'Interfere, I mean. You're here and they're – wherever. Gone. I suppose your father thought it was the last thing he could do for you.'

I thought I was saying what she wanted to hear. Instead her face grew bright red, then crumpled like a little girl's. And all at once I had a girl – a grown up girl – crying in my room.

And I didn't know what to do. Someone was crying and there wasn't even a dead dog to account for it. All I could do was stare at her drooping head, and the curls at the base of her neck – and wait.

Without warning she stopped crying and looked up. Her eyelashes were glittering. 'Have you got any biscuits?'

I shook my head helplessly.

'Wait there then,' she instructed me – *as if I was going to abandon my own room!* ' I'll be back.'

And she was. A moment later she had returned with a scuffed Quality Street tin, full of biscuits, all of them home made.

'Tea?' she said. 'Coffee? You must have that?'

Again I had to shake my head. And once again she was away, a little longer this time, coming back with two mugs. Wordlessly I took one and sipped hot, sweet tea. Not the way I used to drink it. She headed for the chair, leaving me with nowhere but the bed. I sat down, awkward, and gazed up and down and around – everywhere except at the girl in my room – tried to think of a single sensible thing to say.

And came up with nothing.

It didn't matter. Carlie did all the talking. She talked about her parents, her town, her school. She told me the books she liked, the music she didn't like, the friends she liked, and the girls who were glad to see the back of her. She sat with her legs curled under her, batting the air as she talked, animated as a kitten let out of a box. Her voice was high and friendly. She looked and sounded completely at home.

And it was an act. Even then I knew. Right from the start I seemed to know my Carlie. I knew she was just showing off, pretending none of this fazed her – not the leaving home, not the being alone. Not even the sitting here with me, a complete stranger. If I had had to guess I would have said it had been practised in front of a mirror, all of it, so she could come up with this: a grown up Carlie. A Carlie who was in control.

A Carlie who was anything but.

How did I know this? I'd never been able to read anyone's mind before. Perhaps it was because I had never looked properly, I mean, just sat there – and looked. She talked, I listened, and we were never so young as on that first day, the day we met. Carlie and I.

She left, taking her mugs and her biscuit tin with her. And that was the last chance I had to speak to her for days. Freshers' week started and she was off and away, doubtless practising the same new skills she had tried out on me. I caught glimpses of her, though, in the distance. Disappearing into coffee shops with other people; once, cycling past me with her skirts flying up, revealing a pair of legs that took me by storm. Before I'd known what I was doing I was running after her. But at the last moment she had turned a corner, pedalling swiftly away from me down a wynd towards the English department. And she was gone.

The next I saw her was in the Union, queuing to sign up for some society or other. Talking, those hands still moving. Another girl was with her, listening intently as if fascinated to see so much energy expended on a simple thing like standing in a line. She had an air of faint disapproval that Carlie seemed not to notice. Five minutes later I was at the head of the same queue, scrawling my name three places below hers. Carlie Hawkins.

'You haven't written down what you want to do.' The girl behind the table, dressed all in black, pointed to the space beside my name.

'What I want to do?' I repeated after her stupidly.

'Acting, stage management, props? What are you interested in? You're nice and tall. Dark, sort of intense looking.
Young, though.' Apparently she considered her position by
the desk gave her permission to pass a verbal commentary on
the appearance of anyone who approached her. Then she
added. 'You'll get parts if you can act.'

I glanced up at the society banner and realised I had just
put my name down for drama soc. 'Oh,' I said, and paused.
'Not acting.'

'Prompting?' She prompted. 'Or lighting?'

'Lighting,' I whispered. 'Maybe.'

'Write it down, then,' she said impatiently. Her eyes had
moved on to the guy standing beside me. I could guess what
she would say about him. Tall as me, but blond with it, with a
proper growth of beard. A natural lead.

I picked up the pen again and watched it hover. Crossed
out my name.

'Sorry,' I muttered. 'Made a mistake.'

But I listened out for her. Tiny movements in her room,
tiny sounds through the wall. Alone, she turned out to be quieter than anyone could have expected. I began to guess that it
took it out of her, all that vivaciousness, all that animation. I
would hear her door close, and that would be it. Silence, pal-
pable in its relief. Sometimes I imagined I could hear pages
turning. I imagined a quiet Carlie, a different Carlie, released
from the show. A happier Carlie?

Turning the pages in my own room, I remembered her
father's words. '*Go knock on our Carlie.*' But how? Some folk
could make the hardest things sound easy. I bought some
mugs and some teabags, and listened for the sound of Carlie
that somehow would say, *knock on my door.*

Until one night, I heard a different kind of sound.

It was hardly anything. To catch it you'd have needed ears
like mine, trained to trap the smallest sounds of a girl I'd only

talked to once. What was it? I didn't know exactly. A series of breaths, too quick and stifled to be normal breathing. An odd, laboured sound that repeated itself over and over. A bad sound that disturbed me, as if I had been a dog with an instinct but no vocabulary to put it into words.

And it electrified me. I went back to my desk with its half written essay on the poems of Horace. Was she crying? I thought how she had cried here that time, in my room. There had been no sound at all then. Tears had simply rolled down her face in a way that seemed effortless, painless. In retrospect, Carlie had made crying look like something almost enjoyable. If she was crying now, then it wasn't like the first time. This was different. This was wrong.

I bent towards the page I had just read, the words I had just quoted. *Odi profanum vulgus et arceo.* Suddenly they didn't seem to mean anything any more, lines in a language I seemed not to recognise. I told myself that in a little while she would stop, the way she had when she was here, and no harm done. I told myself there was nothing I could do. Nothing she would want me to do.

I listened to the fractured sounds through the wall and told myself I couldn't knock on her door, not for this reason. Or any reason. Unless maybe for a fire. Maybe.

Then I thought of Carlie with the excited eyes crying. All by herself. *Go see our Carlie.*

Next thing I knew, I was standing at her door. It gave way without me expecting it, and there was Carlie, kneeling on the floor in front of me. And the sound wasn't tiny after all. That had been the wall getting in the way. She was bent over, taking great whooping breaths as if trying to empty the room of air. Looking up, her eyes, bulging, terrified, fixed me with mute appeal. Her teeth were bared, strands of saliva shining on her chin.

I understood now. Twelve years with other boys, you were

LIMERICK
COUNTY LIBRARY
○○ᒷᒣ ᒍᒣ ᒍᒣᒍᒷ

bound to see it soon or later. A kid – usually one of the fat ones – who'd sit bolt upright in the night, gasping and wheezing. And if throwing slippers at him failed to put him right, someone would have to go running for matron. Asthma, last refuge of the homesick. It happened all the time, until they grew out of it.

Except this was different. This was worse than any chubby boy in the middle of a fright. And no matron now. No one to sit quietly on the bed, quell the panic that constricted the airways, soothe the breath back the way it came. All Carlie had was me.

I got down on the floor, and tried to catch her hands. They flailed around, her fingers catching me on the chin, nicking the skin with her nails. I'd find blood there later. But I struggled until finally I had them, Carlie's two hands held fast in mine.

And those frightened eyes. I kept a grip on these too, in a way. *Look at me*, I said. *Look at me, Carlie.* I was surprised at my voice, how calm it sounded. *Count with me…. One, two, three, four.* A cool calm voice, soft as matron's when she used to say the same thing – softer even than that. I never knew my voice could sound the way it did now. *Five, six, seven. Slowly…breathe slowly, Carlie.* I counted and I talked, and I held her with my hands and my eyes. And gradually, the toiling stopped. Her breathing became regular and open. Easy again.

Even then we kept counting. *Eighty eight, eighty nine, ninety.* Up to a hundred and beyond. Two hundred, long past the point where we could have stopped.

Finally, I loosed her hands, laid them in her lap. Her breath was easy, her breast rising and falling. Her eyes had closed ages ago, way back in the nineties. Now she opened them again, to look at me, half in a daze. 'I'm sorry,' she whispered. 'What did you say your name was?'

'Guy,' I said. 'I'm Guy.' Suddenly I could feel myself blushing. Awkward, I got to my feet. 'Will you be alright?'

She nodded, too tired to speak. I took a step back, felt behind me for the door. 'I'd better go then.' I said, 'Leave you in peace. I've an essay to write, anyway. But I can always be back, if you...' Somehow I couldn't bring myself to say it: *if you need me.* Then I blinked, looked around me in surprise. I was no longer even in the same room as her. Too large a step backwards and somehow I had taken myself right outside again. I was back in the corridor with her door already swinging back into position. I had forced my own exit. I waited a moment, wondering if she would call after me, but she didn't.

I went back to my desk. It was a full hour before I could make the words stand still in front of my eyes. But I got there in the end, by gathering every thought and shovelling it out of my head. Lines of poetry began to make sense again. *Odi profanum vulgus et arceo.* 'I hate ordinary people. They're vulgar and I won't have them near me.'

The words looked different to me now. Half an hour ago I'd thought there'd been something splendid about turning one's back on the world like that. Now they read like the opinions of a lofty snob. I had to start the essay all over again.

I worked, and when I had finished I was pleased because I thought I had managed to forget Carlie. Then I read my essay and saw I hadn't forgotten her at all. She had changed the way I'd thought about something I thought I knew all about – a poem, a poet, an entire world view. Pushing her out of my head, only to realise an essay written in her absence had been transformed by her. Carlie was inside me now.

Chapter Two

Next morning there was a knock on my door. I had slept late after sitting up all night working. Thinking it was the cleaner, I shouted that I was in bed, pulled the covers over my head.

'Can I come in anyway?'

The voice was right above me. I pushed back the cover and there was Carlie standing over me.

'I've brought you some tea.'

There was a jangle of bracelets as she handed me a cup. I had a glimpse of fingernails, all short, gnawed down to the quick, and all of them painted a different colour. She must have done this since last night. I concentrated on these nails of hers, unable to look directly at her face.

'There's blood on your pillow,' she said sadly. She pointed to the scratch on my chin. 'I think that was me. I'm really sorry.'

'I don't suppose you could help it.' I was transported by the closeness of her, yet my voice came out filtered of emotion, icy cool. Almost forbidding. Instantly I was reminded of someone else: my father, at his driest, putting the distance between us.

And hearing it, she drew back, chastened as if I had slapped her down. At once, though, something inside me reached after her, and the words tumbled out in hot pursuit. 'Carlie, why have you brought me tea? This...this *lovely* tea?'

The loveliest I ever tasted. I would drink it sugared from now on, always.

Her eyes grew warm again. 'Because you deserve it, naturally. Because I would have turned completely blue and stiff if it hadn't been for you. Because you talked to me, and calmed me down, so I could breathe again.'

'I'm sure it wasn't as bad as that.'

She frowned and tweaked a curl abstractedly. 'I don't know. It never has been that awful before, the asthma, I mean. I put my inhaler somewhere and couldn't find it. Instead there was you.' She stopped, uncertain. I could see the words becoming difficult. Finally, dramatically, she said, all in a rush: 'I feel that you...that *somehow* you...did something no one else could. Heroic. Like you really did save my life. Sorry, does that make me sound silly?'

I shook my head. Silly wasn't the word. Not for Carlie. Something more specific, more tragic, was required to describe a girl who believed in the crisis of every moment. And I didn't have the word for it, not yet.

She pointed at the mug. 'So there you are. I'm going to bring you tea every morning – as a sign of my gratitude. It's the least I can do.'

It took a moment to sink in, what she was promising. Tea every morning. Carlie coming to my room, every morning. 'You don't have to do that,' I said at last.

'Yes, actually I do – unless of course you don't want me,' she added. She watched my face. 'So, is that alright?'

'You really don't have to,' I said again. And sipped my tea again.

Of course it didn't last. I was up too early most mornings for a start. I would pass Carlie's door knowing from the silence through the wall she hadn't even stirred yet. But once or twice she caught me, knocking on my door just as I was about to leave for lectures; yawning, still in her pyjamas, holding out a mug with tea spilling out of the side, before diving back into her own room, too sleepy to talk. Carlie was a girl who tried hard to keep her word.

And every morning I tried to hang on, leaving at the last moment, in case she appeared.

I thought about asking her to meet for coffee in town, but I never dared. I never saw her out by herself for one thing. Where there was Carlie, there were people. Besides, our lectures never seemed to mesh. I would see her diving into the

English department just as I was walking out of Ancient History. Or cycling towards the library just as I had gathered up my Greek books and come away. And people. There were always people, with Carlie in the middle of them, like the nucleus inside a cell. And talking, talking for England, as if her life depended on it.

Sometimes, though, she would see me, and just for a second the talking would stop. And maybe I imagined it, but a shaded, almost wistful look would pass over her face as if she had glimpsed someone standing where she would like to be, off-stage, in the quiet. Somewhere she didn't have to perform. Then somebody else would say something to her, and that would be her cue. The moment had passed and Carlie was ready to start talking again.

Then one morning, she caught me by surprise, knocking me out of the deepest of sleeps. It was a Sunday, very early. I woke to find her standing over me with two mugs, her face glowing.

'I haven't been to bed,' she announced before I could speak. 'Not the whole, entire night.'

'Oh?' I said casually. Although equally I could have said 'I know'. I had fallen asleep waiting for the creak of the fire door. Reading and re-reading Ovid half the night. At first the rhythms had kept me awake; later they had galloped through my dreams. *Lente lente currite equi noctis.* What was she doing? When would she be coming home? What did it mean, Carlie staying out so late? Slow down, slow down, you horses of the night.

'Well?' I pressed her. And this time she heard it in my voice – over-arching curiosity, and something else. Jealousy? Her lips quivered with delight. She might have been up all night but there were rivers of pink in her cheeks. Carlie was a girl who glowed when she felt the world's approval.

'Walking, if you want to know. Along the East Sands. Right

the way to the estuary.'

'All night? You were walking all that time?' I pulled myself up on my pillow.

'Just about.'

'*All night* by yourself?'

'No.' She laughed as if I had said something stupid. 'No of course not. I was with someone.'

I had the urge to turn my face to the wall. Stop this conversation.

'That's how long it took, to let him down lightly.' Carlie stretched, smothered a yawn I wasn't even sure was real. I saw her glance at me under her lashes, measuring, testing. 'There's this really nice guy who wants to go out with me – *sooo* badly. Last night he finally came out with it. I had to find a way to be kind, seeing as I had to disappoint him.'

I watched her carefully. 'Do you want to tell me about it?' I said slowly. Guessing and knowing at the same time.

She giggled at the question, then looked troubled. Then delighted. 'Oh I couldn't possibly,' she said. A moment later she had plumped herself on the bed and was telling me everything. How he had held her hand, how he had quoted poetry, some of it his own. How, before coming out, he had phoned up his girlfriend (who was still back home, at sixth form college) and finished with her, just so as to be free for Carlie.

'Isn't it awful?' she said, wondering and ecstatic. 'That someone would do that for me? And I don't even want to go out with him. Do you think his girlfriend will take him back?' She hugged her knees, tried to keep the exultation out of her voice.

(A few days later she would solemnly point him out to me, the boy she had walked with all night along the beach. He was shorter than me, younger looking, and he must have made a virtue out of the necessity of finishing with his old girl friend. Now he was hand in hand with a girl in the same year as us. She was taller than him, big thighed in tight jeans; nothing like

Carlie, who nudged me and gave me a dramatic look.)

Half an hour into the story though and even Carlie had managed to tire herself out. She talked non-stop until at last there came a pause. I sat up. Curled at the end of my bed, with the sun shining full on her face, Carlie was snoring, smiling in her sleep.

I looked at her in something close to awe. It would happen again and again, this: Carlie dropping suddenly off to sleep in front of me. But this was the first time and I was nonplussed. There was something animal in it, this sudden yielding to her body, her arms and legs gone limp, her face smudged against the duvet cover. I stared, almost put out. I had never even heard a girl snore before. Carlie snored faintly, happily – reminiscent of a cat purring. And to think that all I felt was mild surprise! I didn't know about the future then, what it was going to mean to me in the months and years to come – Carlie falling asleep. My recompense, my reward. My consolation. Birds, animals and Carlie – they only sleep when they know they are safe, and Carlie would fall asleep in front of me all the time. I would come to love it when Carlie slept.

The first time though, and all I knew was what the last half hour had taught me: don't make the same mistake that boy had made. Never quote poetry to her (at least not any of my own making), never try to hold her hand. And never, ever, tell her what I felt about her. Wasn't this the way to keep her coming, to have her knock on my door, drink tea and talk?

She slept and it dawned on me that I could make myself a permanent fixture in Carlie's world. I remembered the glance from under her lashes. Testing, measuring. *Inviting*. If I had acted upon that look, I would have gone the same way as the boy on the beach. But I'd passed the test and what she was offering was more than just a letting down lightly. She was offering me friendship.

I was right. Making friends with Carlie seemed to happen

in the snap of a moment. She woke up and it was as if it was a done deal, made when she was sleeping. As if both of us had agreed at the same time, but for different reasons.

After that she always knocked on my door when she went to meet her other friends. Sometimes I went with her, and sometimes I didn't, knowing she would tell me everything when she came back, in the same way she had told me every-thing that happened on the beach. She stored it all up for me. If she didn't tell me, it would feel to her as if it never hap-pened.

If I didn't go with her, it was usually because I had work to do. It even came to irk her, the fact I never lost sight of why I was here: to know my subject. Yet she was happy to ignore the fact that she worked hard too, reading voraciously, scribbling down her thoughts in lengthy essays that earned her excellent marks, along with the odd dry comment about the length and the untidiness of her writing. She fell in love with the people that she met in the quiet of her room – Barry Lyndon, Gilbert Osmond – cads and sadists who didn't exist. Men I was quite happy to hear her talk about, for whose sake she covered her fingers with ink.

Soon I was meeting people in the street who stopped and spoke to me as if I were one of them, the crowd she went around with. Noisy, clever people from the English department who somehow didn't know half of what they were talking about. Most of them seemed to forget I was doing Classics, and thought because I was in the street I was missing lectures, like them. Carlie was putting me so much in the centre of things, people were beginning to think I belonged there. But I never said much, not to them. If I'd disappeared from the scene no one would ever have noticed. And that was alright. I was only there to be with Carlie, marvel at the show.

Is this how they had brought her up, those quiet people I'd seen that first day? I doubted it. Her father had come to my door to tell me about his daughter who was terrified to step out of her room. Was this the same girl, running around in a never ending succession of thrift shop clothes, laughing, wriggling, arguing? If so they would have been dazzled at how she pulled it off. She was like electricity, something wired for instant flash. Disarming, apt to talk herself hoarse.

Maybe they *had* brought her up to do just this. Maybe they were proud of a daughter who could sit terrified one moment, and centre stage the next. Maybe they knew that shyness runs to extremes and trusted that in time she'd find a middle ground, and all this could stop, and Carlie could be quiet at last, trust herself to be still.

Meanwhile, did they know how much it cost her, here at the extreme end?

I did. Sitting in a crowd, listening to her talk, I'd suddenly find I couldn't bear to watch. I had thought people were born more cunning than this, that instinct taught everyone to keep something back. A sensible reserve. But this – the total commitment to the moment, total donation of the self, keeping nothing for herself – you'd welcome it in puppies and small animals. But in human beings...? Sometimes, sitting beside Carlie was like being tossed someone's vital organ to hold, feeling it twitch with the life force that kept it going, feeling it use and consume itself. Sometimes I had to come away.

Occasionally, then, I had to be alone. In my room, holding a book, touching something that did not tremble. Something solid, not chaotic and moving. Something not Carlie. I would hide in the library, between the cools spaces of the words in the poems of Horace, amongst the other Classicists in my year. My crowd.

All that energy, all that use. You could see how she could tire herself out just pretending to be herself. And it threatened to drive me away almost as much as it drew me to her. I'd come home and tell myself I wouldn't do this again: I would not watch her perform. I told myself she was irritating and self-centred, too quaint to be attractive, too childish to be taken seriously.

Then she would turn up in my room to tell me what I had missed. And sooner or later, she would fall asleep in front of me.

I would wait for it. Wait until the pauses became longer, and her breathing had grown even. Finally I'd see her eyes close and listen to her sigh as the tension loosed its hold. And when her breathing had grown deep as well as even I would watch her, lay my wrist against the back of her wrist, and marvel at the smoothness of it. Or touch the pulse in the crook of her arm. Carlie slept and I'd compare her hand with mine, and consider how alike they were. How young they both looked, one hand lying alongside the other. I'd look at the glow in her cheeks and gaze at our two hands and wonder at how much time we had, both of us. Watching Carlie sleep convinced me there was all the time in the world, that we were cocooned in a present that could last for ever.

And sometimes I would even dare to believe the unbelievable: how there might come a time when the time was right. When she'd see there was no need to perform, not in front of me. She could read her books and dream her dreams. And lie with me, awake, not sleeping. Carlie and I, the two of us – meant to be.

Chapter Three

There were others that I spent time with, the people in my class, the ones who talked about Latin and Greek, whose sentences I could have finished. I kept them separate from her, though. I had the feeling Carlie would not approve of them. Or they of her. Compared to her crowd, they were quiet, but I liked that. After Carlie, being with them was like stepping into a cool room out of a hot wind that excites – then blows sand in your eyes.

On the first day of lectures, twenty of us had sat down and looked about us in awe. Most of us hadn't been in a classroom with so many people since we were fifteen. And yet we all seemed to recognise each other – the odd ones out, people whose schooling at some point had peeled away from the norm. The ones who'd got used to spending hours alone with a teacher while everyone else did science, or rugby, or simply messed around in free periods.

We were the Classicists. And we knew more than half of what we were talking about. That was the problem. It ruined us for everyone else.

And being Classicists, most of us had arrived at the university looking like clones of the people who taught us. Boys wearing tweed jackets that already looked as if they had seen better days. Girls wearing skirts with generous waists and bobbly jumpers. Despite that, we all seemed absurdly young – ironically, since at school we must have all seemed absurdly old. Not quite like everybody else. And no wonder. Take a child and teach it that nothing properly worth the mention has happened since the Goths took over the Forum – that's sixteen hundred years to feel sniffy about. A well schooled Classicist ends up cynical and naïve in equal measure. Herodotus is king; there's nothing new under the sun.

I was like that, right down to the tweed jacket. I walked

into the Classics department, breathed in the chalk dust air and felt completely at home.

Hardly surprising, then, that he stood out, the first person I saw who broke the mould.

I was waiting to go into a lecture when he passed me in a corridor, talking to the head of Greek. There couldn't have been two men more different. The professor – head down, elderly, catching billows of air in his academic gown; and Walsh, gownless, slouching beside him in jeans and a tee shirt, his head shaggy with thick black curls. He looked like a care-taker, someone who moved furniture. Then I heard mention of Euripides and knew I was wrong.

The next day I turned up for a Greek tutorial and he was waiting for me.

'Dr. Walsh?' I closed the door and sat down.

'Yeah. Call me John.'

He flopped back into his chair and stared at me. 'So, you're the *really* bright one.'

'Sorry?'

'The one I was told to look out for.' He pushed a file towards me. 'Want to see what it says about you?'

I shook my head.

He looked at me a moment then laughed. 'You don't look like you'd care anyway. Don't be too sure of yourself though – you're in a clever year, and you've got a rival in Jennifer...whatshername...Saunders. Smoke?'

I shook my head again. I knew Jennifer, a tall, quiet girl who never said much, all but invisible inside her sensible clothes. I watched Walsh roll a wadge of Old Holborn and light up.

'I suppose I should tell you, we're both new. This is my first teaching post. I got it over somebody's dead body. Literally.'

I nodded. We all knew about Dr. Mack who was to have

taught Greek poetry. He had been found curled up in bed with a, now indelibly stained, copy of *Archilochus* at the beginning of September. He had been there the entire summer. *Aneurysm* – a suitably Greek name for what killed him. Everyone thought he had been lecturing to tourists on a Swann Hellenic Cruise through the Aegean Islands.

Walsh said, 'So how do you want to play this? Tutorials I mean. The old fashioned way with sherry and all that crap, me doing all the talking? Maybe you would. I've had kids in this room this morning who haven't learnt to speak. Incredible. Eighteen, nineteen years old, and all they could do was stare at me. That was a kind of hell. You going to do that to me too?'

For answer I stared, not at him, but at the opposite wall with its Free Nelson Mandela poster. He gave a grin and blew out smoke. 'Oh I get it, you're only going to speak if you have something to say. Is that the way you always operate?'

I said nothing.

'Right then,' he said reaching for Pindar's Odes. 'In that case, let's get to work. Proper, serious, grown up work. Give you something to talk about.'

When I came out, Carlie was sitting on the wall.

'God,' she said. 'I've just had an Anglo Saxon tutorial with an old fart who fell asleep on me. His head actually ended up on my shoulder. Guy, he was snoring. He must have been eighty if he was a day. And I don't think he'd washed since the war. Sometimes I wonder if I've come to the wrong place.'

I sat down on the wall beside her. 'I think *I* might just have come to the right place.' The door to the Classics department opened and Walsh walked out. I nodded to him.

'Who's that?' Said Carlie.

'He's teaching Pindar – and Euripides. I think he may be clever.'

'Cleverer than you even?' There was no irony in her voice.

'Everyone's cleverer than me.'

She shook her head, pushed her hand into a large knitted bag. 'For you.' She slapped a doughnut into my hand. 'For last night.'

Last night she'd had another asthma attack. Coming home coughing from an audition which she didn't get. Not so bad at first, then suddenly a lot worse. I had done what I had the first time, held her hands and counted, held her eyes till the panic subsided. Then, as always, she had fallen asleep, exhausted.

We shared the doughnut. For once Carlie wasn't talking. Autumn sun warmed the wall we were sitting on. Through the open window of the music department behind us we could hear someone playing the violin. That must have been what silenced Carlie. Spiralling crescendos of notes, interspersed with gaps and swear words. Someone as young as her, wrestling with perfection, never satisfied. Something Carlie understood – all too well.

'Carlie,' I said abruptly. 'I think you do too much.'

'What do you mean?' she said, her mouth full. But interested – as she always was whenever we talked about herself.

'I think you put too much into things. Of yourself. You think everything's important. That audition, for instance. It didn't matter, not really...'

She swallowed her mouthful of doughnut, unchewed. 'Of course it mattered. It was the main part.'

'Exactly. Carlie, admit it. You'd hate it. Being on stage. Everything...You choose the thing that scares you most and dash off and do it. Then you end up, well, like last night. All I'm saying is, you don't have to. Don't try so hard...'

She stopped protesting and looked at me, mystified. It was as if I had started speaking in tongues.

I rushed on. 'I think you could slow down, stop thinking you've got to shine every day of the week. You treat everything too...too seriously, Carlie. Don't you see?'

'No I don't.' To my surprise, she was calm as she answered

me, her voice reasoned. Thoughtful. 'If you want to know, I don't think *you* don't treat anything seriously enough.'

'What do you mean?' It was my turn for bewilderment.

'Oh you work hard. You work too hard. But you don't take it seriously, even though it's what you love more than anything on earth. You told me yourself what happens when you're finished here. Your life is all planned. You're doing the bit you enjoy now, getting your *liberal* education – isn't that the word for it? Then it's off for the real stuff, the stuff grown ups do – law, the Bar. Wigs and gowns and money. All of that. And all of *this...*' she waved her hand airily, dismissing – on my behalf – the buildings, the books inside them, the music cascading through the window. Herself '...To you, this is all just playtime.'

I stared at her. She raised the last bit of doughnut to her mouth, then at the last moment rammed it into mine.

'I'm not treating this place as school,' her voice was crisp suddenly. 'This is life, where the big things happen. You should treat it...treat *yourself* more seriously.'

She nudged me. At the end of the lane Walsh was coming back. He planted himself in front of us, stocky in his jeans, ran a hand through his curls.

'I'm thinking of having a party,' he said to me. 'See if I can get those children to lighten up. Do you think it's a good idea?'

I shrugged.

He looked at me, glanced at Carlie. It was impossible to tell if she had made an impression. He threw his roll-up on the ground. 'I'll take that as a yes, then.'

'*Children?* Who does he mean by children?' said Carlie, indignant, as she watched him walk away.

'Not you,' I assured her. 'You talk.' I nodded to the door of the Classics department. 'Them. Those are who he means.'

Coming down the steps were the others in my year, girls

and boys. The girls carried their books in duffle bags hung with mascot key rings, and wore thick brown tights disappearing inside sensible shoes. I was aware of Carlie smiling to herself, reaching down to smooth the fishnet stockings under the layers of skirt and underskirt she was wearing. One of the boys stopped, reached into a waistcoat pocket and took out a pipe, and with some ceremony commenced to light it. Straight away he began to cough.

She began to rock silently on the wall beside me. I had to put my arm around her to drag her away. 'Did you see,' she hissed in my ear as we went. 'Did you see that girl in the fluffy cardigan scowling at me?'

I glanced over my shoulder, and sure enough, Jennifer – my so called rival – was staring after us. Not scowling though. That was unfair. She was looking at Carlie, taking in the skirts and fishnets and the button-up boots. Not mocking or disapproving. Just interested.

Chapter Four

Halfway through the term, Carlie's parents came up to visit. We all went out to tea together, then walked along the West Beach with the wind whipping up the waves and the sand like soft fudge beneath our feet. As we walked, we passed a blackened pile of ashes and I found myself smiling. This was where Carlie and I had been busy last night, hauling driftwood up the beach and then setting fire to it. Carlie's idea to build it; mine to sit and watch it until the wind burned it up and reduced it to embers that lay like a small galaxy of hot red stars in the sand.

After that we had tried to dam a stream where it trickled out of the dunes down to the sea, piling up sand using flat stones for shovels. The water always found a way through, but it didn't put us off. We had been busy half the night, and afterwards Carlie had fallen asleep at the end of my bed, her cheeks flushed with the wind, snoring gently while I watched.

Mrs. Hawkins asked about my parents, if they were missing me.

'On and off,' I told her, or rather shouted, over the noise of the sea. The wind snatched the words from my lips so quickly they hardly seemed to count as a lie.

'Your poor mother,' she said comfortably. 'I'll bet not a day goes by when she's not worrying about you. Mothers do, you know.' She nudged me, like a conspirator. 'I worry about *her* all the time.'

Ahead of us, Carlie and her father were walking like a pair of kids, jostling against each other, trying to stamp on each other's toes. Carlie was screaming with laughter. Mrs. Hawkins nodded towards them. 'Like peas in a pod they are. That girl used to follow him around like a little puppy when she was young. And when she was a good sight older. It's the way it goes, isn't it? Dads and their daughters. He's the same.

He'd walk through fire for her, he would.'

She didn't have any sons, I knew that. One of the first things Carlie told me: how there had been an older brother who had died of a heart condition when he was three. No children after that – until Carlie came along, late in their lives, their accident. Their precious, eccentric girl. Whose father would walk through fire for her. Not thinking what I was doing, I offered Mrs. Hawkins my arm to hold, and she took it. An act as natural as breathing.

She leaned towards me. 'You and Carlie' she said. 'I don't think that the two of you are…?'

I shook my head. She stopped walking and searched me with her eyes. Nice eyes, grey green like the sea all around us. I found I could meet her stare and not want to look away. After a moment she nodded. 'Give her time, Guy, love. She'll find her feet. She thinks she's old as the hills, and the truth is she's a big silly baby. Don't you tell her that, mind! We sheltered her – too much, I used to think. You watch, though, one day she'll stop jumping around and see what's right under her nose – if you've the patience to wait that long.'

She smiled. I took her arm again and we carried on walking.

The end of another tutorial. Walsh closed the book and scribbled something down on a piece of paper. This was how assignments were usually given – a pencilled scrawl I'd need to pass back to him to decipher. Sometimes he'd be demanding an essay three times the length of normal, other times, setting books I'd have said had nothing to do with Greek. Once it was *The Divided Self*. 'Madness and the families that cause it,' he had explained cheerfully. 'Required reading for Oedipus Rex'. Another time, it was the *Dice Man* which he explained as: 'All about chance and necessity. Socrates would have hated it, so it's got to be a good thing.'

Today I glanced at the scrawl and discovered that not only

was half of it neatly printed in capital letters, but had nothing to do with work.

'This is an address,' I said.

'*My* address. I'm having that party I mentioned. I wanted it here, in the Classics Department. We could have put our drinks down on the display cabinets in the archaeology rooms. Boogied on down to Chaka Khan in the library – but the Prof's not up for it. So it's got to be at my place.'

I squinted at rest of the scrawl. Walsh's handwriting had collapsed again.

' "Dress, classical." ' Walsh translated for me. 'Good idea, yeah? Get the girls and boys into something more casual.'

'You're having a toga party?' I said. And there it was again: the dry note of my father creeping in.

Walsh bridled. 'Fuck togas! That's for the suburbs. Tight arsed bloody Romans. No. You tell your young friends it's *chiton* party. Greek garb. Only Greek. No imitations. Give me that.' He grabbed the piece of paper off me and scrubbed out the *classical* to replace it with *Hellenic* – in capital letters.

'There,' he said. 'Go get them, tiger. And write me a piece about cross dressing in tragedy. That's got to be a good three thousand words. Start with transvestism in *The Bacchae* and take it from there. OK?'

I lifted my briefcase off the floor. 'Can I bring a friend?'

Walsh frowned. 'What do you want to do that for? You'll have friends there. This is meant to be exclusive.'

'I'd just like to, that's all.'

He rolled his eyes. 'Go on then, if you must. Me, I think we should keep it all in the family.' He threw himself back in his seat and drummed the desk. 'Next!' He shouted, the signal for whoever had been waiting to begin the next hour with him.

I shut the door behind me. *If I must!* Cassandra like, he'd made it sound like a warning. As if something bad could come out of bringing an outsider to a party thrown for classicists.

'Hello, Guy.' It was Jennifer. She was sitting by the door playing with a long dark plait.

'I didn't know you had Walsh too,' I said.

'I got switched, didn't I? Don't know if I want him. I've heard he's a bit, you know – off centre.'

'I don't know if those are the words for him,' I said. 'Not that he'd mind. He wants to be thought off centre. Just make sure you talk while you're in there. Lots. He doesn't like people doing their thinking in silence.'

She laughed at this. A nice sound – husky, making the plaits seem suddenly like a disguise .

'He's having a party,' I added. 'He wants to break the ice.'

'What ice?'

I shrugged. 'He thinks everyone is shy, uptight. Something. Not like him, anyway. And it's to be fancy dress. Classical.'

'You mean a toga party!'

'*Chitons*. I'll let him explain.'

'So, are you going?' She held my gaze, looking as she had that day with Carlie. Interested.

'Probably. You?'

She thought a moment, and nodded.

I told Carlie about the party, then immediately wished I hadn't.

I'd never done this before. Taken her to spend time with my own friends. Would I even have called them friends, exactly? What would she think of them? What would she think of me? I was one of them. They would claim me as one of them. They always did. She'd look at what we were wearing, listen to what we talked about. She'd think I was like them. And she'd be right.

Not cool. Not trendy. Just classicists.

But now that I had mentioned it, she really wanted to go. It was the idea of fancy dress. Another role to play. 'I'll be Diana,' she said happily. 'Goddess of the moon.'

'Diana was Roman. He wants everything Greek. You'd have to be Selene. Or Hecate, the triple crowned goddess – more of a witch, really. A moon hag. Do you think you could be a hag, Carlie?'

'Of course. But tell me what else I could be.'

'Everything's more complicated in Greek. Messier.' I thought a moment. 'You could be Eurydice.'

'Who's she? I've heard of her.'

'A nymph. Orpheus the musician loved her so much he followed her into Hades to bring her back when the serpent bit her. You must know the story – he was allowed to lead her out of the underworld, but on condition that he never turned to look at her or help in any way. They had almost made it to the light, when he couldn't help himself and he turned around. He lost her for good then, and she was dragged back into the dark for ever.'

'And what happened to him?'

'He went mad. The Maenads tore him into pieces.'

'That's good. That's who I'll be, then. Eurydice.'

She looked smug. And very young. And suddenly, more than anything, I didn't want to go to this party, not with her; something I couldn't have explained even to myself. I heard myself say. 'We could do something else. Or nothing at all.'

'Why?' she said, surprised. 'Don't you want to?'

'I've got a cold coming on.' I coughed to prove my point.

But I was talking to a girl who could die coughing and she was not impressed. She tossed her head. 'I'm going to make a costume.'

The night of the party and Carlie was at my door.

'You're not dressed up,' she said accusingly.

'I don't do fancy dress,' I said. I was trying not to stare at her. She had taken the swathe of gold material that usually covered her bed, folded it and pinned it – and turned herself into a goddess. A young, white-limbed goddess, eyes liquid with ambrosia. There was gold ribbon threaded through her hair. A goddess who laughed at me in my ordinary clothes.

'You look…' I had to pause, swallow. 'Wonderful.'

More miraculous than a goddess because she was the real thing. A girl, pink and breathing – pleased with her costume. A stage goddess, straight out of the eighteenth century, the sort who came from nowhere to pirouette through Handel operas, the toast of the town. Briefly exquisite before age and fate took everything away and she disappeared forever.

I shivered for no reason I could think of. 'You'll get cold,' I said.

'I'll keep moving,' she replied.

Walsh's house was on the outskirts, at the end of a terrace with a river running opposite. We reached it by crossing a small bridge, barely lit. The house stood well back from the road, screened by laburnum and rhododendron bushes, with a short path in the dark leading to the front door. A cold night, we stood shivering, waiting for someone to hear the bell and let us in.

But we were late and the house was full of people and music. Nobody heard us and for a full five minutes we knocked and rang, until Carlie would have come away when I suggested going to sit in a pub instead. I could see her warming to the idea: of her glowing by the light of a pub fire, drawing the eyes of everybody in her goddess clothes.

Then just as I was catching her hand, Walsh opened the door.

'Finally.' He stepped aside to let us in, swaying slightly – with the drink, I supposed.

'Good grief,' I said looking at him. He was dressed as a woman, rouged up and bedecked in robes not much different from Carlie's. He had plastic flowers in his hair.

'I'm Pentheus,' he said 'Remember him?'

'A famous drag artist,' I explained to Carlie. 'A prince who got dressed up in women's clothes so he could watch what the women got up to in the worship of Bacchus.'

'Sex and drugs,' interrupted Walsh. 'That's what they got up to.'

'What happened to him?' said Carlie.

'He was torn to pieces by the women he was spying upon,' I told her. 'Including his own mother. She only recognised him after the deed was done and bits of him were hanging off the trees. Lots of people seem to get to torn to pieces in Greek myth. Have you noticed that yet? Close the door, Walsh, we're freezing.'

'I don't see why,' he said. 'You're not even in fancy dress. But your friend's got the right idea.'

He batted his false eyelashes at Carlie, who laughed.

'You're pretty,' he said. Carlie stopped laughing and blushed.

We followed him into a room filled with people I didn't recognise. Or did I? Walsh had placed candles everywhere, on every surface. Their flames swayed and flickered with the draught, and it was only as the light moved over the faces I realised in fact I knew everybody here. It was the bodies I had failed to recognise – young bodies normally hidden beneath tweed and sensible skirts. Now they stood about the room as if in their true colours, with the amazing grace of exotic birds.

These were my year, Walsh's so-called children. Be Greek, they had been told. And like children, obedient to a fault, they had taken Walsh at his word. Now they stood, draped and arranged like figures on the side of a Grecian vase. No trace of awkwardness, they spread their bare shoulders and basked in the candlelight as if it was the warmth of an Aegean sun. As if they had been in disguise all this time, only now allowed to show who they really were.

I looked for something that took away from the effect – a pair of spectacles, a sensible shoe or a sock. And there was nothing. If they had come in shoes, they had taken them off. Only the paper cups they clutched in their hands gave them away.

'Here,' said Walsh handing us two paper cups of our own. 'Excuse the lack of goblets. The Thessalonians raided the last of the Corinthian ware.'

I took a sip. It was only some kind of punch, terribly sweet, hardly alcoholic. What had I expected? Something stronger to explain the atmosphere, perhaps; the new, softer shapes of the girls' bodies as they leant towards the boys with down on their cheeks. The sort of boys the Greeks would have loved. Walsh stood and watched me take it all in – the odd one out in my everyday clothes. Immediately I was struck by two of my classmates – Rhona and Gordon, the quietest and shyest of all of them. They were standing in a corner, fingers touching, and their quietness now came from concentration, an intensity of studying the other.

'Will you look at them all,' said Walsh in a low voice. 'They arrived in a gang, all at the same time in their duffle coats. Like there was safety in numbers. Tripped through the door as if they were here for a seminar. I thought it was going to be one hell of a long evening. Then they took off their coats, kicked off their shoes, and lo and behold!'

He pointed to a girl standing by the fire, beside a looking glass that hung over the mantelpiece. Her arms gleamed in the candlelight, contrasting with the shadows in her hair hanging heavy to her waist.

It was Jennifer. Sensing the attention, she turned and looked at us gravely, her eyes lingering a moment as they met mine. Grey, clever eyes, like a young Athene's. I stared back, entranced by the difference.

'What's the music?' said Carlie almost sharply. As if suddenly she didn't like the fact that my eyes were elsewhere. I listened for a moment, and then wondered the same thing myself. Long plangent notes that found their way inside your head before you registered them. Like music in a dream.

'Eno,' said Walsh. He frowned. 'Or is it *Fripp* and Eno? Used to play it all the time at Cambridge. *I* didn't put it on, though. Magnus must have done it. I'd have kept to Bach for this crowd. But it's good. Good for the ambience, don't you think? Music to get stoned to.'

He smiled, his eyes vague behind the mascara. I remembered Walsh, too, was young, only nine, ten years older than us. He looked like a proper Pentheus, so obviously a man in drag, so obviously drunk when it would have been wiser to stay sober. I glanced over his shoulder. And glanced again. Gordon's hands had crept tentatively inside Rhona's robe, and she hadn't stopped him. Now, holding on to a breast, he stood staring at her with a look of astonished joy on his face.

'Walsh,' I said, startled. 'What's happening? Have you got everyone pissed?'

He shook his head, indignant. 'No one's even had that much to drink. Just the punch, and I know what's in that.' All the same, suddenly he lurched forward, and had to steady himself, frowning, genuinely bemused at his own state. He glanced across the room and, seeing Gordon's hands at work, looked away hurriedly. I would swear he was blushing. He muttered. 'I was going to get them to play spin the bottle. I don't think it's necessary now, do you?'

'Who's Magnus?' I asked.

'Magnus? A Maths post doctorate. Does a bit of lecturing. Rents a room from me. Wasn't going to let him come – but when *you* insisted on bringing someone from outside...' He frowned and looked around. 'Where's he got to, though? I thought he'd stick around. Last I saw of him he was closing in on wee Jennifer over there.'

Again, he had drawn our eyes to the girl by the mirror, complete in her stillness. I couldn't imagine how anyone would dare approach her uninvited. Then I remembered all the times I had plumped myself beside her in class without giving it a thought.

Things were different tonight. Everything was different tonight.

Carlie stirred. As if once again to bring me away from Jennifer she said, 'Who's got the best costume, then – out of the whole room?'

I looked at her, as she wanted me too. 'You,' I said. The best costume – but not the most authentic. A beautiful opera dancer, but not the real thing. When it came to authenticity every person in the room had the edge over her. Every fold authentically Greek. While over there, in the mirror, Jennifer with the grey Athene eyes had turned away from us to study her reflection...

Strangers all of them to me now – except for Carlie. She had become the most familiar thing in the room, the person I was closest to. The one person I could catch by the waist, and say *dance with me*. There was a sense in which we didn't belong here, not me in my normal clothes nor Carlie in her not quite Greek dress, and this made us a pair. She gasped as I seized hold of her and for a moment, I felt her body tense. Closet Carlie, shy Carlie. But only for a moment. She relaxed, and I let go of her so we could move, easily, to the music. We seemed to dance for hours, not quite touching, but close, closer than we had ever been, until dizzy, finally we stopped and looked around us.

'Oh,' said Carlie faintly, taking in the scene.

One by one the candles had begun to go out. A strange kind of peace had fallen over the room. In the semi darkness, people were moving slowly, as if rehearsing the movements of a Greek play, or the silhouetted meetings on the belly of an urn. Folds of dresses and tunics had slipped aside, revealing the glimmer of flesh. My classmates had divided into pairs.

Now quietly, dreamily, they were sitting, standing, lying around the room, doing what Rhona and Gordon were doing.

Two boys, both called Peter and both from the same school in Arbroath, were entwined on the sofa. As I watched, Peter leaned forward and kissed Peter on the mouth. As their lips met they closed their eyes and sighed, for sheer happiness, found at last. At that moment, the record ended leaving space for other sounds all around us, soft gasps and whispered laughs. A newer, simpler language than I had heard any of them speak.

Something had happened to us all. I looked round for Walsh. He was sitting on a piano stool, left out of everything, confusion in his face. A man who had dressed up as a woman to watch a spectacle he didn't understand. Catching my eye, he gave me a wry, slightly haggard smile and shrugged, and went to put on more music.

The shrug said it all. Walsh could explain nothing. I turned back to Carlie. This time, scarcely daring to think what I was doing, I pulled her to me. She came without resisting and stayed, put her head upon my shoulder. Not knowing if she could feel it, I brushed her hair with my lips; and we began to dance again. This was like a dream. Carlie was in my arms, the one still point while the room moved slowly round us.

In the looking glass Jennifer's eyes watched us, thoughtful. Unreadable. As if she too was part of the dream.

'Guy.' I felt my own name whispered, warm against my neck. Warmth that made me realise that she was, that we both were, real. This was no dream. Carlie was in my arms. I could smell her, the burnt sugar smell of her. Not sleeping, but awake.

A night of true colours. I put my mouth to her ear.

'Carlie,' I whispered. 'Remember that day you told me I wasn't serious? You're wrong. I am serious. I am so serious. There is something that matters to me, more than anything in the world. Is it safe to tell you, Carlie? Because if I tell you everything will change, and I'm afraid.'

She lifted her head from my shoulder. As if by agreement we took a step back and stared at one another. I saw Carlie's lips part, she was about to answer me. And the strange thing was, she almost didn't have to. On this, the night when suddenly all colours seemed to become true, I swear I knew what she was going to say.

For this was the moment. It had arrived out of the blue when neither of us had expected it. Now here we were, staring at one another. A moment in which Time was ours only. Even the music seemed to die away, and I marvelled to think that it should have come so quickly, this moment, our time. *Wait,* her mother had said, and I'd hardly waited any time at all. Simple, suddenly so simple.

But still I told myself I needed a word. A single word from Carlie. It was all I needed to hear.

I watched it forming on her lips. One word. *Yes.*

But then, falling through the silence – one thought, cold and clean as a knife. Makes me catch my breath, threatens to choke me. I remember the boy on the beach. The letting down lightly. *What if I were wrong?* What if *yes* isn't what she is about to say? Or what if it's just the strangeness of the evening, strange behaviour having its effect, somehow catching? But only temporary. How do I know if this is not what she wants, not what she wants at all? And if not now, then tomorrow, she says no?

If Carlie says *no,* that would be that. Not even a friendship any more, not after tonight. No more Carlie. Yet all I wanted was Carlie for ever. I took another step back, alone this time.

'I'm thirsty,' I said briskly. 'Shall I get us another drink?'

Carlie blinked. Her mouth closed. She began to shake her head, then nodded uncertainly. But her eyes were saying something different. Her eyes were asking me to stay.

'I'll wait,' she said aloud. In silence her eyes were still talking to me, not wanting me to go.

I ignored her eyes, and everything they were saying. I walked over to the punch table, taking my time as I ladled the warm sweet stuff into another pair of paper cups. Then stopped and stared at my hands and their unwanted cups of punch. There, with my back to her, I froze, overwhelmed by what I had done. I had walked away from Carlie, from everything I wanted, from our time. And with that, I felt it sweep over me, a dizzying sense of loss...

...Which melted instantly into an equally dizzying euphoria for what was still there, ours for the taking. *I'll wait,* she had said. And of course she would. She was still there. It was all still there. This was no dream – she had touched my cheek and the warmth in her fingers had told me that I was, that we both were, completely real. I seized the cups and turned, back to Carlie...

Too late. I turned, only to find that someone else had taken it. Our moment. Our future. Our Time.

Why, when I look back, do I see things as they cannot possibly have been? A rearing out of the ground, black horses plunging, black manes, black hoofs flailing. A black chariot and a man descending, black hair, black eyes. A long arm reaching and taking Carlie, who stands helpless as he comes. All in a silence created by a black magic, so she would disappear without a scream, back with him where he came from. The Underworld.

That's how I see it in my dreams. Like a fool in the meadow, I watch him carry her away. My Carlie. Dreams that come night after night. They still come, all these years later.

It wasn't like that, of course.

I turned from the punch table, and a man was talking to Carlie. Tall, snake hipped in narrow denim. Black hair, black eyes. He bent over her, casting a shadow, even by failing candlelight. And older, so much older than us. There were lines on his face, etched deep – running either side of a mouth that was wide, thin lipped. Ravenous. What was he saying to her? I couldn't tell, but his hands shaped the air as he talked, creating an invisible cage around her, around Carlie.

Not yet complete though, this cage. I saw her face tilted to his, and I saw the bewilderment there, resistance even. Not quite taken with him, not yet. There was still an air about her, of holding something back as if she remembered she had been waiting for something else. Someone else.

Me. She had been waiting for me. I had to remind her, before he made her forget. I strode towards them, spilling the punch. But it was like being in slow motion, and a couple of yards seemed suddenly to turn to miles. A body got in my way, solid, colliding with mine. There was a grapple of arms and legs, sending the remainder of the punch flying.

'What's the rush?' It was Walsh, sounding irritated. He bent to examine the mess on the floor, his body massive suddenly. I couldn't get past him. I moved and he moved. Seconds wasted.

The man said something, and she laughed, then frowned. Not certain.

'Carlie.' I called out over Walsh's shoulder. But she didn't seem to hear me. Half laughing, half frowning she stared at this new face. I try to reach her, but Walsh is still in my way.

Tell him, Carlie. Tell him you were waiting.

Not laughing at all now. Carlie continues to stare. She is beginning to forget, I can tell. You can see the thought dawning, the idea taking hold. She looks at him, looks away. Then looks again, curiosity overcoming resistance. He says something and without warning, places his hand on her arm.

Makes her shiver. Startled she stares at the hand on her bare skin. I can see it happening.

Carlie, no.

Too late. Her eyes move from his hand to his face. Slowly her own face clears, the last of the doubt is leaving her. Now it has happened. She thinks she has remembered what she was waiting for. *Who* she was waiting for. Not me. Him, this man who has appeared from nowhere.

His hands have stopped moving. The cage around her is all finished. Now it is closed. With Carlie locked up inside. In the moment she had been about to be mine, I'd lost her. I'd lost Carlie.

Not able to believe it, though. Not yet. I side-stepped Walsh and came to stand beside them.

'Who's this, Carlie?'

But my words vanished the moment they left my lips, contentless. No one had noticed me.

A gap of seconds. Then she gave a start. 'Guy! I didn't see you. This is Magnus. Magnus, this is Guy, Guy Latimer – a friend of mine.'

Magnus's eyes flickered once in my direction, and looked away. In that very moment I became invisible. Magnus had made me vanish, robbed me of substance. I turned again to Carlie, tried to make her see me. But she was staring up at him, into black eyes that swallowed up every last vestige of memory. I touched her arm, but nerveless from his touch, she couldn't feel me. *Carlie*, I whispered again, but she couldn't hear me. If Carlie couldn't see me, feel me or hear me, then who would?

Dully I turned away, and in turning met another gaze reflected in the mirror. Jennifer was staring at me with her grey Athene eyes. *She* could see me. She had seen everything, perhaps even the inevitability of it. Now, in the mirror, she smiled, gently inviting me to step away from lost ground, to join her, there in the glass.

I didn't go. I continued to stand beside them, waiting for Carlie to see me and remember. Yet I could have walked away from her then. It was another moment where we could all have gone one way or the other, another of those between-places, where the future peels away from the past. A young woman was looking at me and smiling. Another young woman no longer saw me at all; I had a choice. A promise of everything or nothing.

I had a choice and I chose the one who didn't see me, who from now on wouldn't see anything unless it was Magnus. Who promised me nothing.

I chose Carlie. I had no choice.

Even then, it's possible it was not too late. If I had stepped between them, made myself present, I might have forced her to see me again, before her eyes became cemented for good. Forced her to remember me. Somehow I might have done it.

But in that same moment, over in the corner, came a small liquid explosion. Rhona had started to be sick. In another corner, someone else started to wail; not cry or sob but wail, like a child waking in the night not knowing where he was. On the sofa, Peter suddenly pushed Peter away and fled from the room. Walsh stood up from examining the punch stain on the floor and looked at me in alarm.

'What the...?'

Someone else had started crying. In another room, a boy screamed.

Both of us spoke at the same time.

'You spiked the punch.' I said.

'Fuck no. I swear.' Walsh's eyes were wild. He grabbed my arm. 'You think that's what's happened?'

I nodded. Twelve years in the company of boys. Homesickness, asthma, drugs. Lots of drugs. The better the school, the better the drugs. Everyone knows that.

Over in the corner Gordon choked on a scream. 'Flies! There are flies crawling out of her mouth.'

Together we ran across the room. There were no flies in

Rhona's mouth. But she was crying, hard, her face slippery with regurgitated punch.

Walsh said, 'I'll look after these two. See what's happening to the others.'

It was clear what was happening. Everyone was crying, or being sick, or both, as if it were an infection. Throwing up where they stood, drenching their clothes. Over by the mirror only Jennifer continued to stand, not sick or crying. But her eyes were closed, not watching any more. Keeping the infection at bay.

I ran from couple to couple, wherever the fear was most. None of it lasted long. And to tell the truth, it was over in a few minutes. Already one or two were beginning to recover. The others weren't far behind. Whatever had been in the punch, it can't have been much. Just enough to explain every strange turn in the evening. Gradually they stopped being sick and began to pull themselves together, quietly mopped themselves up, too dazed to ask what had happened to them. Or too polite.

My classmates amazed me. One by one they took positions, bolt upright on the edges of the chairs, trying to find some semblance of normal; couples who had been entwined careful not to catch each other by the eye. Every one of them seemed calm. Only one of the two Peters was missing. I went in search and found him in the kitchen, sobbing. He wasn't calm. I had to bend in close to hear what he was saying: *now he'll never, now he'll never, now he'll never.*

He thought he had found his moment. Only to have it snatched away. As I had.

And Carlie. Where was Carlie?

I ran back into the sitting room. There was no sign of her. Or Magnus.

I went to look for Walsh and found him on the stairs with his head in his hands. 'Fuck,' he said over and over again.

'Fuck. This will get out and I'm going to lose everything. They won't even let me teach fucking table tennis in fucking schools after this.'

I shook his shoulder. 'Who did it?' I said. 'Who spiked the punch?' But already I knew the answer. *Magnus.* I breathed the name aloud.

Walsh nodded. 'I should have realised,' he said heavily. 'He was after Jennifer. She'd given him the brush off, and when he told me about it, I just laughed. I said they all just needed to loosen up a bit. I shouldn't have spoken a fucking word, not to him. I knew he'd already dropped a tab or two himself.'

'And you? Had you taken anything?'

He avoided my eyes. 'I'd never have let him do it to them, never. Not if I'd known.'

There came the sound of stirrings from the next room. My class were moving, making ready to leave, in a group, the way they arrived, as if there was safety in numbers. I saw them help each other into their coats, careful with each other. Gentle. Was it possible they had no inkling of what had happened?

No. They knew something, but they weren't complaining. They gathered by the front door. Still fragile, but calm. These were the Classicists, not quite like other people. They reminded me of devout Athenians after the excesses of the Mysteries, ready to be respectable again, the initiation over. It was folly for Walsh to call them children.

'I think you may be safe, Walsh,' I said in wonder.

He glanced at them putting on their shoes. And the same thought must have struck him. He gave a sigh of relief. He counted them silently then said, 'Where's your friend? The one you came with?'

I heard the question and felt a weight on my neck, like a hand pressing down. 'She's with *your* friend, Magnus.'

'Oh,' he said. He looked embarrassed, but that was all. 'I'm sorry. I hope she wasn't...that you weren't...' He saw my face and stopped. 'Ah.' There was no more he could say.

'Where is his room?'

He nodded upstairs. I drew a breath and went to stand outside a door that was shut fast.

'Carlie, if you can hear me...I'm going home. Are you coming?' Without thinking, I laid my hand on the door, felt the wood blocking my fingers. There was no answer. Of course.

I closed my eyes. Maybe she was sleeping, that was all. Carlie fell asleep so easily, when she felt it was safe.

Safe? Here? With him?

Carlie! This time I couldn't help myself. I shouted her name, but the door was a sponge soaking up sound.

A hand fell on my arm. It was Walsh. He had seen everybody out. They had left as they had come – together. I didn't want to look at him now, the makeup smeared over his face. In a low voice he said, 'Come away Guy. Come away, man.' I had the urge to hit him in the mouth.

Instead I let him lead me downstairs. Not everyone had gone. Jennifer was still standing near the mirror, her eyes open now.

I went over to her. 'I'll walk you home.'

She nodded. We put on our coats and left, over the bridge and into the streetlight. Somewhere along the way, our hands met and caught hold of each other. But outside her hall we parted and went our separate ways.

On the road back to my own hall I passed a couple in a doorway. From out of the dark that cocooned them I heard a small laugh of pure happiness. Straight away I knew who they were. Peter and Peter, together after all. They had taken their moment and held on to it.

The way I should have done.

Chapter Five

Back in my room I took a book down off the shelf and sat, waiting for the creak of the fire door.

It didn't come. As I knew it wouldn't. Eventually I climbed into bed in my clothes and listened to the silence on the other side of the wall. The silence of Carlie's empty room.

I must have slept, only to wake in an instant, listening. Daylight now, but still there was only silence from next door. Upstairs, in the dining room I looked for her amongst the few students who appeared for early breakfast. As if she would possibly be amongst them.

I went back to my room and spread my books out in front of me on the desk. But the pages could have been so many dead leaves blown in from outside. The person who could have made sense of them was absent. I had lost my centre – the worker, the reader inside me.

Instead of words, I saw Carlie. In a room behind a door shut fast, I saw Carlie being undressed, the slow unwinding of her golden robe. I saw Carlie naked. I saw her moving beneath his hands, catching her breath. I saw her the way a fly would see her, flown out of Rhona's mouth to settle on the wall of Magnus's room. I saw Carlie's cheeks burn and her lips bruise. I saw her breasts and belly glow. I saw the shock of the final moment and heard her gasp.

And I saw him, moulding and shaping her, stamping his mark on her.

And all of it happening, not last night but here, now, in the light of day, as I sat in my chair. I had eyes that could see through walls. I could see it all.

How did I know? Because Magnus was a cage shaper. Last night he wooed her. This morning he took her. Every move considered, every gesture practised. Ancient clockwork. He'd know when the time was right. He would have read Carlie like a book.

I knew this to be true. I'd only met him once and already I felt I'd known him all my life.

I fell asleep in my chair.

...To wake suddenly with the words on my lips. *Tell her.* This was all I had to do: tell her about Magnus, what he had done to a roomful of children in fancy dress. She would stare at me in disbelief, and then horror. Horror at Magnus, horror at his deed. Followed by disgust because then she had let him...

I felt the smile spreading across my chops. Relishing it, the look on Carlie's face. Because what else should she feel but horror? She deserved it. She should have recognised him the moment she set eyes on him. She should have seen the intention in his smile, in the movements of his hands.

And that wasn't even everything. Because after the horror and disgust would come the humiliation when I told her: how he only did it to get Jennifer. Pale, clever Jennifer who would not let him near her. She had been the one he was after. I would tell Carlie because she needed to know that she was the second choice. Because it was true.

Poor Carlie. She would turn to me and I would take her in my arms and see, it would happen all over again, the process. Carlie in my arms, Carlie naked, crying and moving at the same time Only this time I wouldn't be the fly on the wall. This time it would be my hands moulding and shaping...

...To wake suddenly with the words on my lips. *Tell her.*

I knew it wouldn't work like that. I knew my Carlie.

This was the worst of it. I couldn't tell her what I knew about Magnus. She wouldn't believe me.

Later, much later, I heard the creak of the fire door. Then came the opening and closing of her own door. Quietly. Carlie was trying to come home without letting anyone know.

Without letting me know.

Even then I waited for the knock on my door, telling

myself that sooner or later she would have to come. If she didn't talk about what happened it would be as if it never happened. Carlie was her own recording angel. She needed me to hear.

Surely.

But she didn't come. And she didn't come. I sat with my empty books and waited. And she didn't come.

Until suddenly: *Go knock on our Carlie.* The words, so real they made me jump, came out of empty air. A moment later I pulled myself from my chair and knocked on Carlie's door. There was a space of seconds before her voice reached me.

'Who is it?'

'It's me, Guy.' Again there was silence. 'Carlie, are you going to let me in?'

Yet another pause, then I heard her move. The door opened.

'Hi,' she said. She was trying so hard to sound normal, but her fingers trembled on the edge of the door, at the same time gripping as if otherwise she might begin to rise, weightless. We stared, and I felt we had become the finished opposites of each other. Carlie flushed and shaking with the excitement in her limbs, and me with arms weighed down by lead. Hot and cold. Fast and slow. Carlie and Guy.

I forced a smile to my lips. 'Hello Carlie,' I said.

What was it about my voice that fooled her, made her think everything was alright? I don't know, but I saw her relax, saw her come back to me. She grasped me by both my hands and pulled me into her room.

'I haven't slept,' she said exultantly, closing the door. 'Not the whole, entire night.'

How could she have told me that? Because she couldn't see me. Only the smile, which was all she wanted to see. Carlie still needed an ear.

So I kept the smile on my face. Smiled so much it ached.

And even the ache wore a smile of its own – wry, resigned. So this was love, just as I'd always suspected. *Odi et amo.* I hate and love. I listened to Carlie and smiled and ached in every part of my body.

Monday and in the lecture room I stared around at my year. The girls drifted in with their duffle bags and bobbly jumpers, the boys in their jackets musty with pipe smoke like old professors. As usual, Peter and Peter sat together. Only Jennifer was late.

Halfway through the lecture, she appeared in the door. I saw her hesitate then make her way to the seat beside me. Our year was whole again, all of us present. Intact.

After, I sat with Jennifer on the wall outside – where Carlie and I had once sat.

'Why were you late?' I asked her.

'I was arranging not to have Walsh take me for poetry any more.'

'It wasn't his fault,' I said dully. 'Someone spiked the punch.'

'The same man who took your girlfriend.' She spoke with confidence. So she knew. She truly had recognised Magnus. As Carlie should have.

'She's not my girlfriend. She never was. Anyway,' I added. 'It was you he was after.'

She didn't bother to answer this. I imagined Magnus thwarted by that grey Athene stare, cut down to size. She laughed out loud suddenly.

'What?' I knew she wasn't thinking about Magnus.

'It's Walsh. I told you I saw him this morning. He's had all his hair cut off. It must have been the first thing he did when he got out of bed – run to the barbers. He looks almost respectable. It didn't last long, did it, all that determination not to be like the others?'

'He's frightened,' I said. 'He wants to keep his job.'

'I don't think he's in much danger of losing it, do you? Not because of them.'

As she spoke there was a clattering on the steps in front of us, and here they were again, Walsh's so-called boys and girls. They saw us as they trooped out of the Classics Building, and beckoned.

Jennifer smiled at me, slid off the wall and joined them. I stayed where I was.

Chapter Six

I woke to find Carlie sitting on the desk, watching me.

'I haven't slept…'

'…the whole entire night,' I finished for her. I sat up in bed and tried not to stare too hard. Two weeks since they had met. There were shadows like caves beneath her eyes. Carlie looked as if she hadn't slept in far more than a single night.

'Term ends tomorrow,' she said, as if somehow it had escaped me.

'That's good, Carlie. You can have a rest. You need a rest.'

'You don't understand. You don't know what it will be like, not seeing him.'

'You can see your parents. You'll like that won't you?'

'My parents!' She grimaced, and for the first time it came to me. I wasn't the only one to have lost Carlie. For a moment I imagined a misery to match my own. Which died in a second; my own misery was all I could feel. I spoke up, though, weakly on their behalf, Carlie's parents.

'Oh, come on,' I said. 'You're tired. It will be good for you. You'll have time to catch up with yourself, being with your mum and dad.'

She shook her head. Her shoulders had slumped as if she was too tired to sit up straight. Carlie was in love, but she wasn't stupid. A month away from *him* was a long time. Anything could happen. Already she had learned to watch him, watch where his eyes went. I knew all about this. I'd watched Carlie while she watched him.

Oh Carlie, you were so tired and it was only the beginning.

When I didn't say anything, she slipped off the desk and sank down on the end of my bed, put her head beside my feet. She stared at the ceiling a moment, then slowly her eyes began to close.

'Carlie,' I whispered, half in wonder. 'Are you going to fall asleep?'

She didn't answer. I watched her, afraid to say any more. This was the first time she had fallen asleep in front of me since they had met. I watched her body relax, her hand unfurling beside her cheek. I watched, listened, till the only sound was Carlie breathing. Then I sat up and bent over her.

'Carlie,' I whispered. 'Do you remember how we danced, just a little while ago. You and me?'

She stirred, half in sleep, half in assent. Already dreaming.

I laid my head next to hers on my bed. 'Carlie, I loved dancing with you. I loved it.'

Again she stirred. In dreams you can say anything.

'Carlie...' I breathed against her cheek. Closer still. 'Can you hear me, Carlie?'

Then, drilling through the quiet, came the creak of the fire door, and footsteps that could belong to one person only. A long confident stride, which made the breeze blocks ring. I stared down in horror at Carlie, knowing what this noise would do. An instant in which my hands hovered over her – to do what? Keep her, there on my bed, no matter what? Yet all I wanted was for her to sleep. In sleep Carlie stayed with me.

But no. Carlie's eyes snapped open. Her cheeks were already flooding with pink. I doubt Magnus ever saw her pale – at least in those first weeks.

And now she was off the bed, hand reaching for the door.

I couldn't help myself. I was there before her, blocking the way. Words spilling out of me, out of my control.

'Carlie, listen to me. You have to know this. Magnus – he put drugs into the punch at that party. Acid. Do you know about acid? It's LSD, Carlie, LSD for a bunch of children who've never had anything worse than sherry. He did it so he could get to Jennifer – remember the girl by the fireplace? – because she wouldn't have him, not unless he'd drugged her.' I made a grab for her hand. 'Doesn't that make a difference,

Carlie? Doesn't it make you see?'

I saw Carlie's eyes flicker. She pulled her hand away from mine. My voice sank. 'OK forget it. I'm sorry, I didn't mean to tell you. Forget it, Carlie. Forget I ever spoke.'

But Carlie was gone. I heard her voice next door, indignant. I heard Magnus laugh. Then a little after that, I began to hear other noises. Noises to drive me out of my room, scrambling out of my window, sending me running across the grass towards the sand dunes and the sea, gathering speed. Crying.

The night I arrived home, I told my father I had changed my mind. I wanted to go to his old college after all.

He was oiling the lock to our old oak front door as he did every year. After this he would oil the hinges. Winter would make them rusty, he said, and noisy. For now, though, he put down the oil can and looked at me. 'I thought that might happen,' he said after a moment. We stood in the hall, in silence, as he waited for anything more I might need to say. Then he picked up his oil can again.

So that was that. St Leonards sent the paperwork which I filled in on Christmas day with the fat black Mont Blanc ink pen I had unwrapped that morning. Boxing day it began to snow, settling in drifts piled up in the lanes, cutting us off from the village – and the post office. When the snow stopped, I went for a tramp with my father through the blanketed country side while we discussed Balliol and, after that, reading for the Bar. We talked about suitable Chambers for pupillage, but really there was no need for any of it. Both of us knew where I would end up. In his Chambers.

That was the first year I noticed a walk could make him breathless. We stopped, pretending it was so he could retie the laces on his boots. Meanwhile I turned to look behind me and saw our foot steps trailing us in the snow. Yet no matter how hard I looked, I could only seem to make out my father's prints. I had followed him so closely, my own were nowhere to be seen.

Back in the house, we took off our boots. My father went into his study. Down the corridor in the back kitchen I could hear my mother, chatting softly to the dogs as she fed them. I supposed there was a time when she would have talked to me like that, long ago when I was very small. But I couldn't remember. I couldn't remember a time when anyone in this house talked for the sake of talking, for the sake of contact, to set a happening in stone. To be his or her own recording angel, to comfort herself.

What would I do without Carlie and her talk, telling me everything, even if I didn't want to hear?

I went upstairs, ripped up the leaving form for St Leonards, then went to tell my father. He touched the objects on his desk and said: 'You won't take my advice in this?'

I didn't answer.

Two weeks after that I went back to St Leonards. And Carlie.

I got a shock when I saw her. She had dyed her hair bright red and strung it with ribbons. Neither the colour nor the ribbons suited her, but they made her stand out. Carlie wouldn't have to open her mouth now to be noticeable. Besides there was Magnus. They made a pair – good-looking, exotic. An older man and a beautiful girl. Youth and experience. She must have known what they looked like, how they drew the eye.

She wouldn't talk to me. That first week I only ever saw her from a distance. The fire door creaked, but she never came to my room. Sometimes in the corridor I caught the scent of her just having come or gone – Carlie's own burnt sugar smell overlaid with something else, smoky and acrid. Rank. I tried to breathe in the scent of one, only to end up coughing on the other.

Days empty of Carlie, and yet filled with Carlie. Her absence gave shape and substance to everything else. Nothing

I touched failed to be touched by her, by the absence of her. This is what I had done. This is what I had come back for.

I asked Walsh where Magnus had gone to live after moving out of his house.

He looked confused. 'Move out? What are you talking about?'

I stared at him. 'Walsh, are you still renting him a room?'

'I gave him notice, naturally...' He halted, his face guilty. He had done nothing more than that. Magnus was still there in Walsh's house.

I murmured, 'You're seeing more of her than I am, then.'

'Who?'

I looked away. 'No one. Forget it.'

He looked at me sharply. 'You're not still thinking about her – that girl, the one who visits him?' When I didn't answer he pushed his book away. 'Don't, Guy,' he said. 'Don't waste your time. Take my word in this – she's sweet and everything, but she's – how can I put this? – she's only got eyes for him. First love and all that.'

'And Magnus?'

'Magnus?' Walsh's voice lost some of its force. 'He's very fond of her, of course. Why shouldn't he be? *I* like her. Always glad to see her. It's like having a kitten, actually, padding about the house.'

Not a kitten, Walsh, a girl. A living, breathing girl – until age and fate change everything. I closed my book and stood up.

Walsh sighed. 'Guy, listen to me. Keep away from her – or have her as a friend – whatever works for you. But don't let it affect your work. She's too...' He shook his head, despairing of what he had been about to say. He started again. 'You know what she reminds me of? Really?'

'A kitten,' I said drily.

He had the grace to look uncomfortable. 'To be serious – I'm talking psychology here, Pavlov and all that. The girl is like a bloody duckling, fresh out of the egg. She takes one look at him and thinks this is it, he's the daddy, and off she goes after him. Conditioning, a case of pure conditioning. It helps that he's probably twice her age.'

He's the Daddy. A rain of distaste falling over me. Out of my mouth, my own father speaks, his voice icy: 'You should stick to Classics, Walsh.'

Walsh's lips pursed. 'All I'm saying is, it's hopeless. You've got to think about your work. I heard about the application to leave, by the way. I'd have been sorry but it might have been a good thing. But if you're going to stay, get the most out of this place. This is a good department. Use it.' His eyes met mine. 'I'll give him notice, Guy. Proper notice. I'll get him out of my house.'

'Don't,' I said, and meant it.

Let him stay in Walsh's house. Walsh could be the fly on the wall, the only contact with Carlie I had left.

Days and weeks of absence. Then Carlie came back to me.

I had worked late, deep into the night until, finally, I was tired enough for there to be a chance of sleep. Outside my window seagulls cried as I fell into bed, but everything else was quiet.

Then the fire door creaked and put an end to it.

I pulled the pillow over my head. But still I could hear through the wall – Magnus's voice rising and falling. Not a whisper from Carlie. I imagined her watching him, listening. Drinking him in like water, like wine.

It was no use, I took the pillow off my head, thought about getting up and going for a walk in the dark, along the beach, let the sound of the waves drive every other sound out of my head.

But then I heard it: the familiar half cough, half sob through the wall. Something not heard in so long. It had never occurred to me to wonder why, since Magnus, Carlie had suffered no more asthma attacks. But now she was having one – a bad one, I could tell. I froze, listening for Magnus's response – and heard something fall. The soft slide of a young body collapsing. I heard Magnus call out her name.

He didn't know what to do. His ignorance made itself heard through the wall. He was shouting at her now, ordering her to get up, to breathe. Not to fuck around. I heard the fear in his voice and knew exactly who he was frightened for.

A moment later I was driving through the door. It might even have been locked, but it gave way before me like paper.

She was so far gone this time – on the floor, her fists pulsing against the carpet. Foam flecked lips stained with a new, blue tinge I'd never seen before. Magnus was standing over her, shouting into her face, using up the oxygen.

He sprang back when he saw me, almost guilty, as if afraid to look like the reason she was struck down.

'She's having some kind of a fit, fuck it. Nothing to do with me. I don't know what's happening. What's she playing at?'

'She's not playing at anything. It's asthma.' I got down on my knees beside her.

'Asthma?' He repeated the word, trying it out, seeing what difference it made. Cautiously he said, 'Like kids get, right?'

I shrugged. He stepped back, threw himself back onto Carlie's bed, relaxed, almost smiling now. Asthma – nothing to pin on him. 'So she's going to be alright. Asthma, you don't die of that.'

'People die,' I said. I put my mouth to her ear. 'Carlie,' I whispered. 'It's me, Guy. Open your eyes. Look at me, Carlie. Count with me.'

Her eyes squeezed open – only to stare past me. Terrified, she was looking for him, for Magnus. I took her hand in mine, tried to keep the urgency out of my voice. 'Come on Carlie, we've done this before, remember. This is me, Guy. Count with me, Carlie. One, two, three…

But still she wouldn't look at me. She was looking for Magnus, and I was losing her all over again. We were all losing her. For good this time.

'*Carlie!*'

In panic I had shouted her name at her. And this time the shock of hearing it made her turn her eyes to me, just for the instant. But it was enough. Because now, having caught it, I kept it – Carlie's gaze, trapped in my own.

And little by little I brought her back. Or rather she came back; only barely alive, following my eyes and the sound of my voice, putting her faith in me. The truth is, I didn't bring her; she came.

We counted to a thousand and beyond, until she fell asleep.

I smoothed the hair from her face. Silly red hair with its silly ribbons. Then I heard a sound. It was Magnus, I had forgotten he was there. He put down the book he had in his hands and yawned.

'You were reading,' I said in wonder. 'All the time she was…'

'Hey – not at all. I only picked up the book when the two of you started counting. Had to do something to stay awake. Is that what you do?'

'When?'

'When people have asthma. You count?'

'I don't know,' I said. 'It's what *we* do, Carlie and me.'

He yawned again. 'So…she's going to be alright, yeah?'

I nodded. Then aloud, I cried, 'Don't!'

He had been reaching for the stub in one of Carlie's saucers. A fat ended roach which explained the sweet, acrid smell that filled the room. He raised his eyebrows. 'Don't approve of the weed, is that it?' His eyes, heavy lidded, were amused.

'It's the smoke. It's probably what set it off, the attack.'

He shrugged, and produced a small pretty tin decorated with flowers, slipped the joint under the lid. His fingers were long, delicate as a violinist's. The fingers of a fiddler. He snapped it shut and stared at the lid, bored. 'So,' he said at length. 'You a friend of Carlie's?'

'I'm Guy. We've met before. At the party – where you...where you met Carlie. And yes, she's a friend of mine.'

His eyes mocked me again. 'Can't say she's mentioned you.' He swung his legs off the bed and stood up. 'Anyway, I'll see you around.' He looked down at Carlie on the floor, slanting his long, lean body over her. 'Night night, honeysuckle.' Then stepped across her to the door. I heard the clatter of his footsteps in the corridor.

I waited until both footsteps and disbelief had faded. Then I bent towards Carlie again. 'He's gone,' I whispered. 'Carlie, he didn't even stay to look after you.'

This time, she didn't stir. Now would have been the time to tell her about Magnus.

Except what could I have told her that she hadn't been learning for herself all these weeks and months? Instead, I stroked her head, her cheeks, let my fingers brush her lips. 'I've missed you, Carlie.' I said. I took hold of her hand and laid it flat against mine.

Carlie slept and the night settled down around us. Time slowed to the pace of her breathing and I wanted her to stay like this forever, with me. If this was the only way to keep her, I didn't want Carlie to wake up. Ever.

Carlie's parents came to visit. Their car had broken down so they made the trek by train, cross-country, changing from one line to another, hauling cases as their daughter had never had to do. I was there with Carlie when she met them at the station.

'Come with me,' she had said. 'They like you.'

I had been seeing a lot of Carlie since the asthma attack.

Not that either of us had ever mentioned it – or the fact that he had left her to recover by herself. In the morning she had woken up and looked around for him, tried to hide her disappointment when she found there was only me. But she was back – as much of Carlie as I was allowed to have.

I saw her parents as the train drew in, craning their necks for the first glimpse of their daughter. It was possible Christmas had warned them what to expect and that was already two months ago. All the same, I wanted to jump on to the train before it stopped and warn them anyway. They would see a change in Carlie.

Two months and Carlie was whittled down. Infatuation had been working like an engine inside her. Combustion, heat, burning up flesh. She had covered the result with layer upon layer of multi-coloured clothes. But these were her parents; they would step off the train and know that their daughter was vanishing.

Carlie pulled the sleeves over her narrowing wrists and smiled a bright, forced smile. They stared at their daughter and you could see the words fail them. And Carlie did nothing to help. After the smile, she seemed as bereft of words as they were. Before the silence became too much to bear, I stepped in.

'Let me take your case, Mrs. Hawkins. You're looking very well, both of you. And not such bad weather for the journey. Now all we need is to find a taxi, get us into town...'

I did my best for them, laboured to fill in the gaps. Small talk to flesh out a reunion that should been solid and warm and breathing. But Mr. and Mrs. Hawkins were no more fooled by me than they were by the layers of Carlie's clothes. Something terrible had happened. Their daughter, the apple of their eye, was only half there, unwilling even to look them.

Heart breaking, the speed with which they adjusted, resetting their sights. After the first shock I watched them smile and hug their daughter as if the awkwardness was nothing new. As if they were used to a Carlie who sat, silent between them, in the back seat of the taxi.

In the tea shop, though, Carlie seemed to spring back to life. The colour came into her cheeks and she began to talk fast and furiously. For a moment I thought everything was normal again; then I spotted the trembling in her hands. Instinctively I turned. Across the room, Magnus was sitting at a table, his legs sprawled in front of him, arms trailed by his sides. In the presence of her parents, this what he was here to remind her, she belonged to him now.

Who's the daddy?

Next to the wall, the waitress, a Spanish student with long curling hair, sucked her pen and watched him, and wondered the same thing. I saw her catch his eye, and his attention wander from Carlie. Magnus and student, they were smiling at each other. I began to gag on the cake the Hawkinses had bought for me.

I couldn't keep it up, fleshing out the bones. But still I couldn't bear to leave them, the three of them trying so hard to act as if nothing had changed.

The next day I was with them again, back at the station, this time to see them off. On the platform Carlie and her father were saying goodbye, awkwardly, politely. Mrs. Hawkins turned to me, touched my cheek quickly, her fingers warm like Carlie's.

'Guy, love,' she whispered. 'Make sure you look after *your-self* now.'

Look after myself. She knew what it was like. She could see right through me. I felt the wet come into my eyes.

'I'll look after Carlie, too,' I whispered. 'I'll do everything I can, I promise. And…' I took a breath '…I'll write you a letter, explaining all this. So you understand why Carlie is…like she is.'

'Do that, Guy,' she said. Her eyes were pleading.

Chapter Seven

The train disappeared up the track to Edinburgh and Carlie gave a sigh of relief. Followed by a giggle.

'Did you see him, Guy? In the tea shop? Wasn't he *naughty?* Staring at me like that.' Except he hadn't been staring, not the whole time. Not once he'd found somewhere else to look.

'You haven't told them, then, about Magnus?' But of course I knew the answer to that.

Ignoring the question, she began dragging me towards the station café. 'Come with me. I need a cake. Two cakes. I'm starving.'

I watched her devour an iced bun almost whole.

'Why couldn't you have done that when your parents were here?' I asked her. 'It would have done them good to see you eat something.'

She swallowed vigorously. 'I know, wasn't it awful? I was all nerves, did you see? I couldn't have eaten a thing. Not in front of them.'

'Nervous? With your own parents?'

'God, they've changed. Didn't you think so too? It's the first thing I noticed. They just...stared at me.' This wasn't true. After that first moment of stepping off the train, they had avoided anything that resembled a stare. She gave a dramatic sigh. 'I suppose it must be difficult for them, finally realising I'm an adult.' Then she giggled again. 'And it didn't help, Magnus threatening to introduce himself to them all weekend.'

'Well, why didn't he?' I said.

She gave a small scream of laughter. 'Magnus, meet my parents? Can you imagine?'

'What would have been so wrong about it?' I watched her. 'Why shouldn't they meet him, Carlie?'

She stopped smiling. She knew what I was up to, trying to make her admit the truth. *If they met him they would hate him. Worse than that, they would fear him.* Carlie's eyes suddenly were stony, avoiding mine.

Abruptly I stood up. 'I'll see you back in hall.' There was already a distance between us, created by Carlie. Better to make the distance physical than sit, waiting for her to relent and come back to me – as she always did come back. As she was learning about Magnus, I was learning too, about Carlie: how much she needed me. I was learning that it was safe to walk away from her.

'Guy...' she began more softly, so that for a moment I thought I would be staying after all. Then her eyes slid past me and her face lit up. 'OK,' she said simply. 'See you.'

I didn't even have to turn round. One look at her face and I knew who had stepped into the café. I passed him on my way out. As always, he looked straight through me, as if he genuinely didn't know me. As if there was nothing about me to know.

I didn't see her after that, not for days. She came and she went but mostly her room stayed empty, so I thought he was keeping her with him. Perhaps he'd decided to stamp himself all over again, making sure. Early one evening though, I heard her come back – alone. I knocked on her door, but there was no answer.

The next two days were the same. She was in her room, but she never came to the door when I knocked. I thought she was punishing me. I had almost expected it.

Walsh invited me round for dinner. And still I didn't expect to see her. Walsh was always careful this way, making sure our paths never crossed in his house. I followed the road across the bridge to his front door where laburnum trailed its blossoms across my face. Poisonous laburnum. Walsh should cut it back.

Just before the porch, I stopped dead, heart lurching the way it always did...

...Heart lurching the way it always did when I saw them together. Their bodies filled the space in front of the door. All I could see was Magnus's back. His hands were busy, working out of sight, in the dark. I heard the sound of a soft choked laugh, and turned on my heel. Anything rather than pass them like this.

Too late, the garden gate, closing behind me, rattled shut and startled them. They fell apart and now I could see them both, Magnus and...

...Magnus and not Carlie. It was the waitress, the Spanish student, from the tea shop, her mass of hair silhouetted against the door. Magnus leant out of the porch, trying to make out who was there.

'It's me – Guy.'

'Guy?' It seemed he had forgotten me yet again.

'Carlie's friend.' I let the significance sink in.

There was a pause. 'Guy – yeah. Right. You seeing her later, Guy?'

'I might do.'

'Then say that her worshipful Prince bids his lady sweet dreams.'

The Spanish student giggled softly. Then gave him a cynical look. She had the measure of him. Not like Carlie. The door opened and Walsh ushered me in.

'He's out there,' I said. 'With somebody else. Not Carlie. He didn't even care that I saw him. How am I going to tell her, Walsh?'

At the same time, a shiver of excitement. What would she say? What could she say?

Walsh shrugged. 'Tell her any way you like. It won't make any difference.' He handed me a glass of wine and took me into the sitting room.

'But...'

'She knows. She found him with that particular one a couple of days ago. They were in bed together. Your friend had run upstairs before I could stop her. She'd almost caught him a week before that. I suppose it's all over between them now.'

I took this in, not trusting myself to speak. Out in the hall the door opened and closed, followed by a scuffle on the stairs.

Walsh walked over to the turntable and put on a record, louder than usual. Presently he ladled over-cooked spaghetti onto plates, and watched me struggle to eat. There were sounds filtering down through the ceiling – rhythmical, unmistakable – which Walsh stolidly ignored. I imagined Carlie hearing them, what they would do to her.

'Sorry,' I said as he took my plate away, hardly touched.

'Your loss.' He kicked open an already overflowing bin. 'Just for that, though, I'm going to give the class medal to Jennifer. She's got more sense and *lots* more poetry in her translations.' He glanced at me. 'Why aren't the two of you together, you and Jennifer? You've got a lot in common. You even remind me of each other. Same cool heads. A union made in heaven, I'd say. And that's the last thing I'd ever say about you and other one. You want the rest of this wine?'

I shook my head. At the same moment the record ended, quickly followed by an ending of another kind upstairs. The Spanish student was screaming, calling out for her mother. Walsh winced. *'Madre de dio.'*

'I've got to go,' I said and stood up.

He nodded and looked gloomy. I could imagine him ten years from now, no longer tolerant, banging on the ceiling with a stick. Leather patches on his sleeves.

Carlie's door was locked.

'Carlie, let me in.'

Silence.

'Open this door, Carlie or I'll break it down.'

I heard a sound. Carlie was dragging herself across the room. Arms and legs like lead. Carlie who had been almost weightless. She opened the door then stepped back to let me in.

'Oh Carlie,' I whispered.

Her eyes flickered briefly then went dead again. Her hair was lank, her face the colour of whey. She had a cold sore in the corner of her mouth. She looked as if she hadn't eaten or slept in days.

She sat on the bed, ignoring me as I made her some tea and found the tin of cake that had travelled halfway across the country with her mother.

'Eat,' I said. She stared at me blankly. 'Eat,' I said again. Then I went to run her a bath. When I came back she was sitting in a mess of crumbs – as if she hadn't even been able to find her mouth.

'The bath's ready for you.'

But she made no move. She didn't even look at me. Her eyes were somewhere else, taking in a scene, a fly on the wall. Carlie was trapped in her imagination, forced to watch the same thing over and over again. I knew exactly what was happening to her.

I touched her arm to rouse her but she didn't seem to feel it. Carlie would have continued to sit there as if I had never found her.

So I took her clothes off for her, slowly, as gently as I could. Breathing in the warm unwashed smell of her body. Carlie's own scent, intensified, making my heart, my head and my cock ache.

'You're too thin.' I murmured. 'Too thin, Carlie.'

She didn't seem to hear me. She didn't even seem to know she was standing naked. I wrapped a towel round her and led her to the bathroom. She sat in the bath, her shoulders hunched, staring straight ahead of her. I took a cup and poured water over her shoulders and her breasts and washed her hair. Handed her a toothbrush.

'Teeth now, Carlie.'

I took her back to my room and dried her, wrapped a rug around her and lay her down on the bed.

'Sleep now, Carlie.'

I got the blankets from her room and lay down on the floor. In the small hours I woke to the sound of crying. I lay down on the bed and put my arms around her.

'What happened, Carlie?' I whispered. 'Are you going to tell me about it?'

After a moment she took a breath, and I knew she was going to talk. But I should have put on the light as she began to tell me. Because for the first time Carlie told me everything – what it was like to be with Magnus, to be spell bound, to be trapped. He wove a spell around us even here. In the dark, Magnus had free rein. She talked and we clung to each other while he filled the room. *I should have put on the light.* In the dark, he fucked everything, he fucked the walls, the doors. Greedy, he fucked anything that moved. Ravenous, he fucked the dark itself. I wrapped myself around Carlie, tried to keep him out, but he was there, fucking her inside her head.

Fucking Carlie.

She told me everything, until there was nothing left inside to tell.

When I woke up she had gone back to her own room. I could hear noises, though. Encouraging noises. Carlie was moving again. I went to her door and found it open. She was dressed in clean clothes and her window was wide, letting in light and air. I went to the dining hall and came back with slices of buttery toast, still hot, wrapped in a napkin.

'First day of spring, Carlie,' I said, pointing to her calendar.

We ate in the sunshine, sitting on the grass below our windows watching the sea twinkle blue in the distance. A salt breeze stroked her curls, as I would have liked to do, and brushed the colour back into her cheeks. Then a thought struck me.

'Have you done any work, recently, Carlie?'

She shook her head.

'Don't you have exams coming up?'

I had exams, every one of them important. I thought of the books lying with their covers closed in her room and suddenly I saw a new danger looming. A new way of losing Carlie.

'Carlie, you have to work!' For the first time I heard the panic in my voice. 'Fail and they throw you out.'

No sooner had I spoken than I was scrambling back into her room, picking all the books and papers off her desk, tossing them out of the window to the ground beside her.

'Work, Carlie. You mustn't get thrown out. Get on with it.'

I sounded so wild that she stared at me. Then, unbelievably, she smiled, and I knew she was there, still able to be saved. She began to sort through her papers, ruling margins, rearranging her pens. All the things she normally did when she was getting ready for a task. Then she looked up.

'What about you?'

She waited while I climbed through my own window. I hardly liked to tell her that I was up to date, that the one thing I always came back to was work. I pulled down my Catullus from the shelf and pretended it was work instead. Pretended that I didn't know every line by heart. That it was not, in fact, a conspiracy on the page holding the words I couldn't say to Carlie. *Si quicquam cupido optantique optigit umquam* – 'What happens if you'd lost hope, and suddenly it's back – the thing you wanted most? Joy, reaching right to the soul.'

But keep the joy inside, keep it from Carlie. Don't lose it again. Don't lose *her* again.

I was a hard task master. When her eyes drifted from her book, when her fingers began tremble, I'd see it. 'Work, Carlie.' I said. 'Don't think, work.'

Do as I've done, all these months, and I'll lead you out of this. Don't look back.

A week, two weeks. Exams came and went. Jennifer and I tied for first place, but Walsh was as good as his word and awarded her the class medal. Amazingly Carlie scraped through. Each morning I had walked her hollow eyed to the actual door of the exam. And after, I'd be there when she came out, fretting that she had just been sitting there for three hours, the paper staying empty in front of her.

But I was wrong about that. If she was hollow eyed, it was because I'd bullied her, kept her up all the night with the books. *Don't think. Work.*

The night she got her results she appeared in my room. 'I want to go out,' she said. 'I've passed my exams. Now I want to go dancing.'

'Carlie,' I said. 'Are you sure?' The hollows were still there under her eyes.

But Carlie smiled and there she was in front of me, the old Carlie. Older in every way, thinner, wiser. And only I knew about the girl who had sat in the bath, staring at nothing.

We had done it. We had come through. *She* had come through. Clever Carlie, resilient Carlie, ready to bounce back.

We ran all the way to the Union where there would be music. Neither of us said so, but this would be our Victory dance. Only at the door to the hall did she pause, taking in the mass of bodies moving to the music. Carlie hadn't been in a crowd like this for weeks. Worse, there were all the old crowd, the people she used to know, and who for so long had only seen her with him, made more glamorous by him.

'Come on, Carlie,' I said. 'They're playing your song.'

And it was true, an old Blondie track from years ago, thrumming across the floor with the urgency of an ice cream van's chime. *Heart of Glass*, Carlie's favourite song. I followed her on to the floor, moved a little, but more than anything, I watched her. I had almost forgotten how Carlie used to dance. She had not an iota of grace. She was too enthusiastic, used up too much energy, like a child with no respect for rhythm. A clumsy beautiful child, the sort that falls off a stage into your lap.

But not tonight. For the first time since I had known her, Carlie seemed to have found a way of accommodating herself to the music. The DJ noticed her and cut a beam of light towards her, casting everyone else into shadow. Dazzled, she twisted in the beam like a huge moth hypnotised by light. And that, suddenly, was how I saw her – fragile as a moth, with no more than a moth's sense that light can be dangerous. In other words, no sense.

But I had sense – a sixth sense, warning me. I felt before I saw it – the movement in the dark, the shadow separating itself from the other shadows, making its way towards her.

She smiled at me out of the spotlight, then frowned, noticing that my face had become frozen. Behind her the shadow was close now and I watched her body stiffen as the hand lighted on her shoulder. I saw her face change, saw her half turn towards the touch. I watched as Carlie forgot all about me.

The music carried on, but Carlie had stopped dancing. She stared up at him, at Magnus. Her arms had fallen to her sides. Without a word, he put his own long arm around her, and began to draw her away, back into the mass of shadows, back the way he came, into the dark. And she went. But this time she knew what lay ahead; on the point of disappearing, she turned and threw me a last smile, brilliant and hopeless.

I walked home by myself.

Why was I so calm, as if nothing surprised me? Because I had known this would happen. He had never intended to let her go.

I knew this about Magnus: I knew it from that slow, cynical look of the Spanish student in the porch. Carlie would never look at him like that. Carlie's look was never measuring. It only enlarged, the reason he came back for her and would keep coming back. He was greedy for enlargement, for tumescence. Carlie was the lens through which to see himself, making him bigger, harder, younger. He would stray but he would always come back to claim her. She was the ideal mirror, he was never going to let her go.

I caught sight of myself in my own mirror – and turned away. Waited for the knock on my door which meant Carlie had returned, needing to tell me everything.

Chapter Eight

That was the end of the beginning, the first full turn of the screw.

In the summer vacation my grandmother died. My father read the lesson in the church, pausing only once to clear his throat. After the funeral, he explained the terms under which she had left me her estate, in trust until I was twenty-five. He told me I could draw on the funds by way of advancement and maintenance, that they would get me through the rest of university and beyond to what came after. He used words already familiar to me: *probate, accumulation, advancement* and *maintenance,* the language of Equity. Roman words held in check now by the law.

I bought a house in St Leonards and filled it with people from my course, two girls and two boys – Peter and Peter. They were neat and tidy, and paid their rent promptly every week. They pinned posters of Greek ruins and statues to the walls. They drank cocoa far into the night, pooled the use of Homeric dictionaries – and every now and then, they got rip-roaringly drunk on sherry and acted out the more obscene sections of Aristophanes. There was no censorship and no harm done. We were the Classicists. The house had a pleasant reek of pipe smoke and freshly laundered woolly jumpers.

I didn't ask Carlie to come and live there.

I fretted about how I would tell her I had a house which I would not be asking her to share. Because it was impossible to have her there. Because sharing a roof with Carlie would mean sharing a roof with *him.* But I didn't have to worry; before the start of term she wrote to tell me she was going into a flat with three other girls, members of the old crowd. And in the event, there was hardly any distance between us. My house was four doors down in the same terrace as Walsh's. In the night, I could hear the sound of the little river trickling over stones –

the same noise Carlie would hear when she lay in bed with
Magnus.

Close enough, so when she walked into the house and
found him lying there with someone else, for her to find her
way blindly down to me. As happened once, twice, a third
time. Then more times than either of us could count.

Halfway through second year, though, and she was back in
hall. At first the girls in her flat had been thrilled by Magnus.
When he darkened their door, they had felt a frisson, a virgin's
shudder when his long body pressed them to the wall as he
made his way inside. Carlie said they were jealous, and she
might have been right. She said this was the reason they were
so quick to tell her when they saw Magnus with other women.
She told them she didn't believe them, and let them draw their
own conclusions about what she thought about them.
Indignant, then angry, they began to leave her alone.

It turned out that Carlie didn't want to spend any time
with them anyway. Not if Magnus was going to come knocking. She didn't want to cook when it was her turn, or sit
around a two bar electric fire, discussing boys their own age.
She didn't want to swap clothes, she didn't want to sit and
revise in the same room sharing bags of liquorice all sorts. She
didn't want any of the things she used to want. She didn't
want friends. Not when there was Magnus. In the end they
asked her to leave, and replaced her with someone else.
Someone willing to join in.

But nothing changed between Carlie and me. I never threw
her out because I had never asked her to stay in the first place.

And still she told me everything. It became a ritual – the
knock on my door, the silent walk from my house to the
beach, always the beach, careful not to talk until we had
reached the sea, and the wind could safely whip away the
words as fast as she uttered them. That way words couldn't
haunt us as they had done that first night when his shadow

flickered in the dark beside us. Words we could leave amongst the flotsam to be bleached by sea and sand, like bones.

We never made the same mistake as last time, talking about him in the dark, closed in by walls. Back home we talked about other things until she fell asleep. Carlie was so tired, it happened all the time.

Even here, though, in my house, she wasn't safe from him. He would come to my door looking for her, leaning on the bell until one of us would answer it. But he never changed his attitude to me, never seemed to recognise me. He must have seen me every other day and he still had difficulty remembering my name.

Only once did I turn him away.

'She's working.'

He raised his eyebrows, leaned against the side of the door. 'Yeah?'

'She's got to hand in an assignment. A ten thousand word essay. She's been warned that if she doesn't, she won't get into third year.'

'And if she still wants to come with me?'

'She can't,' I said shortly.

He gave me a quizzical look, then his eyes came alive with laughter. 'You've got her under lock and key, you bastard. Fucking brilliant.' And you could see it; how the idea appealed to him – keeping Carlie prisoner.

But it was true. Carlie was upstairs with her books and I had the key to my bedroom door in my pocket. It was an arrangement we had made, half joke, half serious. I was the gatekeeper, guarding her from distraction until the essay was done.

I began to close the door.

'Wait,' Magnus said. He felt about him for some paper and a pen. 'Give her this.'

He scribbled out a note, then handed it to me before

sauntering back to Walsh's house. I unfolded the message, as he must have known I would.

My sweet honeysuckle princess – the Tall One whose eyebrows meet in the middle is standing guard. Stop what you is doing and get your ass down the road to Maison Walsh where your cosmic lord waits with a prick as strong and sturdy as the tool of the Prince of Darkness Himself.

I will say it again. She was studying English, for God's sake. And he wrote like this, he talked like this. And she fell for it. And kept on falling. Time and time again.

I unlocked the door to my room. Carlie was stretched out on my bed. She had fallen asleep. But neatly piled beside her were the pages of the essay she was meant to have handed in a month ago. I had no reason to keep her. She was free to go.

I crouched down beside her, gently placing the note in the curl of her fingers. She was breathing deeply, sleeping the sleep of the exhausted. I thought nothing would wake her. And I was wrong. Her eyes snapped open the moment the paper touched her skin.

A moment later she was gone.

This was how it was. This was how things were. Events repeated themselves. We stumbled to the sea. Carlie cried and talked and slept. Months turned to years.

End of our last year. Almost the end of finals.

And, while Carlie was busy revising, Magnus finally found someone else, someone serious, a first year. It shouldn't have been a surprise. I had seen her act in a play before I knew anything about her, and thought even while she was on stage how she had the same look that Carlie had when she'd first arrived. Small and vivid and lively – and very, very young.

This time was different, this time he was careful. Carlie wasn't meant know anything about it, at least not yet. He took precautions, trying to keep his options open in case he was forced to choose. It must have suited him. Two Carlies instead of one, multiplying that flattering, enlarging gaze. His prick must have been like iron during those last weeks.

A prick like iron. Is *that* what kept Carlie hanging on, all those years? I had thought of all the reasons, but I never let myself think of this one – *a prick like iron.* I told myself I had no illusions about her, but maybe I was wrong. I told myself I had no fantasy about her, and perhaps it was all fantasy, the one belief I allowed myself.

Because I told myself that Carlie never did anything but submit. That in submitting she suffered, hating what happened on Magnus's bed; sacrificing tender flesh on the altar she called Love. I told myself it was all part of the agony, *the prick like iron.* I never let myself think of a Carlie who took everything he gave her because she wanted it, because she liked it and even when it was over she wanted more. I couldn't think of that being the reason she never gave him up. I couldn't think of Carlie as anything but a victim of it – *a prick like iron.*

What did I close my eyes to, Carlie? What did I take away from you?

I found out about the other girl when I saw them together.

I had taken up running in second year, coming back one vacation with some worn out school shorts and a pair of tennis shoes. A new remedy to an old problem. I had remembered Xenophon and his army of Greeks running across Persia towards the sea that would take them home. *Thalassa, thalassa* – an end to the agony of homesickness. I wondered if running could provide a pause in another kind of sickness. And it did. I put on my tennis shoes and became the running man from Marathon, bringing word of victory to Athens. Or one of Xenophon's own men, racing to the sea and home. *Thalassa, thalassa.* Don't laugh – I was a Classicist. I ran as a Classicist. For an hour a day, I ran away from everything. Even

Carlie.

Until, nearly done with finals, I saw them. Seven in the morning on the West Sands, and here were two figures walking hand in hand towards me, miles from anywhere. Students of course, their silhouettes wavering, almost transparent in the sunlight. Up all night, probably, like so many. I ran towards them, full of good will.

Only to falter, heart lurching as it always did when I saw them together. Heart lurching, even now, in the final year. It was Magnus and Carlie – in the distance still, framed by the sea. Here, even here, no getting away from them.

And too late, they had seen me too. Nothing to do but carry on towards them. I tried to concentrate on her, on the small slight figure, made slighter still by the expanse of sand and sea and sky. Tried to ignore the longer, leaner shape that strode beside her, setting the pace. A fast walker, Magnus, always in a hurry. How many times had I seen Carlie having to trot to keep up?

I speeded up, the sooner so as to pass them. But as the distance closed, something in the picture changed, and the smaller, slighter figure came into focus. Not Carlie after all, but someone like her – the small dark student I had seen on stage. Prettier than Carlie, more graceful than Carlie. Younger than Carlie.

And this time it was different. I saw the girl look up at Magnus as she walked. Her face glowed. She would never be as young as she was now, never so innocent – until he took it all away And suddenly I knew: finally it was someone else's turn. This wasn't just another girl. Carlie was redundant. This was her replacement.

Magnus was frowning, a man caught out. This time he had recognised me. Deliberately I stopped. And so did they. He covered the frown with a smile that was meant to bring me on side, man to man. For a moment we stood, while the girl stared curiously from Magnus to me, wondering why neither of us spoke.

And still without a word, I turned on my heel to run back the way I had come. I had to get to Carlie before he did. Warn her of what was coming. Tell her it was finally over.

But I couldn't find her. Not in hall, not in the library, not in my own house. I ran from one end of town to the other, and the seconds ticked away. I wasted time, precious time.

It was an hour before I arrived where I should have gone first of all, at Walsh's. He wrenched open the door the moment I knocked, as if he had been waiting for me.

'Thank God,' he began as I pushed past him. 'There's all hell to pay. Your friend Carlie – she's lost it. She's trashing my house, Guy. Throwing things around.' There was a note of pettishness in his voice. The outrage of a homeowner. You never saw him without his tweed jacket nowadays.

From inside I could hear Carlie, shouting, screaming with rage. And more than anything I felt a kind of pride, joy even. Here was Carlie – angry at last, finally letting loose as she should have done years ago. Accusing, abusing. Hating. I opened the door – and with a jolt saw exactly who Carlie was screaming at. Carlie was jabbing, shreaking into the face of the other one, the younger girl who was trying to fend her off weakly with her hands, terrified.

'Carlie…' I stepped up behind her, unseen, put my hand on her shoulder. Instantly she was still, lulled by the touch. She thought I was Magnus. But when she saw who was touching her, the rage flooded back. She tried to shake off my hands and when I hung on she screamed at me, squirming and tearing at my hands till she had torn strips off the backs of them. But I didn't let her go. I held her through all the transformations – anger, violence, and finally, exhaustion. At last, panting, she stared at me, and came back. Carlie was quiet again. Slowly, unwillingly, she turned her head and looked at the other girl, her younger self.

She tried to say something to her, but the girl backed away, the horror still in her eyes. Seeing it Carlie swayed, about to fall, but I caught her. And held her. Held her closer still when, as we walked out of the front door, Magnus was there.

'Hey pumpkin…'

I felt her body quiver, but we didn't stop. I took her back to my house with its comforting reek of smoke and laundry, sat beside her on the bed.

Carlie was limp. I took her hands in mine. They were chilled, boneless. Something you could roll and shape between your palms like putty. They couldn't hurt anyone now, these hands. Her head lolled against the pillow, eyes closed.

I said, 'It wasn't your fault, Carlie. He did this. He's the one who's going to hurt her, not you.'

At once her hands slid out from under mine. Not willing to hear anything against him, not even now.

'Carlie,' I whispered. 'Didn't you see? He was watching, enjoying it all. He never tried to stop you…'

Her eyes shot open, and I saw what I had done. In attacking him, I had given her something to kick against, wiping out the exhaustion that would have kept her, here on my bed. Safe. She leapt up, unbending like a spring. In long swift strides, she headed for the door.

'Carlie! What are you going to do?'

She turned. To my amazement, her face was calm. 'What you always said I should do. Work. I've got a final tomorrow – like you , remember? It's the last one. I can't give up now. *Don't think, work.* That's what you've always said.'

'But Carlie,' I faltered. 'How are you going to be able to work – after this?'

She gave me a smile that made me shiver. Carlie's mouth was old suddenly. As if a lifetime had come and gone.

'Oh, I'll manage,' she said. 'Just like you do.'

I stared at her, defeated by my own advice. Falteringly I said, 'Alright then, Carlie. Go and work. Get tomorrow over with, then we can think about this. Together.'

I shouldn't have believed her. I should have made her stay with me. I never should have let her go. But I wanted to believe her. Because last week I had broken it to my father: I wouldn't be reading for the Bar. I wouldn't be going into Chambers. I had decided to stay here in the department, first to do research, and then, if all went well, to teach. But it all depended on me getting a First. One more night to work, then my life would be my own. This is was what Carlie had done for me. She had broken my mould. But I needed my First.

So I let Carlie go.

Chapter Nine

My final paper was set all around the Roman love poets. I stared at the questions and almost laughed out loud. Because I never needed that final night alone. I could have written this paper any time in the last three years. *Odi et amo.*

And now I was finished. And Carlie would be too.

Before starting, I had searched for her amongst the other students entering the examination halls, then remembered that the English final was in the main hall, a quarter of a mile away. That was where I needed to find her now. As I rushed out of our own exam, the two Peters caught me and tried to drag me on to the lawns with the others where they were laying out a picnic. Jennifer was already there, kneeling with a basket of strawberries beside her. She sat back on her haunches and looked at me, slowly picked up a strawberry and put it in her mouth. And suddenly, even in my rush, I saw myself, in a different life, strolling over and sitting beside her, taking a strawberry and eating it. Smiling at her. A different life. We held each other's eyes a moment and then I turned away, tore round to the other building, praying I hadn't missed Carlie.

The English students had already made their way out. There was a lot of noise with people opening champagne, laughing and crying at the same time. Over on the exam hall steps, Carlie's former flatmates were doing a kind of improvised can can, revealing suspenders and stockings, put on just for this occasion – the closest they had come to decadence in all these years. Suddenly I wondered how I could have let Carlie live with them.

I shouted into their faces, their silly young faces. 'Carlie? Where's Carlie?'

They frowned at me and carried on the dance. I went from group to group asking the same question until it began to dawn on me. No one had seen Carlie.

Racing towards her hall, I stumbled across the drive, making a bike and its rider swerve. It was Jennifer already on her way back. She had left the picnickers on the lawns. And like me, she was alone.

'Carlie,' I said. 'I can't find Carlie.'

I didn't have to say any more. She was behind me as I ran inside, down corridors that were echoing and empty. And here was Carlie's door. Locked, with no one answering.

'The caretaker,' said Jennifer and disappeared. But I wasn't about to wait. I threw myself against the door, again and again, bringing curious first years out of their rooms. The door gave way, and creaked open. The room was empty. Carlie's books were lying on the floor, the pages torn out of them, hundreds, thousands of pages fluttering up in the draft.

A girl stepped into the space behind me. 'If you're looking for Carlie, she's in the bath. She's been there all morning and no one else has had a look in, selfish cow.' Then she saw the state of Carlie's room, the ruined books, and her mouth fell open.

The bathroom. Years ago I had bathed Carlie myself. Washed and warmed her with water, and brought her back to life. 'Carlie!' I hurled myself against the bathroom door, this time with such a force it gave way straight away.

Carlie was lying in the bath, scarlet waters lapping her body. Behind me the first year girl began to squawk.

'Carlie,' I whispered. I saw her eyelids move.

Suddenly Jennifer was there too. 'Call an ambulance,' she snapped at the girl, And when she didn't move, she slapped her.

The girl disappeared and we tore up towels, turning them into tourniquets. Carlie drifted in and out of consciousness. We drained the water but, afraid to move her, we kept her in the bath, wrapped in blankets. And still it didn't seem enough. When the ambulance arrived they found me in the bath, curled around her, still trying to bring her back. Carlie, my Carlie.

Chapter Ten

At the hospital they thought I was her boyfriend. They thought I was the reason she had done it. Unfaithful, untrustworthy, undeserving, but they had to let me stay, because she said so.

I could have told them about Magnus, but I didn't. The more they treated me with veiled contempt, the closer to her it made me feel. I wanted the closeness. I wanted it in any way I could have it. And when Carlie forbade them to inform her parents, they had to turn to me instead, because who else was there?

For two days I sat by her bed and held her hand. No one had seen fit to bathe her since that last scarlet bath. There were crescents of rust under her nails and I couldn't bear it. So I put her fingers in my mouth and sucked the blood out from under them. Carlie didn't know. Carlie slept, not her usual kind of sleep – but heavy and helpless, weighed down by drugs.

Towards evening of the second day, she forced her eyes to open and stared into mine. 'Don't ..' she whispered.

'Don't what?'

'Don't let him...Don't let me...' She stopped. A tear ran down her face and into the pillow.

'I understand, Carlie.'

She sighed and went back to sleep.

Next morning, I went out into the corridor, and there was Magnus. He was bending across the ward desk, talking to the nurse, closer than he should be, bringing the pink to her cheeks. Seeing me, he pulled himself back. Yet again, I saw him frown trying to remember if I was who he thought I was.

'Hey,' he said. 'They won't let me see her. There's been some kind of mistake.'

'No mistake,' I said. 'She doesn't want to see anyone. Not yet.'

He hesitated, darted a glance at the nurse who shook her head regretfully. Then here he was again, back on the case, hunting for paper and pen. The nurse, seeing his trouble, dived into her desk and found both for him, gave them to him with a warm look. Scowled at me.

He wrote what he had to say, folded the paper over and handed it to me.

'You'll give this to her? Yeah'

I took the paper, put it in my pocket. Magnus looked at me squarely. 'You gotta give it to her. All this, it's made me realise. She's the one, fuck it. She's the One.'

Of course. Who else would actually kill herself for him? How much bigger would he ever feel than this?

Behind the desk, the nurse sighed wistfully.

I went back to Carlie. She was still asleep. I took the paper out and read it.

My Lady of light, my honeysuckle starlit girl – the demons got ya, while another demon had your demon eater by the throat. But he'll always be there from now on. He wants to marry ya, take you for his bride and nuzzle your starry cunt forever.

I went over to the basin and began to wretch. Then washing my face and drying my hands, I took the note and placed it gently in the sleeping curl of her fingers.

And straight away she began to stir. Even with the drugs, she began to stir at the touch of his words. Before I thought what I was doing, I reached out and snatched the note away. Thrust it deep into my pocket.

Carlie's eyelashes fluttered, she stared dully at her empty hand. 'I thought...'

'Thought what, Carlie?' I said hoarsely.

She lay, seeming to listen, searching through unseen space for something she half knew was there. Nothing. In her soundproofed room she could hear, see – nothing.

She shook her head, and closed her eyes again.

When I was sure she was asleep I went and threw the note down the lavatory, watched the water carry it away.

Chapter Eleven

When she came out of hospital I took her to my family's holiday cottage in the Lakes. While we were there, the exam results came out. I had my double first. Carlie, not having sat the last exam, had failed everything.

'You can appeal, Carlie,' I told her. 'You must.' But she was adamant. If she appealed it would all come out and then her parents would know how close she had come. 'They *should* know,' I told her. 'They would understand. They would want to know, Carlie.'

But there was no persuading her. And so Carlie, who once had written meticulous essays, who had been intimate with every character of every novel she had read, who had loved her course, had nothing to show for it. Only a fail. Failed Carlie.

When she was stronger, we tramped up Scafell Pike, and down into the valleys I had known since I was a child. Early summer and it was still possible to be by ourselves on the fells. Clouds moved slow as glaciers above us, making the sheep-shorn hills sit like bald giants waiting for the sun. At the top of Skidaw she opened up her arms and tried to breathe it all in, filling her lungs with something larger than herself.

She tried. She tried so hard.

One night, she found me crying in the bathroom. Crying for her, crying for me, crying for us both. Unseen, her arms came around me. And, just as once I had undressed her, she undressed me and led me quietly to her bed. I followed blind, and stepped into a dream with Carlie there to guide me. Carlie leading, then letting me lose myself in her. A dark Carlie, a hidden Carlie, with no stamp or mark on her. My Carlie.

Dreamlike, but not a dream. Just Carlie and Carlie and Carlie. She touched me and her touch was warm, showing me that she was, that we both were, still real.

She fell asleep beside me, and for the first time in weeks she

LIMERICK
COUNTY LIBRARY

smiled in her sleep. I put my head into the curve of her neck, smelt the burnt sugar smell of her skin. For the space of an hour, a night, Carlie was here, with me.

If I lost her now, after this, how would I live?

I touched her face with my fingers, her eyes, her cheek, her mouth, the cleft in her chin. I traced the line of her neck to the base where, in the dark light of dawn, there beat a single pulse. I wrapped my hands around her throat, gently, to feel the life in Carlie.

All her life depending on that one rhythm. Mine until she woke up.

Three years of watching her with someone else, watching her give herself away. And now here we were, the two of us, as if everything had happened simply to bring us to this place. Carlie slept. But what should I do now?

Keep her, or kill her.

Words so real, I could hear them whispered in my ear. In terror I jumped out of bed and cowered by the window. No one had spoken but the air shivered as if in the aftermath. In panic, I called to her from her across the room. 'Carlie.'

She opened her eyes, frowned to see me so far away.

'What is it?'

Still from the window, keeping my distance, I said, 'Marry me.'

For a moment, she said nothing, but her hands moved slowly up her body to touch her throat, curious, as if she knew that only a minute ago my hands had been there, thinking of gathering up her pulse and stopping it for ever.

Mine for ever.

Carlie touches her throat and looks at me, her eyes calm. Makes me wonder if she ever was asleep.

PART TWO

Princeofdarkness100@hotmail.com
Received 9.47am 27th January

Hey you! After all these years! Fuck, I should have married you my lady of light, you know that. We have to meet. You know that also. Contact me.

Chapter Twelve

Hey you…

I stared at the message until I thought my eyes would melt. *My lady of light…*

Only the one person used to write to her like this. *I should have married you.* I used to read the notes he'd leave for her in her room years ago – and wonder how she could have been impressed. She'd been studying English for God's sake. He wrote, talked, in superannuated hippie speak and still she had fallen for it. And kept on falling, deeper and deeper, until there was nothing there to catch her. Only me. I stopped her from falling. I picked her up and put her together. I held her together like glue that takes an age to bind. I kept on holding her.

Fifteen years we've been married, Carlie and I.

Now he's back. A Blast from the Past. *We have to meet.*

She must have put herself on the website everyone seems to be talking about. That's even the name of it – *Blastfromthepast.com.* There hasn't been a dinner party in months where someone hasn't mentioned it, harking back to the old days, as if the present just isn't enough. She must have put her name in, made herself a sitting target. She must have known the danger. What was she thinking of?

Who was she thinking of?

Contact me

Outside the window, I hear the car door slam. She's back, bringing David home from football practice. He's jumped out of the car as if he were on springs, is already on the lawn kicking the ball. Carlie, however, is all stillness, standing as she often stands, gazing up into the trees. I don't have to see her expression. Inward-looking, features calm, giving nothing away. If I were to ask her what she was thinking – and sometimes I still do – she would smile and touch the side of her face. As if to check there's nothing there, nothing that tells a story.

And 'Nothing,' is what she would say to me. 'Nothing worth the mention.' My enigmatic Carlie, who used to tell me everything. Yet, after touching her face, she will invariably touch me, her fingers warm on my cheek; and the warmth will be a reminder that I am, that we are, still real. The reason I still ask Carlie what she is thinking.

David is kicking his ball perilously close to the windows of the summer house. I should call out and tell him to stop. One word – it's all it would take. Our son listens to me. It grieves me how he listens to me.

But the message is there on the screen. *Hey you!* The backs of my hands are tingling and I don't care to think about windows or anything else. Except Carlie. And *him*, the blast from the past. Besides, if I shouted out of this window I would be giving myself away. I am in Carlie's room, next to her desk, staring at her computer. I only came up here because a small smiley face suddenly leapt on to the screen of mine, and started gobbling up the words of the Opinion I was writing. A virus eating away at a morning's work. I should have gone into Chambers and done it there, with a library of law books around me. But I wanted to be home. With them, Carlie and David. It's the weekend.

And now I have to cut off the machine and pretend I've never been here. And hurry. Carlie has given herself that little waking shake I've seen so many times. She has come back, really come back. She is calling to David to come away from the summer house with the ball. And he, with the attentiveness of all twelve year olds, is fondly ignoring her. As he never ignores me.

I watch her walk towards the house, the composed sway of her hips, my beautiful Carlie. Who has made herself a sitting target.

What is she thinking of?

Who is she thinking of? Is she going to tell me about this, the blast from the past?

The old Carlie never walked like this. She ran, stumbled, tripped, danced, but the old Carlie is gone. I was there when it happened, when Carlie took the girl she was and folded her up like a rag doll and hid her out of sight. I watched her re-make herself, and marvelled at the result.

So where is the Carlie I fell in love with? Gone. And where is the Carlie I fell in love with? Here. Quiet Carlie, composed Carlie. Who occasionally touches my face and reminds me she is, that we still are, real. Qualities like *quiet* and *composed* can be donned like masks. In the dark, we recognise each other by touch, like blind people. Like lovers.

Somewhere Carlie is, old or new. Fifteen years. We are still here.

And now this.

Hey you!

When I come downstairs she is cutting up salad for lunch. She tilts her head as I enter, smiles at me. He has found a way back in and yet I can see no change in her, no ripple in her universe.

'I'm going to have to go into Chambers,' I say.

Her hands continue to chop. The hair swings away from the face. Longer now, the curls, like everything else, kept under control.

'Why?'

'My computer's on the blink. I can't access a file I need.'

Now, now would be the moment for her to tell me to use her computer instead. I watch the knife pause above a piece of cucumber and hold my breath.

And Carlie says, 'Don't be late coming back, will you. We're out for dinner tonight.'

A soft fall inside me.

I take her car with its scents of Carlie and of mud and grass from David's football boots *why didn't Carlie invite me to use her computer* and head towards the M 40. But first I have to drive through Patersfield.

There are small mounds of dirty snow left over from last week's fall, banked up beside the road like rubbish no one has bothered to collect. It never amounted to anything much here, this winter's snow. Weather in general never seems to amount to much in Patersfield, too far away from sea or mountains for serious precipitations. Too temperate for drought or flood. Today, though, we see a change. Patersfield is going through the motions of Saturday morning.

You can see it's a Saturday just from the number of men. In the week, says Carlie, it's as if there's a war on. The men are all absent, up in town or further afield, leaving the wives to their own devices. It's a time warp, says Carlie *why didn't she invite me to use her computer.* Large, serviced houses with women who don't work. People who have lived overseas, who have got used to the ex pat life, choose here to live when they come back. The rhythms are the same. There are bridge parties and charity auctions, book clubs whose memberships are vetted and controlled by the few as surely as by MI5. There are as many au pairs on the street as there are teenagers. Slovakian is fast becoming the second language of Patersfield.

Did we know this when we came here? I can't remember. I know we chose it, Carlie and I, because we thought it was safe, as far as it was possible to be from sea and skies and words whipped away by the wind *why didn't Carlie tell me to use her computer.*

The traffic moves so slowly that the passenger in the car ahead of me has time to jump out, dash into the Italian deli, and return with a large parcel wrapped up in wax paper. It is Jonathan Stackpole who with his wife Lydia will be giving us supper tonight. He spots me behind my wheel and waves.

I wave back. And in that instant I am able to breathe again.

Everything is familiar – whether it's the faces in the street, or the known scents of Carlie and David all around me. This is Patersfield. This is where we are. The Past is a place of old stone and sea, and brief intense summer nights. We are not the children that we were.

In contrast to Patersfield, there's barely a soul about in Lincoln's Inn. I walk into Chambers and let myself into my room. The work I lost on my home computer reshapes itself on the screen and an hour later it's a job well done. I can spare everyone an expense of a trial on this one if they listen to me, which they probably will. People tend to listen to me, the way they listened to my father. He died thirteen years ago, just before David was born. He only met Carlie once, after the wedding. And what he thought of her, he kept to himself.

This was his room. On the facing wall is the poster I pinned up years ago – a young Graeco-Roman girl, her living portrait preserved on the lid of her coffin. She stares out at me, sucking the end of her pen, her dark hair curly, threaded through with ribbon. She's been dead these two thousand years, but here she is today, lively and studious, a sparkle in her eyes. Forever young.

She has the look of Carlie to her. The Carlie I used to know.

Apart from the poster, the room is exactly as my father left it. The heavy oak desk was his desk. The prints on the wall are pictures he chose when he was young – drawings of classical ruins he visited while doing Greats, before he followed his own father into law. I always meant to change it, bring in some modern furniture, but I never did get round to it. In the meantime other people made changes for themselves. Six months after my father died, my mother phoned to tell me she had married Barry, the local painter and decorator who had done odd jobs for her all through the years they had lived in the village. I used to play with his son when I came home in the holidays, until he dropped me for other boys who were there all the year round.

'You don't mind *too* much, do you darling?' she said to me, not about the marriage, but her other news – that she was selling the house I grew up in. I went down to pick up my father's law library, and his oil can for oiling the locks – and listened to my mother showing a footballer and his wife around the house. She and Barry moved to the Costa Blanca, where Barry does odd jobs for elderly Brits. My mother runs a donkey sanctuary. The rare times I see her, she wears a sarong – and a faintly sheepish, happy look that she tries to hide from me. She doesn't keep dogs any more.

Somewhere else in Chambers a chair scrapes across the floor. I am not alone. I put my head outside the room.

'Gary?'

Only the one person it could be. Gary the senior clerk appears round the door of the office. Does he never go home? Does he even have a home to go to?

'Mr. Latimer.' His thin face smiles, approving. He likes his briefs to be hard at work, even on Saturdays, like he is now. He's been here from the day he left school. Something else left over from my father.

'You should be at home, Mr Latimer, enjoying the weekend.' But he doesn't mean it.

'You look nice, Carlie.'

I mean beautiful. Carlie's eyes flicker carelessly towards the mirror. Years ago the old Carlie took an hour to dress and still looked as if she had thrown the contents of a drawer together in the dark. Now she takes no time at all, and the result is...this. Clothes that leave you noticing the woman, and only then what she is wearing.

Of course I mean beautiful. But she knows that.

Doesn't she?

Hey you...

Lydia Stackpole has wrapped wedges of dolcelatte in

swathes of Parma ham, waxy as the paper it came home in. It's the sort of thing we would serve to her and Jonathan – and have done time and time again. Carlie and Lydia met during NCT classes and have been friends ever since.

I like Lydia. She reminds me of the girls I grew up with. Big jolly county girls who stepped on your feet during dancing lessons, who walked like ducks and never quite turned into swans. She is large-boned, wholesome as the hockey player she used to be. And generous, the sort of woman who should have had a brood of children following her round like a litter of puppies. As it is, she and Jonathan have only the one son, Angus.

Over the years, Patersfield - or perhaps repeated miscarriages - have toned her down, made her sleeker, quieter than I remember her. But she can still honk like a tug boat if you make her laugh. And she's probably the only woman I know who cuts her own hair. Some of it has ended up amongst my ham, which with a little effort I manage to remove without her seeing. Lydia has many virtues, including warmth, loyalty and a kind of headgirl sweetness that has never gone away - but cooking is not amongst them.

Jonathan Stackpole is a solicitor, and briefs me sometimes. It happens a lot in Patersfield; the wives meet and the husbands send work in each other's direction. He is short and used to be slight, although lately he has been growing increasingly pear shaped. He has carved out a small area of expertise in planning law and is completely comfortable with what he knows. Everything about Jonathan seems comfortable, smoothed out by use, including his relationship with Lydia.. Since his waistline increased he has started wearing his father's old suits which naturally no one has ever thought to throw away. Perhaps it's the clothes that keep him looking - even at the age of forty and broad in the beam - still boyish.

He is comfortable with his son, too. Angus was born at the same time as David, and would be in the same class if they

were at the same school. But David goes to the local comprehensive and Angus attends a prep school just up the road.
Next year Angus will sit his common entrance and their paths
will widen still further. This is something Carlie held out for:
a state school, the sort she went to – and in which she thrived.
I remembered my own days and entirely agreed – except it
grieves me that they offer Latin, but not Greek.

Lydia says we can afford to send him to a state school
because he is clever and would do well anywhere. Strange,
what people mean when they say *afford*.

The other couple here we try to avoid, but there is no
escaping them tonight, or any time. This is Patersfield where
the orbits are as established as the solar system, and Vanessa
and Miles are regular as the stars that come out at night. We
have known them almost as long as Lydia and Jonathan.
Vanessa is blonde - or pretends to be - pencil thin and wears
low, close-fitting tops, loud in the sense that they speak vol-
umes. Unlike Lydia, she was never sweet. The lean lines of her
face are airbrushed, eyes rimmed with black, and she has a
mouth that could be any shape under the lipstick. At this
moment she is smirking, having watched me remove the rogue
hair from my plate.

Smirking and avoiding having to look at her husband. Miles
is overweight and sullen, watches her all the time – when he's
not covertly eyeing Carlie. It can't be food that has bulked
him out. Tonight, as always, he is ignoring what is on his plate,
committing himself instead to the wine. He attacks it with a
dedication that reminds me of boys I knew at school, the ones
who were bullied, relentlessly; who raided their tuck boxes
and those of others for the only comfort available. Miles and
Vanessa, naturally, have no children.

I have the feeling the Lydia and Jonathan have only asked
us so as to smooth what would otherwise be a difficult
evening. This is fine. We've done the same to them in the past.

We are comfortable with Jonathan and Lydia; and David and Angus are close despite their diverging education. Lydia is the nearest Carlie has to a best friend.

Yet Lydia, oddly, is the one I have to blame. She started it all. Lydia is the reason that an email has appeared on Carlie's computer, searing a hole in the present.

But it only comes clear to me now, tonight, as she chortles over the latest news from Cassandra and Cressida and Saskia – women, like Lydia herself, whose names have the cadences of nymphs from a Classical landscape, but turn out to be big strapping girls last seen in the Upper Sixth, twenty years ago.

'Honestly it's *incredible*. People you haven't seen in yonks – suddenly there they are, at the other end of the machine. You just bash in *Blastfromthepast* and hey presto! It's fantastic, you can catch up with absolutely everybody. Some have been through the mill though, bless them. Divorces and all that. Cassandra's had both breasts removed, but God, she's cheerful. She sounds just like when she had the accident with the thresher during the hols and was bandaged right up to her thighs all term. I can't wait to see her. We're going to have a meeting, all of us, a proper reunion.'

She pauses for breath, panting slightly.

'Why on earth would you want to do that?' says Miles, eyeing his glass which has become empty. 'If you didn't care what happened to them years ago, why go overboard now?'

Lydia squeals and rocks in her chair. 'Because you're *wrong*. Of course I cared. We all cared. It's life that gets in the way. You leave school swearing to keep in touch and next thing you know, you're running around some appalling office for some awful boss who only wants to grope your breasts. Then you meet someone and it's all nappies and kids. Downhill from then on.' Jonathan pretends to look put out at this, but Lydia ignores him. 'Now there's this fantastic site, and everybody's getting on to it.'

'Well, you won't catch me going near it,' says Miles heavily. 'Worst bloody days of my life, school. Too pretty for my own good, that was my problem.' He smirks as he speaks, and Carlie catches my eye. She's thinking the same as me: Miles was never pretty.

Lydia shakes her head. She's counting names on her fingers, of people we know who have been drawn to the website. 'There's Tony and Tanya, Roberta and George…there's even Carlie, though we all had to nag her. Remember that evening, Carlie, when you tried to have nothing to do with it? We practically had to arm-wrestle you into going on line.'

Vanessa says smoothly, '*I* didn't nag you, Carlie. Leave the past alone, that's what I say.'

Lydia clears her throat. 'You weren't there, Vanessa.'

Vanessa raises one thin, well plucked brow and yawns. 'Wasn't I? Oh well, I forget. Evenings do tend to merge into one another, don't you find?'

I am watching Carlie from across the table. Her eyes are downcast, hidden from me. Can you actually arm-wrestle someone into doing something they don't want to do, to tap a name where anyone could find it? Just how reluctant was Carlie? Really?

'Can't it be rather dangerous,' I say mildly. 'Getting involved in something like this? *Isn't* the past sometimes better left alone?'

And still I watch Carlie, wanting her to speak. Instead it's Vanessa who answers: 'Why's that, Guy? Too many skeletons in the cupboards? Scared the past will come back and bite you?'

'*I'm* not scared,' says Lydia. 'I loved my life back then. Loved it. I'd love it to come back and bite me,' she stops and darts a glance at Jonathan, colours slightly and giggles.

'I just think sometimes things are better left alone.' My words sound lame to my own ears, and I can't seem to make Carlie look at me.

'Oh?' says Vanessa. She leans towards me, her voice smooth. I can see the pulse in the base of her neck beating a rhythm, like someone tapping their fingers on a table. 'Can you give us an example?'

I shrug and Vanessa throws back her head. 'Typical man! Laying down the law then refusing to give reasons. Why shouldn't people visit the past? Isn't that what we're supposed to do? Work for closure and all that? If there's unfinished business, then finish it. Put those bad old ghosts to bed. Or, failing that...' she pauses and her eyes glitter – is this woman stroking my foot with hers? '...you could just climb into bed again with them yourself. Talk about closure! That should put an end to something.'

Miles sniggers, then frowns, gives her sharp glance.

Lydia says hotly. 'That's *not* what the website is about, Vanessa. It's just a way of finding out about people who meant something to you...'

'Oh,' says Vanessa triumphantly. 'You mean curiosity. Well, of course. Who doesn't want to find out what happened to the poor sod you left bleeding – or better still, who left *you* bleeding in a puddle of gore yourself?'

Lydia makes an impatient noise. Vanessa waves a hand tipped with nails like small, stiffened red flags. 'Don't look so cross, Lydia. I'm sure *your* motives are perfectly pure. But Guy has just mentioned that he thinks the site might be dangerous, and I'm simply saying – despite what the agony aunties tell us – that maybe I agree with him. What's so wonderful about the past? Unless of course it's the present you really can't stand. Remember – some folk you lost touch with because they were just plain nasty, or worse still – *boring.* And I haven't even said a word, *yet,* about the biggest danger of all, the thing that will really get you – if you don't look out.'

She looks around the dinner table, holding her fire, waiting for the moment. This woman would make an excellent barrister.

A voice makes itself heard. Smooth, curious. Composed. 'And what is that, Vanessa? What's the biggest danger of all?' Finally Carlie has spoken.

Vanessa allows herself a small triumphant smile.

'Why, the *scavengers,* darling. Wolves and hyenas. Blood suckers. People who remember they once had something good...and let it go. Not so choosy now, though – how could they be after all these years? So back they crawl to pick over the bones, see what they can find. This website is a feast for the likes of them. They're out there, just you watch. Look out for the scavengers. And don't say I didn't warn you.'

There's a silence round the table. Lydia murmurs, 'For goodness sakes, Vanessa, I'm talking about getting in touch with some old friends, that's all. Girls I absolutely adored at the time...'

'...Red hot chums in the dorm eh?' chimes in Miles. 'I'll drink to that.' Tired of waiting to be asked, he reaches out and helps himself to another glass of wine.

There follows an unspoken agreement to concentrate on our food.

Lydia gives us a pleading look as we leave, but we've done our duty. In the car, I say to Carlie, 'Did you know that Vanessa was stroking my foot all evening?'

She laughs, but says nothing. What was I hoping for? That by making one pseudo-confession to her, I could make her come up with one, real, confession to me?

But Carlie, who used to tell me everything, has nothing to say, not about this. She leans her head back against the seat and shuts her eyes. It's as if it never happened; no email, no history, no blast from the past. But it has happened. It's happening now.

Hey you...

Where are the ripples in Carlie's world? Is she going to answer him?

Chapter Thirteen

David wants to know if he can take his skateboard down to Angus's house.

Normally he would ask Carlie, but she's out. It's something I'm noticing more and more: if David has anything to say, he says it to Carlie. For a moment I can only look at him and frown as if I've barely understood the question. He's found me sitting at my desk, staring at the wall. A new way of working, he'll think.

Hey…you

Eventually I manage to answer him. 'Where are you thinking of going with them, your skateboards?' Boarding has been banned from the pavements of Patersfield, having a tendency to knock the feet out of the people loading up their 4 x 4s by the sides of the road. Or else they plough straight out into traffic. Bull bars get scuffed.

He names a skate park about six miles away, adding, 'Jonathan will take us. He always does if you ask him.'

My son has eyes like Carlie's, but in all other respects looks as I did at twelve. This means he's smaller than other boys, almost fragile looking. His growth spurt won't kick in till later, when he will shoot up past his contemporaries. For a while, he won't know what to do with his arms and legs which will suddenly seem too long for his body, or feet that have a mind of their own; and all of it happening at a time long after other boys have already settled into their own bodies. I would like to tell him this, give him some warning, but what can you say to a boy who lately seems to find every conversation awkward?

Only with me, though. Never with Carlie. Until last year he was as much mine as hers, slotting himself beside me, friendly, badgering, making the weekends his, time to be spent with him. Never taking *no* or *later* for an answer. My boy too, from the moment he was born. Now, this recent awkwardness that's come with his age, I recognise this in him too. It happened with me and my father, whom I never disliked for any reason; yet still the distance grew up between us, deepening and widening as the years went by. A matter for regret, never discussed.

'I could take you to the skate park, if you like. You and Angus…'

But my son is looking embarrassed, and I know why. They could ignore Jonathan, pretend he wasn't there. Not me, though. Somehow not me.

Better if I went with him though. Better not to be left alone in the house, with only one thing on my mind. But the front door slams behind him, and here I am – alone.

What is Carlie going to do about the message? How can I know if she won't tell me?

Easily.

All I have to do is switch it on – Carlie's computer, Carlie's mailbox. Carlie's things. And that is why it would be so much better if I had gone with David. Because this is Carlie who for fifteen years has never failed to notice when I walk into a room, who touches my cheek when she thinks I am asleep; and this is Carlie's computer. If I switched it on I would be searching through Carlie's things. Like a thief, like a husband admitting he doesn't trust his wife.

Hey you…

Downstairs the front door slams again. Carlie is back. She looks up as I enter the kitchen, as she always does, and something makes me march straight over to her and take her in my arms. *Could I do this if I had just been sniffing through the contents of her computer?* She smiles at me and puts her own arms around my neck. Where are the ripples in Carlie's world?

'David not here?'

'He's gone rollerblading with Angus. Or do I mean skateboarding? He'll be gone for hours.'

I lead her upstairs again and we undress and lie down together. We make love quickly, quietly, as if David could still return at any moment. Afterwards, with the urgency past, Carlie stares at the ceiling, drowsy, so I wonder if she is about to fall asleep. But that doesn't happen nowadays. She always finds a reason to rouse herself, a reason to be busy. And yet I am happy. Her fingers, her touch, were warm on my body, reminding me that I am, we both are, still real. *Do you love me, Carlie?* I know the answer. Without a word spoken Carlie tells me every day.

It's only as I watch her dress, covering herself again, that it occurs to me. We both have a secret, Carlie and I. We both know something we think the other doesn't. And just now we have managed to hide it completely from the other. Neither of us has given ourselves away.

Next day, I watch Carlie at breakfast, sitting at the table, her lips resting against the rim of her cup. All night long I listened to her breathe, softly, regularly. I watch her now, her eyes a little dreamy, but rested. Sleep came easily to Carlie, unlike me.

David gulps the last of his tea and leaves the room – and Carlie doesn't seem to notice. She has put down her cup, is staring at the small beads of coffee grounds, frowning slightly.

'*What are you thinking, Carlie?*'

She doesn't look up, never bats an eyelid. Then it occurs to me that I hadn't actually spoken the words aloud. Carlie's things, Carlie's thoughts. Suddenly I need to know. How do I begin to ask her to speak to me again the way she used to speak, every thought, every ripple accounted for?

'*What are you thinking, Carlie?*'

This time I have said the words aloud, and she looks up. Her forehead clears. 'I was thinking I didn't like this coffee this morning. It's too…bitter.'

She smiles, and at the same time reaches for the pot, pours

herself another cup. She is carrying it as she follows me to the door and kisses me goodbye.

And what will she do then, when the door closes behind me, and David has left for school? What will Carlie do with her day?

Jonathan comes jogging on to the platform just as the train is moving out. He catches a door as it's closing and hauls himself aboard, plumps himself beside me, sweating, and exuding scents of bacon and egg. He grins and shakes out his newspaper before turning to the law reports. In less than five minutes his head will nod into his chest and he will spend the rest of the journey asleep, breathing heavily. I know quite a lot of what Jonathan does with his day.

'So what's Lydia planning on doing?'

There's a pause. He looks up from his paper. 'What did you say?'

'Today. Lydia – what will she do with herself today?'

He gives me another, doubtful, look. The question has thrown him. 'God I don't know. This and that. Manages to keep herself busy, *she says*. Always going on about how she's worn out – that much I know. Too tired for much of the old you-know-what.'

'Tired from doing what, though?'

'Christ! Don't ask me. The house is always a mess so I know that's something she *doesn't* do. Probably playing around on that bloody website. She's hardly been off it recently. Ask her where supper was last night. Ask what happened to cooking as a way of wearing herself out.'

He sounds irritated, holds the newspaper up in front of his face, his arms stiff. He doesn't want any more questions like these. Perhaps he has no real sense of Lydia existing, except when he is there. Or maybe it's just the website that's annoying him, taking up Lydia's time, taking her back in time.

There was a time that Carlie was never so real as in her

absence. I knew what she did with her day: what she did with *him*. She told me, everything, whether I wanted to hear it or not. Thanks to Carlie, I used to see her, so clearly, and in outlines so hard I had to run away from them – images of Carlie with *him*, a Carlie too real to be denied. She made me follow her through walls and doors, unable to turn away from what I saw.

And when it stopped, when Carlie became mine, she stopped telling me. Carlie's day became Carlie's business. There was no need to tell me anything. Not in words. In the dark we found each other, like blind people, like lovers. There were no hidden places in our house, nothing the other needed to know.

Until now.

I know where Carlie is. Carlie is at home. And I have absolutely no idea what she does with her day.

I phone her at ten in the morning, and there's no answer. I spend the morning in court and phone her again during the lunchtime adjournment. She answers. We talk, I tell her how the case is going. She listens patiently, without mentioning the obvious – that I never usually discuss cases with her the way I'm doing now. Why should I? It's too dry what I do, questions of law too abstract for normal conversation.

I phone again when I come out of the courtroom at four, with the client at my shoulder and the solicitor expecting to hear the plan for the next day. All I want is to hear her voice, to know what she is doing. She tells me she's busy, someone has come to the door. She promises to phone me back. And she doesn't.

Back in my room the Graeco Roman girl in the poster sucks her pen and watches me. I tell myself to trust her, trust Carlie. I tell myself she is past thinking about the Past. She is past thinking about *him*. That's why there are no visible ripples in Carlie's world. He is done and dusted and put away.

The girl in the poster looks quizzical and I drag my eyes

away, back to the papers on my desk. And look what I've done – while telling myself to trust Carlie, I have doodled *his* name all over the cover of a brief. I can't make myself believe a word I've been saying.

Hey you...

At home, Carlie comes off the phone from her mother.

'How is she?' I ask.

She shakes her head. Carlie's father died last year after a short intense illness that no one was prepared for. We travelled north to look after Carlie's mother – only to find ourselves looked after. In fact she barely ever came out of the kitchen.

'Eight cigarettes a day, that's all he ever smoked. Where's the justice?' she said to me once, wearily from the stove. She sighed then squared her shoulders. 'Listen to me complaining, we had a good long time – longer than your poor mum and dad. How is she, anyway, your mother?'

'Fine,' I said, embarrassed to say how very fine. On the Costa Blanca, in addition to the donkey sanctuary, she and Barry were now taking in paying guests, with full English breakfasts a speciality.

'And Carlie? How's she?'

'She's here...' I was surprised by the question. 'You can see for yourself...'

'No, Guy, I can't. I can't see anything with Carlie. Neither of us could – not me, nor Jack, not since the day she left home. She never told us...' There was a silence in the kitchen. We were both thinking about the faint white tramlines on Carlie's wrists. Never asked about, never explained – therefore never the need for her to hear Carlie lie. 'You're the only one who knows what's going on in that head of hers. How many years is it now – since the two of you were wed? You tell me how she is.'

She saw the look on my face.

'Ah well. Maybe time doesn't mean a thing. Maybe none of us knows anything for sure, not even about the folk we know best. Take my Jack. That day they told him about the cancer, he didn't look surprised. Not a bit of it. He pretended to be shocked, but he couldn't do anything about that first look of his. He must have guessed long ago, it was right there in the bones and he knew it – and he'd never said a word. And there was me thinking I knew the man, inside and out. And it was the bones that killed him.'

She wiped her eyes fiercely with the back of an oven glove. 'So there we are. We tell ourselves we know a person, and in the end all we have is what they want us to have.' She turned away from me to put the lid on a saucepan. Then suddenly she turned back again. '*Watch her* though, Guy,' her voice was fierce, almost hissing the words. 'Watch Carlie. She buries things. Too deep. She'll end up not knowing there's a difference between secrets and lies. Don't let her do it, Guy, love.'

She blinked, as if shaken by her own vehemence. I touched her arm. 'Come on.' I said gently. 'Come away from the stove. Come into the sitting room with Carlie and David. Be with us.'

She leant against my hand for a moment, then stood up straight. 'No.' Her voice was firm. 'If I step out of the kitchen, I'll see he's not sitting in that bloody armchair of his, and I'll end up crying for a month. Not ready, son. Not ready.'

Asked about her mother now, Carlie shakes her head and leaves the room. I watch her go, the composed sway of her hips. So much I suddenly don't know.

Her computer sits on a desk upstairs.

Now the phone rings again. This time Carlie isn't here to answer it. She's somewhere in the house, busy with David. Or something. It occurs to me I don't even know what Carlie does when she leaves the room.

I pick up to hear Vanessa on the other end. I tell her Carlie is busy, and wait for her to ring off. But she does no such thing. She seems to want to talk to me.

'You really must come round, the two of you. Have dinner with us, just the four of us. Won't that be fun?'

'Of course.'

Again I wait for her to hang up. Instead Vanessa says, 'I hope Miles didn't upset Carlie too much the other night.'

'Upset Carlie?' I say. 'How?'

'Going on and on about that bloody website...like a dog with a bone. He wouldn't let it lie, silly man.'

If memory serves me, it was Vanessa who went on about it. I say, 'I rather think it was Lydia who might have...'

'She just went quiet, didn't she? Carlie I mean. Very...' Vanessa pauses, choosing her words '...Still. That's what made me realise he'd said something to upset her. Although of course it's so difficult to tell with Carlie. She's so awfully deep. I'm sure it must scare the pants off some people. It would send Miles round the bend. I'm the sort who likes to come clean about what's inside her head. If I think it, I say it. He likes that. Most men do, I've found – a woman who's direct about what she's thinking.' She pauses. 'Do *you* like a woman to tell you what she's thinking, Guy?'

I say nothing.

Vanessa laughs. 'Dear God, you're as bad as she is. You must have some awfully silent evenings round your house.'

'We have David,' I say shortly. 'It's hard to be quiet when there's a boy around.'

'Ah yes, David. Mind you, I've always thought he was a silent thing too. Not at all like noisy little whatshisname – Angus. Anyway, ignore me, I'm only teasing. I'm sure your house is chock full of life and laughs. Tell Carlie I phoned, though – next time you talk to her. We'll fix a date for that dinner, just the four of us this time. Lydia and Jonathan are *sooo* sweet, but just a little too jolly for me...'

I hang up.

I tell Carlie and she makes a face.

'We don't have to go,' I say. 'We'll make an excuse.'

'That won't work. She'll just keep asking. There'll be no getting out of it.'

'Can't you stop seeing her?'

She shrugs. 'How? This is Patersfield. This is where we live. She comes with the territory. You can't escape her.'

Suddenly, she has made Patersfield sound like a landscape, a terrain to be inhabited, with all the pitfalls and dangers of the wild. Is *this* what Carlie does with her day, trying to avoid the likes of Vanessa?

'Is it that bad?' I say.

Carlie smiles. 'Just think of Vanessa as a she-fox. You'll know to jump down the nearest hole when you see her.'

'That would make me a rabbit. But what about Miles? If she's a fox, what is he?'

'Prey,' she says promptly. 'Something she carries around with her. Half dead, but always there when there's nothing else to snack on.' She stops, as if surprised by the acid in her tone.

There's a silence between us, a shared sympathy for the lame. Are we among them, Carlie and I, the timid and the lame? Is that why we are here in Patersfield, far from sea and stone? Yet we have been happy. We had a battle to fight, the two of us, and we have won it year by year, little by little. We arrived as walking wounded, but we healed each other, and we did it here in this place. We put our faith in each other.

Whatever the reason, we are here together, the two of us. And suddenly I need her to talk to me.

Faith and trust. Trust me, Carlie.

'Carlie,' I say. 'Vanessa thought Miles upset you the other night, talking about that website. Did he? We were all talking about the past – except for you. Was there something about it – the website – that made you go quiet?'

Another silence. Different this time. I watch Carlie, watch her hand go up to touch her face, testing, making sure she is giving nothing away.

And Carlie says. 'Of course not. It was a silly conversation. Why should it upset me?'

I open my mouth to tell her why. Then close it again. From upstairs David calls for Carlie and she leaves to see what it is he wants.

Carlie has told me nothing. And I know what I have to do. I have no choice.

She's gone out, taking David to Scouts.

I press a key and her computer begins to hum, all the pixels firing. I log in with her password, and there, in her mailbox is...

...Nothing.

The mail box is empty. No message, *and no reply*. Relief sweeps over me, feels like warm rain on my head and hands. I reach to shut the computer down. And then I have a thought. *Don't turn it off. You haven't looked. Not properly.*

My hands shake, but they can't be stopped. I know how to do this. I have lost too much work over the years not to know. Now I can delete whole files in error without having to hang around in Chambers waiting for a technician. I can get what I need and we can all go home.

I *am* home. And on Carlie's computer, amongst Carlie's deleted files, just as I expected – *Hey you...*

And another message. I close my eyes. Open them again to read.

My lady, what is your problem. Why won't you answer me? Has you grown fat? Or bald? If you won't talk to me, then what else can I think? Regent's Park, my fat princess, ten o' clock in the Rose Garden. Tuesday.

I look for Carlie's reply. Somehow I know there will be a

reply. I search through a deleted outbox. And there it is, Carlie's answer – two answers, one sent only moments after the other:

No.

No.

I switch off the machine. Tuesday. Tomorrow. But Carlie has said no, not once but twice. Did she mean to, or was something else at work, making her hit the same button twice over?

Carlie comes home with David, and the three of us eat together. She tells us both she's tired and will go to bed straight after David. I believe her. Tonight she looks tired. Strained.

If she's tired then she should sleep. But when I turn off the light, she lies beside me in the dark, scarcely breathing. What is she thinking?

'Go to sleep, Carlie,' I say at last.

She catches her breath. And yet something seems to ease inside her and presently I hear her breathing again, soft and regular. The sound of Carlie sleeping.

Half past nine in the morning and Gary leans through my door.

'Your preliminary hearing is off, Mr. Latimer. Judge has gone down with food poisoning. Nothing till tomorrow now. Sends his apologies and all that. It's good though. You can get on with that Inland Revenue case...'

I don't answer. Half past nine and I don't have to be in court. For a moment I stare at my desk, then at my Graeco-Roman girl. I reach out and phone home.

And there is no answer.

I cast my mind over Carlie's day. Half past nine. She could be shopping. She could be vacuuming and hasn't heard the phone. She could be sitting in the kitchen with Lydia, picking over the dinner party and Vanessa's body language.

Or she could be on the train to Marylebone, making her way to Regents Park, and the Rose Garden.

Listen to yourself. Carlie said no. Twice.

I open up a set of papers and get to work. But the words on the brief bear no relation to any language I know.

Carlie said.

Carlie said no.

Carlie said no – twice.

I put my head round the clerks' door. They glance up from their computers. Nothing in their faces suggests I am looking anything but normal. 'I'm going home to work. Don't bother to transfer any calls.'

Baker Street, and the sun shines with a leaden February light. Winter, the dead time. The traffic moves between the lights, oddly muted as if the cold has put a lid on the sound. People walk with their heads down, muffled up against the wind and the fumes.

Then I step into the Park and everything changes. The air empties, clarifies so you can hear the clatter of pram wheels from yards away. And there are roses everywhere, all colours, in full bloom. These bushes must have had the same snow we had last week, and still they stand with petals unfurled like summer flags. Here, and only here, winter has lost its grip. Even the air is faintly scented, as if summer has just breezed this way, and we have all trooped in after it. There are people about, lots of them – mothers with their pushchairs, old folk feeding the pigeons, boys on skateboards ducking off school. Makes my mind flit to David.

It's not just Carlie and me now, in danger.

But no sign of *him*. And no sign of her either. On my watch, the hour hand has slid off the ten. And, irrationally, I am outraged on Carlie's behalf. He is late – if he is coming at all. Late for Carlie after all these years, happy to make her think he wasn't going to turn up. Like he always did.

But two minutes later a shape appears, gathering substance behind some adults with a gaggle of foreign children. A head taller than everyone here, walking with that long loping stride I would know anywhere. Hands in his pocket, a scarf around his neck. Closing in.

Magnus. Fifteen years and here he is again. I thought I was prepared, but the sight of him has put me into shock, freezing me to the spot. Instead of moving out of the way, I sink down onto the bench beside the path, watching him come, shivering, waiting to be discovered – only to see him stride straight past me, yards away from where I'm sitting. As always, he hasn't recognised me.

And after the first, a second shock – different this time – of seeing him close up. For in those first few moments, from a distance, he had had me fooled. Same walk, same mane of black hair, same face of a wolf sniffing opportunity on the wind – all making me think he hadn't changed, that time hadn't touched him. Then he walks within ten feet of me, and I see how wrong I was. Time has been hard at work here. The black hair is dyed, not even very well; too matt, too black, evidence of job done on the cheap, by himself probably. And the face, the face is ravaged, every line, every furrow the logical outcome of what was there before, ploughed in by the years. He has the patina of age and use and repair. I see him and something inside me wants to laugh out loud.

Magnus has not aged well.

Now I can watch him, almost admiring the bravado of the walk and the pelt of dyed hair. I notice the clothes he is wearing – good quality, but shabby, obviously picked out second hand. I see all this and know what has happened: the years have passed and he has stood still. Somewhere nearby will be the bedsit he stepped out of this morning, another room in another person's house. And his job? If he has one it won't be in a university. That will have been squandered with everything else. This is a man who has cannibalised his own life. I look at him and I know all this as surely as I've always known him.

And suddenly, maliciously, I find myself wishing that Carlie were here. That she could see him, see what he has become.

Yet we should be careful what we wish for – because suddenly, with another kind of shock, I see her. Carlie has come. She walks with the sun behind her, towards the garden, face turned to one side, unwilling to look ahead. Everything about the way she moves is unwilling. Her body has the flexed, backward lean of someone caught on the end of an invisible thread which is reeling her in, slowly.

Two threads. I wished her here, and here she is. Behind Magnus, there is me. I am not in the least invisible. If she can see past him, she will see me, sitting on the bench.

But Carlie is not using her eyes. She comes to a stop in front of Magnus and still she doesn't look at him. She stands with her gaze fixed on the ground beside him, so he is the one able to take his time and look, take the measure of my wife. Makes me think he has the advantage.

Then slowly, she lifts her head, looks straight at him. And suddenly I understand it's no advantage after all. Because now when Carlie looks up, she is not fooled as I was at a distance. She is able to observe Magnus exactly as he is.

And this is what she does. She gazes at him, intently, absolutely still. Moments pass and not a word is spoken. This is all about seeing: with this first long look, she is capturing him, fixing him onto the cells at the backs her eyes. Taking her time, allowing the new image to overlay the old that has been there all these years. Magnus as he now is.

What can it be like, subjected to that long, diminishing stare? I expect to see him falter, rocked by Carlie's gaze. But I underestimated him. He lets her look; patient, he waits for her to be finished. His expression is enquiring, *amused*.

The amused look says it all. Magnus knows exactly what he looks like. He knows, but he doesn't see it as a problem. He walks over to a bench and sits. Now once again it is his turn to look at Carlie, eyes gliding over the lines of her body, approving what he sees: different clothes, different hair. A polished, composed Carlie. But there's the smile playing about the side of his mouth. As if he can see what I've been looking for all these years. Behind the skin, the old Carlie.

Suddenly, quietly, she says something that makes him

laugh. What did she say to him? Something that has caught him off guard. Because after the laugh he darts a quicker, searching look in her direction. I watch his face: the knowing look has wavered slightly. With just a few words, Carlie has planted the seed of something. *What did she say?* The smile is still there, but more careful now.

He pats the bench beside him and after a second of hesitation, she sits down, keeping a space between them. At once I expect him to move closer, but something in my wife's body language keeps him at bay. How is she doing this? Carlie is talking quietly, and he is watching her, as I am. She is speaking as if to an old friend, relaxed, open. And unbending. And all he can do is observe the side of her face, the fall of her hair, looking for a way in, a way to close the distance. This isn't what he expected.

Again, unbelievably, I feel like laughing. I have seen this so often these last fifteen years: confident men unexpectedly cast in awe of my wife. I have watched them from across tables – QCs, judges used to judging, suddenly suspecting they are being judged. In its most extreme form it's there when Miles looks across at her surreptitiously, in timid desire. It's the enigma of a quiet woman. Carlie's mask.

Something has happened. Now that he has looked, finally noted the change, he can't take his eyes off her. But he daren't touch her. The balance has shifted and Carlie is in control. At last I know why she is here.

Vanessa talked about fighting ghosts. And this is what Carlie is doing. Fighting a ghost, all by herself. Fighting and winning by doing no more than smiling and talking. We watch her, Magnus and I. He, hungry and intimidated, wanting what he cannot have. And me? Spying on my wife, my own Carlie. Suddenly I want to go, but I am afraid of my own visibility, of drawing attention to myself by moving. I don't want Carlie to know I am here, that I have searched through her things. That

I didn't trust her.

So I have to stay, motionless on the bench, ashamed of myself, yet fascinated by my wife and the battle she is winning inch by inch. Watching as Magnus watches her, like a wolf waiting for its prey to drop its guard, but losing hope the while. Hungry, hopeless. Magnus was old when he arrived. Now he is growing older by the minute.

At length she looks at her watch, and rises to her feet. He is trying to make her stay, but Carlie is shaking her head, smiling as she makes her excuses. I recognise that smile. It is the one she would use for Miles, for the drunken husbands of Patersfield, for anyone she cares not to have near her. Charming, impenetrable. And it, too, has its effect. Magnus fumbles the kiss he tries to plant on her cheek. It ends up somewhere in mid air, while she, elusive, has stepped easily away from him. Something he can never catch.

For a moment Carlie stands, almost daring him to try again. But he falls back, keeping the required distance, covering his defeat with a smile. A final goodbye and she is walking away. Magnus can do no more than watch her go.

Or is that not true? As Carlie reaches the edge of the rose garden he is there in front of her again, blocking her way. She stops because there's nothing else she can do, because he seems to have appeared from nowhere. For a moment he stands over her, wordless; then moves again, this time with a sudden sideways lunge to tear a rose from the middle of the bush beside him. Immediately the life in the garden seems to pause around us. People stop talking, walking, stop everything to stare at him and the rose he has snatched. These blooms are sacrosanct. A man might tip one towards his face the way he might tip the chin of a child, nuzzle it gently to breathe in the scent. But not this, never this, tearing a blossom straight from the heart of the bush, tearing his own hand on the thorns, careless.

Carlie stares; not at him, but at the hand proffering the rose. Blood is dripping through his fingers onto the ground between them. Magnus's face is impassive; all expression is in the gesture, in the blood shining on the stem. I hold my breath as silently she takes the rose from him. What will she do now? I watch Carlie, watch my wife.

And Carlie does…nothing. She takes the rose as if it were nothing. Says nothing. Then she turns and continues to walk away from him. This time there is nothing he can do to stop her. He watches her, the composed sway of her hips, watches until she disappears. Then his shoulders slump and he walks over to the bench again. He looks even older now, and knows it – a man feeling his age. After a moment he feels in his pocket for a handkerchief, large and grimy, and wraps it clumsily round his fingers.

This is the man who changed our lives. And what is this? – suddenly I feel sorry for him. If he had looked once in my direction, I might have said something to him: how I remember Carlie, the way she was all those years ago, her talent for being hurt. Maybe wolves don't always choose their prey.

I give her a minute then take off after her, still careful to keep out of sight. She walks with the rose in her hand, unheeding, as if it was nothing. On the Outer Circle of the park, I see her hesitate, pondering her direction. If she turns right, she will be returning to Marylebone and the train. Left and London will be there, to swallow her up.

And as she stands she remembers the rose. She holds it up and gazes at it, every perfect petal. Again I find myself catching my breath. Carlie gazes – then tosses it away into the bin standing next to her. After that she begins to walk again, steadily, in the direction of the station, her steps growing faster and faster until she is almost dancing along the pavement. Nothing composed about her now. This is how the old Carlie would have moved, racing to keep up with her own thoughts, through the streets of St Leonards. Victory Carlie. My Carlie.

She has supper waiting when I come home.

'How was your day, Carlie?'

I tilt her face to mine, as a man might tilt a rose, tenderly. Carlie looks up at me, pale, almost transparent. She smiles, and doesn't answer. She pretends the question is rhetorical, and I pretend with her. What else can I do?

Yet David has noticed the change. I see him observing the slight tremor in her hands as she passes him knives to put on the table. And something else; a small round stain of dark red blood on the tip of her sleeve.

Don't you ask her, David. Don't ask her how it got there.

Carlie has been laying ghosts. But she can't tell him that. She can't tell either of us. And the shame is I can't tell her that I know, grab her by the hand and run with her, the way we ran to the union that night when Carlie danced a victory dance. Where would we run to, anyway, in Patersfield, so far from the sea?

Yet here is Carlie, free at last. We should be celebrating, not sitting here pretending nothing has happened. More than anything I want to take her to bed, fold myself about her, tell I know what she did today. I want to say that I am proud of her, in awe of her. I want to tell her I know why she is exultant and why her fingers shake. I want to tell her I know how the blood came to be on her sleeve.

I can't say anything close to what I want to say. But upstairs, in the bedroom I can say this:

'I love you, Carlie.'

She turns and stares at me. Then the colour rushes into her face, and she is blushing. Her hand touches my cheek, reminding me that she is, we both are, still real. We climb into bed and make love, celebrating a secret neither of us can tell the other. Tonight Carlie comes alive in my arms, and I am weightless above her, like something she has tossed in the air for sheer joy. She stares up into my face and laughs. Afterwards she stops laughing and smiles at me across the pillow, her hand lying on my skin, right above my heart.

Sleep takes us. This is how sailors must feel when they have come through the storm they have dreaded since the beginning of their voyage of many years. Relaxed, finally sure of themselves. Certain of calm weather ahead.

Chapter Fifteen

These are the days following the meeting in the rose garden. Days in which I carry Carlie around with me. She never leaves me. Never so real as in her absence, I watch her, applauding her.

In Chambers, I stare at the law reports and watch her walk away from him. I talk to the clerks and see her side stepping that kiss, tossing away the rose as if it were nothing.

And on the train, on the way home, I hold her as she comes alive in my arms.

We will have a holiday, the three of us. Not in England, in February the dead time. Somewhere far away. Hot, with cool white rooms. In the daytime David and I will swim and fish off the sides of rocks. And we will talk, he and I, chat about nothing, the way we did when he was small. And at night, I will hold her, my Carlie, while a fan circles slowly overhead...

While in some god awful room in someone else's house, Magnus will sit and remember what he lost. Remember how she walked away. Realising how Time and Carlie have finally got the better of him.

This is freedom. This is what I'm thinking as I drive through Patersfield from the station. This is what I will talk about with Carlie when I get home. A holiday, time together. Time for us.

But when I arrive Lydia's car is in the drive, blocking my way in. This is a conversation with Carlie that will have to wait.

Carlie and Lydia are sitting at the kitchen table, an empty bottle of wine between them. Carlie smiles when she sees me, but there's no hiding the fact that the conversation stops the moment I walk through the door. In the silence, Lydia's cheeks grow pink, then scarlet. 'Hello,' I say to her and she loses the battle for control, snorts like a great honking schoolgirl.

I raise an eyebrow at Carlie who says, 'Go and get out of your suit, then maybe Lydia will tell you all about it.'

Lydia slaps the table and howls: 'No, Carlie, how could I possibly.' And dissolves into another fit of snorting.

I duck out of this and make my way upstairs, passing Angus and David on the landing. David darts me a shy smile of greeting that for some reason makes my heart flip. But before I can say a word he disappears with Angus into his room. The door slams and I am staring at the stickers pasted all over it. His entire life seems to be here, glued to the door. A sticker for every stage of his life, from a toddler's passion for Kermit, through Dennis the Menace, to the present day with its football players. My son's years as a collage.

I raise my hand to knock, then lower it again. Because I know exactly how it will be. The door will open and there the two boys will stand, embarrassed, politely waiting for me to explain what I am doing there.

Jonathan wouldn't be like this. Jonathan probably would-n't even knock in the first place. He would barge in, clumsy and intrusive as a large, over-friendly dog who will paddle through everything until bundled out of the room. And he would come away happy, knowing something had been achieved. Contact had been made.

Not me. I am growing shy of David, even faster than he grows shy of me. We need that holiday. What else can I do about my son, whose eyes remind me so much of Carlie's?

Downstairs Lydia takes a swift look at me and gulps her wine, the pink still staining her cheeks. I notice her hands, broad fingered, stained from gardening, are trembling slightly.

'So what's the joke?' I say because it is expected.

Lydia rolls her eyes. If she's going to start snorting again, I will have to make my excuses and leave the room.

Carlie says, 'It's that website – *Blastfromthepast.*'

And suddenly I am alert. I reach into the fridge, fetch out another bottle of wine. 'The one you were talking about, where old flames get back in touch?'

'Not *flames*, Guy,' protests Lydia. *'Friends.'*

'Friends.' I allow myself to be corrected. 'And what's it got to do with this?' By which I mean the pink in Lydia's cheeks and the snorting.

Again it's Carlie who answers. 'Lydia's been having some surprising correspondence from one of her old chums.'

'Saskia,' Lydia interrupts suddenly as if the name was exploding out of her. 'Saskia Jackson. She was captain of sports – big thing at our school. Incredibly responsible position. And of course I adored her. That last term you couldn't have put a cigarette paper between us. We were...terribly close.' She stops. Suddenly she's blushing again. To cover the pause she snatches up her glass of wine and tosses it off in one. Then almost wearily she says, 'You tell him, Carlie.'

Her voice neutral, Carlie turns to me. 'Saskia is gay. That's what she's just told Lydia on the computer today.'

Lydia makes a small convulsive movement, 'Married, tell him – all these years. Four kids, a dog, house in France, everything. But last year she walked away from it all. Not the children of course. But the house, the dog, the husband. She said she'd discovered that she...that she....'

'...Has Sapphic tendencies?' I offer.

Lydia frowns. 'Sapphic what? Carlie, tell your husband I don't know what he's talking about half the time. All I know is we've been emailing all these weeks, Sas and me. Just like the old days really. It's been lovely, so lovely. And now this...' She stops and swallows. Suddenly her eyes are serious, almost panicked. Her final words come out in a small faint rush. 'She says she was scared to tell me, in case I would back off. She says she had to come clean, though, not lie to me any more. She says she's in love with me, can you believe that? Says she always has been, ever since school. She wanted to keep quiet about it, but she couldn't. She had to tell me. Because we're friends and friends don't lie to each other.'

There's a silence. Carlie shakes her head at my offer to refill her glass. 'And Jonathan,' she says softly. What does he say?'

Lydia stares at her glass, 'Jonno? Oh he thinks it's an absolute hoot.'

She tries to laugh – and bursts into tears.

'Don't tell Miles or Vanessa,' says Carlie after she has driven Lydia and Angus home. Lydia has drunk too much and will have to come back for her own car tomorrow.

'God no. Miles would have a field day.'

'I wonder what she'll do,' says Carlie, musing. David is in bed asleep. We are sitting in the kitchen with the second bottle of wine between us.

'Lydia? Nothing, surely. I mean, what is there to do?'

'She was talking about meeting her, having some sort of reunion.'

'And you think – what? That Jonathan wouldn't like it?'

Carlie smiles at this. 'I don't know. And anyway, do you think it matters if Jonathan likes it or not?'

'It might be hard for him. Even if it's only a friendship this woman wants, he might well feel threatened.'

'But Lydia isn't...'

'That's not what I'm talking about. He could see this as being about Lydia and him. He might think he can't compete with that – happy nights with the girls in the dorm...' I stop. 'Now I'm sounding like Miles.'

Carlie stares at her glass. 'I think Lydia *was* happier in the past. I think she was happier five years ago even. At least Jonathan still used to cook occasionally and pick up his own socks. And talk. She misses that. Lydia likes to talk.'

'*We* don't talk much,' I say.

'What are we doing now?' She stands up, carries her glass to the sink, then stretches out her hand. And I take it, forgetting about Lydia and Jonathan, forgetting – almost – about websites and emails that never got mentioned. But then perhaps we don't need words. Or not so many of them.

And actions speak loud, don't they? I saw Carlie walk away, leaving him behind, old and defeated. Carlie doesn't have to tell me anything.

And I remember what I was going to say to her when I came home. 'Carlie,' I say urgently. 'Let's have a holiday. Take David out of school and go off somewhere, just the three of us.'

She looks at me in surprise. Then she laughs. 'Go where?'

'I don't know. Anywhere.' But in my head I see it - the slow revolving fan stirring warm air. White walls and the tick of cicadas outside in the dark.

We've planned holidays before, lots of them. Fortnights in Tuscany, skiing with the Stackpoles. Trips abroad dutifully booked and dutifully enjoyed. More often than not, we'll end up running across people that we know, as if there's no escaping Patersfield.

But somehow this is different. Carlie can hear the excitement in my voice and it's infectious. She catches her breath and laughs aloud, images battling for space in her head. I tighten my arms around her waist. 'Go on, Carlie,' I say. 'You choose. Off the top of your head. Say where you want to go.'

She hesitates, but only for a moment. 'Somewhere cold,' she says softly. 'With sea and sand. And big, *huge* skies with the wind sweeping down on us. Somewhere we have to run to keep warm.'

And now it's my turn to be surprised. 'Cold, Carlie? Are you sure?'

She nods. 'Sky,' she says again. 'Somewhere you can see the stars at night. And I want to run - does that seem odd? Or childish? I want to feel the wind take my breath away, and be deafened by the waves. I want all that. With you.' She adds these last two words and holds my eyes with hers.

This is what Carlie wants. So this must be what I want too. Sea and sand and winds to whip away all words. What will it remind us of? The Past of course. A place we used to know.

I go through the diary with Gary. He has booked me up for all of the next three months.

'You're going to have to wait for that break, Mr. Latimer. I'm sorry. If you'd only told me in good time...'

He sounds disapproving, not even pretending to be regretful. This is his job after all, to make sure every barrister in chambers is working. I am the one trying to buck the trend. For the last ten years I have worked as my father worked, taking my holiday through the month of August when the law term has ended, and judges exert their inalienable right to fall asleep on trimmed lawns with the sun on their heads.

'See what you can do,' I say, and he shrugs.

At home, and in the kitchen, Carlie is standing with her coat on, plainly in a hurry.

'Where are you going?'

'To the school, with you. Parent teachers evening, had you forgotten?'

And I *had* forgotten, something that wouldn't happen, not usually. It's a signal that it's not all over, there are ripples still. We are still in the aftermath. At least I am.

At the school we sit and listen to what we already know, that David is clever, but not working particularly hard. The problem is worst in maths. He is losing interest, that's what his teacher says. He has a mind for numbers, but it's a mind that needs feeding.

'I'll be frank with you, Mr. and Mrs. Latimer.' Mr. Repton, the maths teacher, is a tired looking man, smelling of the staff room. Smoke and sandwiches. Fatigue. 'We are over stretched pupilwise. We can see the bright ones. We certainly don't miss them, but finding the time to give them due attention – well, sometimes it simply isn't there.'

He glances at me. He's wondering why we send David to his

school. This is Patersfield. Why don't we do what the people in Patersfield do, those with money, and pay to send him where the classes are half the size, and the teachers paid twice as much? If he asked (which of course he won't) I would say it is probably for the same reason he is here, tired and smelling of smoke. Faith and trust. Something Carlie taught me.

'Some good news, though. The school is planning to appoint a teaching assistant in the subject, a tutor dedicated to children with special needs. In David's case, of course, that would be a need to be have his talent stretched. There will be the opportunity for special, one-on-one periods out of school time. If you were agreeable.'

'That's wonderful,' says Carlie. 'So when will it start, this special tutoring?'

'Ah, now that I can't say. We're still advertising the position.'

'How long? How long have you been advertising?' I ask.

He hesitates, unable to hide his embarrassment. 'Eighteen months. From before David came to us, actually. Everyone wants maths teachers nowadays. But as soon as we see someone suitable...'

He allows his voice to trail away, meaning to bring our interview to a close.

'By the way,' I say. 'I'm afraid we have to take David out of school for a week. Family commitments that can't be put off.' I feel Carlie's eyes, the faint stirring of surprise beside me. Hadn't she thought I was serious then, about going away together?

Mr. Repton's face gives him away. He doesn't believe there are commitments, family or otherwise. He thinks I'm simply a parent determined to have a holiday when it suits. How could he know, when not even Carlie knows? This is more than a holiday, this is the closing of a circle, a celebration of faith and trust. This is our family. This is our commitment.

Aloud, non-commital, he says, 'You must do as you think best, but like all our boys, David needs to be in school.'

'Do you think we should?' says Carlie, outside in the corridor. 'He might be missing something important - and they'll think we don't care. And they have SATs don't they, coming up?'

'I don't care.'

And Carlie looks at me in wonder. Could it be these are words she hasn't heard in years? She shakes her head and tucks her hand into my arm.

Next day she phones me in chambers. 'That holiday - if you're sure you're serious. I've been on the computer, and found somewhere. It's off the Dorset coast. A lighthouse worker's cottage looking out to sea. Tiny. It'll just about sleep the three of us. What do you think?'

And I am surprised by the relief that whispers to me. She doesn't want to go to Scotland. She doesn't want to go back to *those* beaches and *those* sands. It's not the past she's reaching out to, just a place.

'I think you should book it.'

Which leaves me to deal with Gary who will stare at me in disbelief, wondering what happened to the most dependable man in chambers.

David scowls when we tell him, seems almost as put out as Gary.

'A lighthouse? What will there be to do there?' He has already learned there will be no television, no amusement arcades. There may not even be anywhere flat enough to skateboard.

I say, 'We can walk on the beach, look for stuff that's been washed ashore. Dam a stream where it flows into the sea. Have picnics. We could even build fires out of driftwood.'

As I speak I'm aware that I'm naming the old activities,

things we used to do, not as children but when we were younger still, even less evolved. Children trying to be adults. When Carlie would march along a beach in layers of petticoats and button up boots. When she was still so very young, she hadn't even met *him*.

And David looks utterly unimpressed. 'There won't even be other people. Everyone will be at school.'

'Exactly,' says Carlie, pouncing on this. 'Imagine. Everyone working and you on a beach, with the sun on your back and nothing to do except what you want.'

As usual, it's Carlie who finds the right words. David hears her, and despite himself begins to smile.

I want to talk about it more, but the phone goes. Carlie jumps up to take it. It's Lydia, as usual. It always seem to be lately. And only the one thing on her mind. They'll skirt around this and that, but in the end the conversation will come round again to Saskia, and stay there. Saskia is what Lydia wants to talk about.

'What will she do when you're away?' I say when finally Carlie puts down the phone.

'Who?'

'Lydia. All this on her chest and no one to talk to. There's Jonathan, but all he'll do is laugh. She'll have to bottle it up till you come back.'

Carlie nods, but she's frowning.

'Carlie,' I say softly and hold out my hand. The frown disappears, and Carlie comes to me, only me.

Chapter Sixteen

The cottage is small. Barely more than a lean-to up against a hill where above us an unused lighthouse peers out to sea. There's one bedroom and a put-me-up in the tiny sitting room. We had to leave the car at the bottom of a lane, carrying our bags and boxes of food through the dusk, tracked by a pack of seagulls flying expectantly overhead.

David looks around – at the mantelpiece made from drift wood, the bleached bare boards and the blue painted walls. He shivers, a boy used to central heating and instant warmth. 'It's bloody cold,' he mutters, defying us to scold him for his language.

'Not for long,' says Carlie briskly. She pulls off her gloves. 'Did you see that pile of logs by the front door? Go and bring in as many as you can carry.'

But as soon as he's outside she makes a face. 'He doesn't like it. Do you think I've made us come to the wrong place?' She looks at the room with David's eyes. Everything is threadbare and faded – even the curtains, as if scoured by years of sea and salt.

'Wait till we have a fire,' I tell her. 'And let's get him fed. He's just hungry and a bit chilled. That's what's making him surly.'

The logs are bone dry and in seconds there are flames licking the grate. Carlie heats up soup on the Baby Belling in the kitchen where mouse traps have been laid for our arrival. We eat the soup from our laps watching the fire, aware of the cottage coming alive around us, floorboards heating and creaking, shadows leaping on the walls. The chill is gone, and tomorrow we will wake up to the sea. Carlie looks around her, forgets her soup, preferring the wine warming in her glass. She stares at the beads of red, her mind elsewhere. David picks up a book to read over the edge of his bowl and

I watch her. I watch Carlie.

And as if aware of my gaze she stirs. And smiles. She nods at me to look at David. He is relaxed, all trace of surliness disappeared. He is slurping his soup as he reads, the picture of contentment. And it's enough for Carlie. *We* are enough for Carlie. She is happy, I can tell. Happiness is flickering all around where she is sitting, like the tongues of fire leaping in the hearth. Carlie is here, with us, making me believe there is nowhere else she would rather be.

It's not long before David is yawning. We put him to sleep in the other room where the owners have thoughtfully placed another couple of mousetraps under the bed, and make do with the put-me-up for us, a sofa that straightens, groaning, into a bed just big enough for two. As the cottage creaks around us and the flames crackle in the hearth, we – remembering our son sleeping only feet away – make love, so quietly and carefully that even the ancient springs of the sofa bed are silent. And except that we are slower, quieter as we move, it is like that first night after she came back from *him* and the rose garden. Carlie and I catch and hold each other, still celebrating, still unable to tell the other why.

Afterwards Carlie sleeps with her back curled against my chest, and all the warmth of the room is concentrated here, between us, cocooned in sheets.

Carlie, we have come to the right place.

So where is *he* tonight?

Not here. He is out in the wilderness where she sent him. And Carlie lies asleep in my arms.

The next morning we show David what you have to do beside the sea in winter.

Not as amazing as it sounds – the fact that he's never had the chance to learn.

We have been to so many beaches, the three of us: busied ourselves on hot white sands, too dry to be coaxed into castles or moats; searched for basalt rocks on black vocanic shores; water ski-ed, paraglided, haggled for conch shells under palm trees. Expensive holiday activities. But now it comes home to me how we have never done *this*. Taken our son to a freezing beach with the wind biting his nose. Yet *this* was all we knew for a time, Carlie and I. This and a sky to match the one that is with us now, arching above our heads. A winter sky, like Carlie wanted, reaching to the horizon, like an arc of thin blue glass. All that's there to separate us from...what? Stars and galaxies and winds blowing straight out of the sun.

This is what we ran away from. And now we are back. A place that belongs to us. Only us. And look at Carlie.

This first morning she stands and takes it all in. Then she's off, running down a dune – not like a middle-aged woman, stiff-kneed, splay-heeled – but flat out, hurling herself against the wind. David watches her a moment, then glances at me, unsure how to react – waiting to see what I do. I smile once at him – and run after her, fast as I can. Down by the shore I catch her up, panting, and there we turn to look behind us. Our son is picking his way self consciously down the slope of the dune, leggy as some wading bird, trying to maintain a dignity he feels has been lost.

'*Run,*' shouts Carlie. He stops and stares at us. Rubs his eyes as if confused. '*Run,*' we shout together. A slow grin sweeps across his face and David begins to run, clumsy in his wellingtons – clumsier than we are – towards us. Down by the sea, with waves trickling across his boots, he stops and the look on his face says *what next?*

This is what's next: run, build, dig, climb. Eat. Sleep. Read. Grow cold. Get warm again. All done with the wind lending a leading edge. Things you couldn't think of doing on a tropical beach. Things we haven't done in so many years it's a wonder we still remember how. But we do, Carlie and I. We don't even have to remind each other.

Lunch time and we sit with our backs to the dune in chairs we have hollowed out of sand. We eat doorstep sandwiches and blocks of chocolate, swig tea from a flask, and watch the sea changing colour, until the damp seeps through our clothes and we have to get moving again, get busy on the beach. We don't stay chilly for long. We remember what to do.

Finally, at the end of the day, we shut our door against the wind. It's evening and Carlie and I are on the sofa with David by our feet, poking the wood in the fire. Too tired for Scrabble, too muzzy to read even, our fingers and toes swelling with heat, we are lulled by the flames. David puts down the poker, allows his head to fall first against Carlie's knee, and then – little by little – against mine, the way he used to when he was a little boy. We put him to bed as if he were a little boy, and come back to the sofa, bank up the fire. And reach for each other. Carlie who was too tired to talk comes awake in my arms.

The wind rattles half heartedly against the panes, like a passing neighbour, and nothing can touch us.

The next day is a repeat of the first. Except this time it's David who takes the lead. We've come without buckets and spades, and without consulting us he raids the kitchen drawer for spoons and spatulas that will mould the sand to just the shape he wants. Two hours later we are sitting, trying to look casual, next to the result, secretly delighted there are other people on the beach to stop and stare at the vast Gothic pile we have created with its towers and crenellated walls. Carlie, David and I have been hard at work.

I watch them, my family. A man and his wife have actually stopped to take a photograph. Now Carlie and David are posing next to their work, doing their best to look modest – and failing. Their faces are glowing, making my heart skip a beat. They are so alike. No stamp or mark on them. As if the past never happened.

This is how it might have been if *he* had never been. Magnus. *He* changed us. Carlie's hair whips around her face, her eyes liquid. Nothing composed about her now. This is how she used to be. She could have been like this all the time.

'Guy?' Without warning she has turned to me, and the smile dies away. 'Guy, what's the matter?'

'Matter?' I say feebly.

'You look…' she leaves the couple to chat to David and walks over to me, her eyes fixed on mine. Liquid eyes in which I drown. 'Darling, you look so *sad*.'

I reach down and take her hand. Hold it against my mouth. Close my eyes just for the touch of her. 'Not sad, Carlie,' I am murmuring into the hollow of her hand. 'Happy.'

She looks mystified. Then her face clears, as if somehow she understands everything behind the words. Slowly she nods, takes away her hand and puts her mouth there instead.

'Let's stay this way for ever,' she whispers.

And it makes me realise that we could. We could stay this way for ever. Because it seems the only way we could be.

One morning we wake to find it's raining hard. And, of course, the cottage is cold again.

Carlie jumps up to make tea and runs back to bed with mugs, shivering and pretending to complain. Minutes later, David tiptoes through from the bedroom and tucks himself in next to her. He is shivering too. Carlie tucks the blankets up around his neck, pulls his head against her shoulder. Our feet are all bunched together and our son – too reserved even to speak to me in front of his friends – is practically purring, a young skinny cat who has stolen space under our covers. Part of us.

We don't need to huddle together like this. All I have to do is get up and make a fire. But not yet. We have all the warmth we need here, between the three of us. We could stay this way for ever.

Later, and the cottage is warm, filled with the smell of wet wool drying next to the fire.

Outside it is raining as hard as ever. We have been in Poole all the morning, trailing David round the amusement arcades, watching him racing to eat an ice cream before the rain dissolved it. At lunchtime we followed the scent of fish and chips into a café with red Formica tables. It had windows running with condensation and the steamy hiss of a coffee machine drowning out the sounds of the jukebox. Not much chance of bumping into anyone from Patersfield here.

Carlie and David laughed at me because I ordered Ovaltine to drink, and laughed even more when I told them why: because it reminds me of school, of bread and jam for supper; of boys trying to cram enough into themselves to last till the greasy sausages of morning. It reminds me I am here, not there. With them.

David stops laughing. 'You wouldn't, would you?' He is looking at me.

'Wouldn't...what?'

'Send me away to school? Angus is going next year. He tries to make out he's looking forward to it, but he's not. He's lying, I know he is.'

Carlie and I glance at each other and something unspoken passes between us. Faith. And trust.

'Never,' I tell him. 'Not even if you begged us.'

Satisfied he sits back on his styrofoam bench, concentrates on drawing faces in the mist upon the window, and Carlie watches us both, her eyes soft. I have the feeling she is looking at David and seeing me. A small boy trying to cram the sweetness into himself. Then forgetting how.

Until I met her, Carlie, all those years ago.

And now if I were ever to choose a place to be – and a time – it would be then and there, back in the café with its smell of vinegar, and plastic tables next to the steamy window where Carlie watches us and David draws faces in the mist.

Now we are back in the cottage, dry clothes on our backs, wet ones steaming in front of the fire. And Carlie is standing, staring out of the window. She has been this last half hour. She has stood there so long a mug of coffee has grown cold in her hands. Even David has begun to notice, looks up every now and then from his book, curious, as if he had never seen anyone stay so still. And Carlie continues to stand, not conscious even of him.

I step up and put my arm around her, and she jumps. Then just as quickly relaxes. *What were you thinking of, Carlie?*

As if she'd heard the question, she nods out of the window, at the rain and mist shrouding the sea. 'It's sad, isn't it?'

'Why? Because it's raining?'

'No. Sad that we have to go home. Ever. I wish we could stay here, just the three of us.'

'What here? In this cottage?'

She nods vigorously.

'And sleep on a creaky sofa bed *every* night?'

'Don't you like it then, our sofa bed?' Carlie's eyes are teasing, knowing that I have loved it. Loved her.

'Of course. But *you* didn't like it much when you found the mouse with its skull all smashed in by the mouse trap. What about the mice, Carlie?'

'Not a problem – I'd buy a humane trap. Give them to David to keep as pets.'

'The house then – our house, wouldn't you miss that? I'm not sure I could live in only two rooms.'

'…And a kitchen. Don't forget the kitchen!'

'And what about having to search for driftwood for the fire every day? That pile of logs is only going to last till the end of the week…'

'Guy…' Carlie interrupts me. She pauses, then the words tumble out of her. 'I don't want to go home.'

Suddenly I can see she is serious. Serious as a child coming to the end of the holidays, not looking forward to going back to school. Except Carlie isn't a child.

'Carlie,' I say softly. 'We have to go home.'

She looks at me a moment, then laughs. 'Of course we do. Of course we have to go home. We're having dinner with Vanessa and Miles next week. Won't that be fun?'

And she moves away from the window.

David catches my eye. 'We *are* going home, aren't we? I mean we aren't going to *live* here, are we?'

Carlie's seriousness is catching, and now he has to ask. It's not that he doesn't like this place. Probably he wouldn't even mind another week. But not so much that he wants to stay, never see Patersfield again.

The next day is our last.

As if to make leaving even more of a wrench, the morning dawns clear and bright. And warm. A reminder that we are in the last days of winter. Spring is coming. Even the wind has become still, making the sea seem as smooth as glass.

'We'll pack later,' announces Carlie. 'One last walk. A long one'

David looks reluctant. 'Does it have to be long? Can't we just have a short one, down to the rock pools? Or I tell you what. You could go without me, you and Dad. Far as you like. I'll pack.'

He's ready, you see. Ready to leave the sea and go home. And what's so wrong with that? Isn't it supposed to be the mark of the perfect holiday, when you're content to· leave what you've enjoyed, and look forward to what you left behind?

'No!' Carlie snaps, then colours faintly. More gently she says: 'I just want one last walk, the three of us, together.'

Something in her voice makes David nod, keeps him from arguing.

So off we go, over the dune where we ran the first day. Not

running this time. I have a feeling Carlie will go slowly, as if to make it last, this final walk. David cheers up when he finds a long iron pole, shedding rust, to drag behind him in the sand, making his mark. We let him go ahead of us and walk together, Carlie and I, not talking. Not needing to talk.

'We can come back, Carlie.' I say at length. 'What about buying a cottage down here? We could come back all the time? Now we know...'

I stop. Now we know what exactly? That it's safe? That sand and sea and sun and wind no longer bring back the past? For answer, Carlie puts her hand into mine. And we carry on walking. I'm thinking about the journey home, how, if we left earlier than we planned, there might be time to stop and look into windows of estate agents. We could start the ball rolling...

Carlie breaks my train of thought. 'What's David found?'

She points to our son. He must have sped on ahead faster than we realised. Now he's a hundred yards or so from us, having abandoned the pole, bending over something lying on the sand. As we watch he picks it up and holds it aloft. And Carlie explodes.

'David – put that down!'

He turns, and even from here we can see he is grinning wickedly, dancing, and waving a huge fish by the tail. We can see the wet gleam of its sides catching the sun in its scales.

'Oh for God's sake,' moans Carlie, half laughing. 'It's probably rotting.' She takes a deep breath, all set to shout again.

'Carlie, no.'

She turns and looks at me, surprised by the urgency in my voice.

'Look behind him,' I say softly.

And Carlie looks, and catches her breath. 'Guy...' She stops, tries to reassure herself. 'Oh, but it's just a dog...'

But already we know different. This is not like other dogs.

Half the size of a man, it is moving across the sand in a zig zag sweep, like a wolf following the scent of blood, ears flattened against its skull. Desperately Carlie scans the beach for an owner, but of course there is none. The dog is an outsider, an aberration. No one's to control, like a madness appeared out of nowhere. And it is closing in on David.

Carlie wants to run, but instinctively I stop her. 'Slowly,' I say, whispering, as if it could hear us, even from here. And she understands: if it sees us running, it might attack before we can reach him, before we can reach our son.

And what do we know? It may be harmless, after all, just a dog alone on a beach. Perhaps it's only curious. Why have we assumed the worst? Why are we so sure?

Because of this: the dog has stopped, yards short of David who remains utterly unaware of him. And like us, he watches our son, dancing around on his small spot of sand, a fish swinging from his fist. Watches him – and measures the distance between them. He's not just curious. He is making sure that David is alone, and defenceless. Something that has wandered from the pack. Easy to pick off. This dog preys on things.

And still David hasn't seen him. He just stands there waving the fish and grinning at us. Can't see what's behind him.

And so we smile as we continue to walk towards him, Carlie and I. Forcing ourselves not to run. Already we are feeling as if we know him, this dog, and what he will do. A dog that thrives on fear, only leaps when he's sure. If David turns, sees what's there, if David becomes frightened – then it will be sure. So we try to keep David fixed with our eyes. We try to keep on smiling.

But already he can see something is wrong. Something in our faces that gives us away. He stops grinning and watches us advance. The hand that holds the fish drops slightly as if already he is beginning to forget about it.

'Guy,' says Carlie faintly. 'Oh God, Guy.'

The dog has moved a few yards closer. And stopped again. David is watching us, but his face is tilted to one side, as if confused. He's beginning to frown. I glance at Carlie, amazed to see she is smiling, that she looks completely normal. Yet something is giving him a clue. It must be me, then, giving myself away. David's arm has dropped to his side. He takes one last look at my face, and because of what he sees there, slowly, almost reluctantly, turns to look behind him.

He turns. And like us, David, friend of so many dogs, understands this is not like other dogs. We see his body jerk as the fear takes him. We see it. And the dog, so much closer than us, can smell it.

The fish falls from David's hand, and the dog begins to snarl, crouches down on its haunches, ready to spring.

Now at last we run, faster than we have ever run. Carlie is behind me, but not by much, I can hear her footsteps thumping in the sand. The beach has gone and suddenly my head is full of pictures – of David, limp and new born, a weight on my shoulder, hot mouth gumming my neck. David, just learned to walk, his arms gripping my knees. David, growing up and growing shy, closing the door of his room. Our son. I run towards him and all the images of him, and as if in slow motion the dog leaps.

I arrive where David is at the exact moment the dog lands.

And he lands on me. His weight pushes me backwards and pins me to the ground. Next to my throat a sudden driving pain closes my eyes as my ears fill with the bubbling snarling of the dog with its teeth deep in my neck. I am blind, deafened – and thankful, because I am the one this is happening to, not David. My hands scrabble against fur wrapped round steel. But already I know it's useless. Surprisingly, I can hear the voice of my father, close by, explaining to my mother in matter of fact tones how her son happened to die. A mad dog, slicing through his jugular. Nothing to be done. Sad for them,

David and Carlie.

David. Carlie. I open my eyes. At first I can only see the vibrating skull of grey black hairs that has somehow become fused with me, part of me. But then, in the distance I find him, David, his face hypnotised with horror. My son who never had a stamp or mark on him will be stamped for ever now. Carlie needs to pull him away, stop him from seeing any more.

But Carlie, where is Carlie?

Carlie is nowhere to be seen. Carlie is gone, out of my line of sight. Gone for ever. The dog has me, my father explains impatiently. No good looking for her now.

No more Carlie. Ever.

Then, suddenly the dog jerks, and the force of what makes him jerk drives right through to me. For a moment he seems to be stunned. Then, unbelievably, his teeth loosen their grip and he is moving, snaking off my body to turn, snarling, towards the source of the blow.

Carlie is standing in the sand, the iron pole caught in her two hands, waiting for him. From the ground I watch the dog take stock, shivering on its haunches, adjusting its sights. Ready, it leans back into itself, gathering power, and springs again. Straight at Carlie, a moving mass of muscle driving towards the pale column of her neck.

The pole meets his skull in mid air. Carlie has swung it with a violence that sends the dog flying sideways. It hits the ground, snarling where it rolls briefly – then leaps to its feet again. There's blood matted against his ear, but nothing else seems to be hurt. He is ready to spring again, and this time, he is ready for her, and the pole.

But he hasn't reckoned on Carlie advancing. Before he moves, Carlie runs at him. He flies at her hands, tries to sav-age her arms, but the pole deflects him. And before he can recover she hits him again, and again. His head judders, jaws snapping together. He is still snarling, intent on getting past the pole to Carlie. But the blows are finally having their effect; he is becoming slower. In response, Carlie checks herself, and draws back slightly. She is swinging the pole back, right over her shoulder. Swings it too far, though; she has left her entire body vulnerable. And the dog has seen its chance, is gathering one more time to spring. Carlie has made a terrible mistake.

This time the dog flies with a force that will surely destroy her. But Carlie has stepped aside. The pole flashes from behind her and catches the dog under the jaw. It shudders, but it takes the blow, its own force driving it forward. But when it lands, it is with a limp thud against the sand, like a tossed heap of fur. Carlie watches it a moment, then walks forward. Raises the pole high above her head and brings it down a final time on the motionless skull.

'Dad…' David is bending over me. He touches my neck, then looks to Carlie for help. But Carlie is staring at the dog at her feet, still clutching the pole, as if afraid it could still move.

'Mum…'

And Carlie throws down the pole and runs to us.

The doctor in the A and E finishes with the bandage and stands back. 'You're a lucky man, Mr. Latimer. Very lucky. The dog actually nicked the jugular. A millimetre more and you would have bled to death then and there. You hear about these dogs abandoned on the beaches, becoming feral, but frankly I never really believed it. Not till now.' He looks as if he still doesn't believe it, despite the wound he has just bandaged.

'Mum saved him,' says David, eager. 'She whacked the dog again and again with my pole. It kept coming at her and she just kept on whacking.'

'I'm impressed,' says the doctor. 'You must have been very brave.'

There's a pause. Carlie looks up from her lap, realises he is talking to her.

'He was old,' she says tonelessly. 'I realised after, when I looked at him. He had grey hairs like a human being. He just lay there, old and hungry, looking as if he was asleep.'

'I reckon you broke his windpipe,' says David. 'Whack – just like that. And once more for luck. Like you still wanted to teach it a lesson. She was, like, savage, wasn't she Dad? Awesome.'

The doctor shudders. Perhaps he loves dogs – all dogs, even the ones that appear out of the sand like a wolf in a nightmare. Carlie looks at her lap again, doesn't say another word.

Back in the cottage, we pack swiftly. Carlie locks the door and leads the way back to the car at the bottom of the lane. She fires up the motor and drives us away without a backward glance.

It's beginning to rain, drops smearing the window, dispersing the headlights of oncoming cars, making the driving difficult. I want to stay awake on the way back, keep her company as she drives, but the pain killers kick in and before I know it I am asleep. And dreaming. Carlie is on the beach, the wind whipping her hair, her cheeks bright. She is smiling – no! laughing – at me. *Run*, she shouts, and laughs. *Run to me.* But I am anxious not to. What if she changes her mind? What if I break out into a run and at the last moment, Carlie, finding me too eager, turns away?

So I force myself to walk towards this wind-whipped, laughing girl. Walk when all I want to do is run. With the result that when the wolf lopes into sight, I am too far away. Skinny, ravenous, its black hair shot with grey – it sits and watches her from behind, measures the distance between them. But he doesn't move. He is waiting for her to turn, for the wind to drop. For all smiles to stop.

He is waiting for her to come to him.

I wake with a start. The car is crunching over gravel. We are home. Carlie turns towards me. The drive has made her tired. There are circles under her eyes.

'Are you alright? You were making strange noises just now.'

'I'm fine. Just dreaming. You?'

She stretches, rubs her shoulder. 'I'm stiff,' she says ruefully.

'That will be from hitting that dog over and over,' says David triumphantly from the back seat. 'God, wait till I tell Angus.'

Carlie purses her lips and gets out of the car. Unlocks the front door, and lets David and me go in in front of her. I wait in the hall and watch Carlie walk into her own home, watching how just before the front door she seems to miss a beat, faltering. For the briefest of moment she stands, almost as if she were having to will herself to go forward. Then she squares her shoulders and carries on walking, pausing only to flick the central heating switch as she comes. Quiet Carlie, composed Carlie, smoothing her hair. Back again.

In the kitchen she touches the button on the answer phone to listen to the messages. There's call after call from Lydia, all of them made today when she expected us to be home. Carlie looks at me, resigned, then slowly goes around the house, switching on light after light.

Chapter Seventeen

Saturday and Jonathan phones early, when we are still in bed. He wants me to play golf. Now.

Carlie opens her eyes and looks at me sleepily across the pillow, then reaches for her watch. Holds it up for me to see. It's six-thirty a.m.

'I don't play golf, Jonathan. You know that. And definitely not at this time of the morning. It's not even light yet.' Besides there are the punctures in my neck, nowhere near healed, still making movement difficult a week after it happened.

'It will be in half an hour. I'll pick you up.'

He puts the phone down before I have time to argue.

Jonathan swings and sends a ball soaring into the rough. He swears and strides off after it. We have given up even pretending to have a proper game. My neck is sore, and I haven't stopped wishing I was home, in bed with Carlie. He has been relentlessly cheerful all the way round, hasn't stopped talking once. I have a planning case of his amongst my papers and occasionally we touch on that, making we wonder if this is why he has hauled me out of bed for a game I don't play. I suspect not.

He chips his ball out of the rough and onto the green, keeps a running commentary on his progress. He stops talking only to line up his club for a final putt. For the first time this morning, he seems to relax. His shoulders steady and his backside – broad at the best of times – flattens, and just for a moment he seems at peace.

Suddenly he stiffens and throws down his club. 'Fuck,' he screams over my shoulder. 'Fuck. Why can't you keep off the fucking course? You fucking…'

I spin round to see a woman jogger on the side of the course. She has swerved before the onslaught, all but stumbled and now is looking at Jonathan with a look of shock in her face. She's about to stop – then thinks again. Slowly she lifts a hand towards him, the middle finger sticking straight up. Jonathan makes an explosive sound, attempts a short lumbering run after her.

'This is a golf course, madam,' He is shouting. 'That means *Members* only.'

But she is fleet of foot and Jonathan is – Jonathan. He stops, shambles back towards me, shamefaced, and avoiding my eye. 'Bitch,' he mumbles. 'Shot right across my – what do you call it – peripheral vision. Completely buggered up my shot. They're not supposed to be here, you know, bloody joggers.'

I, meanwhile, am staring at a sign that reads *public footpath*.

Jonathan sees me and snorts. 'You can ignore that. They just do it to assert some God given right they think they have to roam. Did you see the length of that woman's hair? About one fucking inch from her scalp. What does that tell you, eh, Guy? Fucking *lesbian*, that's what. *Asserting* herself.'

So this is what it's all about. Jonathan picks up his club and the fight goes out of him. His shoulders slump. 'Let's go and have a drink.' His voice is pleading.

Ten thirty in the morning and in the club house Jonathan drains a gin and tonic, stares bleakly at the portraits of past chairmen of the club.

'It's a bugger, Guy, no other word for it. Out of the blue, some woman declaring hearts and flowers for my wife. *My wife.*'

'Lydia told us you thought it was funny.'

'I did – at first. But then it carries on, doesn't it, and it doesn't seem quite so funny. *Then* you find out that your wife – who has supposed to have cut off all contact – is still in touch. The two of them are still at it, happily emailing all day long. Like a pair of bloody schoolgirls.'

'Lydia said that she was cutting off from her? She told you?'

He shrugs. 'Not in so many words. But good god alive, what else would you expect her to do? She's a married woman. She's not meant to be carrying on correspondence with some middle aged dyke.'

'But she is carrying on? Talking to her, I mean.'

Jonathan nods. 'Caught her red-handed, didn't I, on the email. Hadn't even waited for me to leave the house. Turned into a right royal row. Do you know what she ends up telling me? That it's none of my business, that she and this Sas were pals before either of them ever knew I existed. Like there's some kind of prior claim here. Can you believe that?'

He stops, nudges my glass towards me.

'Drink up. Look, I don't want to quarrel with her, not with old Lyd. We've been good together all these years, never a cross word spoken. Till now. I don't know what's got into her, frankly. There's no reasoning with her. Carlie, though, she's got her head screwed on. And Lydia likes her. I was thinking...Guy – will you get her to talk to her? Will you do that for me. Fact is, Lydia's planning on meeting up with this bitch. Making no bones about it. It's not on. If Carlie could only make her see sense...'

And I don't know what to say. Who knows what Carlie would tell her? Aloud I say, 'Are you sure there's any need? Maybe it will all die down. Maybe it was just a shock for you, discovering they were still in touch.'

Jonathan bangs his fist down on the table. 'That's it. That's the whole bloody trouble. I didn't even think about it. I thought this woman had blown it with her kinky confession, and after that Lydia would steer clear. I'd even got round to thinking it might have been good for her – a bit of excitement, a bit of attention. The girl's been singing opera in the bath again, for God's sake – just like she used to. It was like having the old Lydia step forward after all these years. Everything was dandy between us. *Then* I find out it's because of this bloody so-called friend, still talking to her. Makes you realise, I tell you. Women! Remember that time on the train when you asked what she does all day? Bloody stupid question, I thought – *at the time.* Now I don't think it's stupid at all. They act like their lives are their own – and we have no bloody idea. Like it's none of our business.'

Jonathan has spoken these last words without any hint of self consciousness. I have to stop myself from smiling. 'The thing is, though – it's not as if she was trying to hide anything.'

Jonathan frowns. 'Don't follow you.'

'Well, the fact they were openly emailing, for a start. If it was something she thought she shouldn't be doing, something she didn't want you to know, she'd have taken precautions, covered her tracks. The fact she does none of that – doesn't it show she has nothing to hide...?'

'I don't know. Why? Is that the sort of thing Carlie would do?' He sounds disbelieving.

I stare at him. Because it is the sort of thing Carlie has done. Quiet Carlie, giving nothing away. For a moment, I am seeing her on the beach again as we walked towards our son. Carlie smiling, utterly normal. Never letting on the danger.

Jonathan is staring at me. 'Well, go on, what are you trying to say?'

I clear my throat. 'She would have deleted her messages, made sure you didn't see them – and she didn't.'

But Carlie did. And if she did it once, how would I know that she wouldn't do it again? Suddenly the air in the club-house has become oppressive, filled with the warm, thick breath of middle aged men and gin. How would I know?

Because she's happy. Happiness flickered around her like flames, all the time we were away - until the dog. Carlie was happy. But then we came home again. And now Carlie is back to the way she was - quiet Carlie, composed Carlie. Which is what happens after a holiday. Everything goes back to normal, the way it was before.

Everything?

I rise to my feet, not quite steady.

'You off?' Says Jonathan, sounding dismayed.

'I'm going to speak to Carlie about Lydia,' I hear myself lie. 'Right now. Like you asked.'

To my shame, I see his face brighten. 'You'll do that, Guy? For me? You're a good friend. That's what you are – a really good friend.'

Carlie has gone shopping, but David steps out of the sitting room, smiles as he sees me.

'Dad,' he says. 'Could you help me do my...?'

And I ignore him, brush past him to get up the stairs. 'Later, David,' I mutter. I'm aware of him watching me before he turns back to whatever it was he was doing. Then I forget him. I switch on Carlie's computer.

Trust her.

I can't, I can't, I can't.

Hit the button that resurrects the deletes. And there it is, another message, one that has been wiped off the face off the machine; but still there if you know where to look.

Hey you! Do I need to tell you? It was like a fucking dream seeing you. No one should have been so beautiful, not after all these years. My lady, you unmanned me. The words I should have told you stayed locked in my bones, and there they burn. They burn me, my honeysuckle girl. Help me. Meet me again. In the rose garden. Tuesday at ten. You owe me. One time pays for all.

One time pays for all. Pays for what? What does she owe him?

Nothing. She owes him nothing. He's the reason she was unhappy, the reason she tried to kill herself, the reason that in the end she turned to me. She's with me because of him. Her life is as it is because of him. Carlie is – happy.

Is that it then? Carlie is happy. Even here she is happy, in Patersfield. Is that what she owes him? One time pays for all. Is that the way she sees it?

I look for her reply on the machine. And there is no reply.

Later, in bed, I hold Carlie in my arms, look into her eyes and I would swear she is hiding nothing from me. Yet the message is there on her machine and she has told me nothing. And once again I see her as she was on the beach, smiling as we walked towards the dog, never giving away the danger.

Maybe she won't go.

I ask Gary what I have on for Tuesday. He tells me a conference with solicitors in the morning. And that is all.

'Cancel the conference. Tell them I'll meet them next week.'

'But Mr. Latimer...'

'Do it, Gary.'

Gary is good at his job. He asks no questions. If I stay in the clerk's office I will hear him on the phone, explaining that Mr. Latimer is on the case, unwilling to commit to an opinion until all options are explored. They will believe him absolutely. I am known for my thoroughness, for my judgement, as my father was before me. Client and solicitors will be reassured.

And I will be in the rose garden at ten o' clock tomorrow morning to see what Carlie does.

This time Carlie sleeps soundly the night before. I am the one who stays awake. Hours pass and I hear the hum of David's hamster in his room, busy on its wheel; the sound of traffic on the M40, of lorries heading into London with deliveries for the dawn. Beside me, Carlie slumbers all night long, her breathing soft and regular. She believes there is nothing to fear. She believes she is in control. And perhaps she is.

But tomorrow she will wake up and go to see him. If I had a wish it would be that she would stay asleep, not wake up at all, not until it's safe for me to let her. If I had a wish it would be to keep her here, never leave my side.

Chapter Eighteen

This time it's raining in the rose garden, a fine mist that condenses almost before it touches the ground. The mothers and the tourists and the schoolchildren have stayed away. Only the roses are still here, soaking up the damp. Roses that bloom no matter what.

Me, I'm like a cartoon spy, sitting on a bench, crouching behind a newspaper. I am hiding, and not hiding. If Carlie were to see me, she would not be fooled for a moment. But only if she sees me, if she has eyes to see. If I were anywhere on her mind.

Magnus certainly doesn't see me, walks past the man behind the newspaper sitting on the bench. Carlie is married but her husband is the last thing on his mind.

I watch him as he lopes over to the same bench as before, takes possession of his ground, ready for her.

Maybe Carlie will not come.

The same thought has occurred to him. He is looking at his watch, noting the hand slipping past the hour. But he has not lost hope, not yet. Magnus has regrouped since the last time when she turned everything around, when she walked away from him. The energy is back, coiled inside him, ready to spring. Energy is all. A well dressed, middle-aged woman – not Carlie – walks past him, and I see her notice him, the long legs stretched across the path. Even now, with the dyed hair and the used clothes, he has the draw. But everything depends upon Carlie turning up to prove it. He runs his fingers through the black mane, nonchalant, yet his shoulders are braced. If Carlie does not come, that energy will drain away and no one will notice him.

How do I know this? Because I know.

Then I see it – the sudden flicker, like a second eyelid coming down. A lizard's blink of satisfaction. And it's all I need to be warned. I don't even have to look.

Carlie has come.

She walks slowly up to the bench in the rain. This time he doesn't get up, makes sure she has to approach under his gaze, a thing observed. But Carlie doesn't falter. With an even stride she arrives and sits, not looking at him. Yet she must feel his eyes on her, making an object of her, something that exists only in so far as he is pleased to notice it.

Don't let him look at you like that, Carlie.

And as if she hears me Carlie, my Carlie, does a clever thing. In a single smooth movement she reaches inside her purse and takes out a small round mirror. It is the mirror I bought her for her last birthday – a tiny silver backed antique. And Carlie holds it up and looks at herself. She looks at herself and negates the gaze beside her. She doesn't need his eyes to convince her she is real.

And the fear, built up over the last two days, drains away from me. My wife knows exactly what she is doing. She has the measure of the man ageing beside her. I sit back and watch, not guilty this time, only grateful to be here, grateful for this glimpse of Carlie keeping the past at bay. Magnus watches her too, but even from where I am sitting I can see the effect. All rules apply the same way. He needs *her* to look at *him*. And she doesn't look. Even though Carlie puts away her mirror, back in her purse, even though she is talking, her eyes only flicker in his direction. There is no enlarging gaze, not any more. He can't exist, he cannot be Magnus if she does not look at him.

And, as if she knows, she does not look at him. Carlie simply talks.

I imagine I even know what she is talking about: David, me, our lives. As if Magnus would want to hear. She allows her pleasure in us to show in her face. Carlie talks and talks, pretending not to notice that the man who sits beside her is disappearing and ageing with every passing minute.

How could I have been so blind? Carlie may have come for all kinds of reasons, but principally she is here for this: revenge. Having laid her ghost, my wife is cruel and I never knew it. Gently letting him know that what she has, he has not. What she is, he is not. I can only watch and marvel at her, my Carlie. Cruel Carlie. This is a revenge so subtle it's like the rain that continues to settle, so fine it turns to mist on contact.

And what is strange is that once again I feel almost sorry for him. I can feel the heaviness setting into his arms, weighing down his hands as if they were my own. Awareness of age and loss and a life that will somehow be different from now on. He thought he could get back what he was in danger of losing, Magnus's own idea of himself. He was so sure it would still be there, kept alive in her for ever. His image stamped in her eyes. He thought this time he would find it.

Instead there is this – Carlie, taking her revenge, not even moved to look at him. He must be realising now he never should have come near her, he should have erased her name from his machine, for his own sake.

Finally Carlie is getting to her feet. Smiling down at him. This will be the last time they meet. And with a jolt that is almost a pang it occurs to me it will be a different Carlie again who comes home. A Carlie I'm not sure I know. The final transformation: the final Carlie, the finished result of what she has been making of herself for years. Nothing like the old Carlie.

Magnus stays sitting on the bench. He has become very still. It occurs to me that he couldn't stand up even if he tried. And Carlie – who was on the very point of walking away – pauses instead and looks at him, curiously, for the last time. I know what she is doing; she is searching for the Magnus of her youth, the Magnus who took her and shook her and stamped himself upon her.

And it's a look that lays her open. Instinctively I know it, feel my hands tighten around my newspaper. Because in that moment I see the shuttered look, the lizard's blink. I want to cry out her name. *Carlie.* I need to warn her, tell her what is coming.

And I can't.

The coil snaps back. Magnus has sprung to his feet.

There is a split second in which Carlie sees what is about to happen. I see her lips part and the step backwards. But it is too late. Magnus seizes her, not by her arms or sides – but by the head, crushing it as his mouth clamps against hers. His thumbs press into her cheeks, his fingers a hard mask of flesh and bone. Her body arches and her fists beat against his sides, but to no effect. Seconds pass and then I see her slump, fists falling away, nerveless, to her sides. Her entire body seems suspended from his hands.

Carlie has stopped struggling, and the kiss continues.

He takes his hands away, releases her. Carlie staggers. She falls away from him, almost loses her balance. The blood is drained from her face, only the lips red, where he kissed her. For a moment she stares at him and he stares back amused, relaxed. He can see his own reflection in her eyes, now – Magnus as he sees himself. He has got exactly what he wanted. Taken away her power. Put himself back where he belonged. Everything is where it should be. He's got Carlie.

And Carlie knows it. She steps away from him and turns, slowly, as if willing herself not to run. Then suddenly she turns back and flies at him, her hand raised, bringing it crashing against his cheek. I hear the slap of flesh on flesh. See her stand, staring at him, before her hand falls, pulsing to her side. Magnus smiles and touches his cheek, tenderly, as if it were the trace of a kiss left there. Carlie shudders, and walks away. But she has lost the evenness of her stride, the composed sway of her hips. She walks like the old Carlie would sometimes walk, years ago, tipsy with shock and grief towards my door.

Magnus watches her go. This is a different way of leaving him – the correct way. He is smiling as he sits down again on the bench. Their bench. Then his hand alights on something and he sees what is still there, lying where Carlie had been, and the smile broadens.

Carlie has left her purse behind, the purse in which she had tucked away the mirror. Magnus picks it up and empties out the contents, careless as a mugger. Carlie's things tumble out: the mirror, money, her cards, photographs, letters, addresses. Our address. Carlie's life is scattered on the bench. Yet he wastes no time over it. He picks out the paper money and folds it into his back pocket, drops the change into his shirt. His hands work fast as a thief's hands. He sorts through the cards, flips through the photographs and glances at them, one by one. Photographs of the three of us, together and separately. And one that makes him linger – our house with its surrounding screen of trees.

She told him everything about us. What she has, and he has not. Now, with all this, he knows where to find us. Where to find Carlie. Magnus runs his fingers through his hair, throws back his head and lets the sky pepper him with warm congratulatory rain.

At Marylebone I find her, sitting on one of the red benches. She has a paper cup of coffee in her hands but she is not drinking it.

'Hey,' I say softly. 'What are you doing here?'

And she doesn't hear me. Her eyes are fixed in front of her, as if she has grown into a fascination with the comings and goings at the cash machines opposite.

'Carlie…' I touch her on the shoulder – and her entire body contracts. A small tidal wave of coffee pours over the rim of her cup and down her legs, surely scalding her – yet she seems not to notice. Eyes wide she looks for who has touched her. Sees that it's me. Only me.

'Guy...' she whispers, and stops. My wife cannot speak. Not now. Not to me.

'Carlie, darling, I'm so sorry, I didn't mean to shock you.'

She stares at me, then down at her legs, touches the skin through the nylon of her stockings.

'Has it scalded you?'

She nods slowly.

'Badly? Are you in pain?'

Again she nods.

'We should get you to casualty. Carlie, what can I say? I'm so sorry.'

But I feel numb as I speak to her. Carlie is in pain and it's because of me. But what do I feel? A numb satisfaction. At what? That Carlie grew limp in his arms, and now she is in pain?

She shakes her head. 'It's alright. I don't want to go anywhere. Except home.'

Home. She has spoken the word so softly, with such a longing. And suddenly I don't feel numb, not any more.

I touch her leg, the soft scalded flesh. 'Forget the train, we'll get a cab. We'll get home quicker that way.'

In the back of the car, Carlie sits as if she is exhausted, stares out of the window.

'I went up to change a blouse that didn't fit,' she says at last. 'I bought it last week. That's why I was at the station.'

I don't mention that she is carrying no bag. Instead I say, 'The solicitors cancelled a conference with a client. That's why I came along. It's lucky we met.'

Lucky? That a touch from me has scalded her? Lucky? Because now we have lied to each other? We have both lied. And not even because we had to. Neither of us had asked what the other was doing there, at the station. We could have come home in this car, saying nothing, and kept clear of the subject.

That would mean silence, though. In lying, we are trying to

avoid the silence. Trying to keep contact, in any way we can. Preparing for what lies ahead.

In bed I reach for Carlie and immediately she responds, open to me, her fingers warm on my body.

And somehow the quickness of her response angers me, makes me come at her harder, more aggressively than she would ever expect. And she responds to this too, and the nature of our love making changes. We struggle with and against each other, forgetting the tender, scalded skin on her legs, taking what we want, forgetting who we are. Forgetting where we are.

Who are we now, Carlie? Who were you thinking I was?

She wouldn't answer me even if I asked. The act has exhausted her, put to sleep the demon that would have kept her awake. Now, she and her demon are both of them asleep, her face still flushed, beads of sweat still there on her forehead. Yet Carlie is shivering.

Why? What is making her shiver? If I could open up her head, reel out her thoughts, whose name would tumble out? It used to be in sleep I protected her. When she slept she became mine.

But now? Carlie is trembling as she sleeps. And while Carlie shivers and sleeps we are not alone. And this is what has happened. He's here, in Carlie's head, in Carlie's dreams. I can feel him, the air is vibrating with him, our bed is straining with the weight of him. What I do have to do, Carlie, to drive him out of your dreams?

Beneath my hand, where her skin is smooth and defenceless as silk, her pulse beats hard. Carlie is panting in her sleep. What is she seeing? What is she doing?

'Wake up Carlie.'

Carlie stirs. 'What?' Now she sits bolt upright. 'What's the matter?'

'You were dreaming,' I tell her coldly. And in the dark, I sense that Carlie is blushing.

Chapter Nineteen

What now? Who will take the next step? Not Carlie.

She is in retreat. I can see it in her. I see it in the carefulness with which she moves, in the way she walks. Willing herself to put one foot in front of the other, to act as if nothing has happened. But something has happened. I walk into rooms to find her staring at her arms, like someone watching for the first sign of a sickness, wondering when it will begin to show. Trying to hide her fascination at her own fate.

Carlie wipes her hands against the sides of her dress, surreptitiously, like a little girl who has come into contact with something dirty, who believes that she herself is somehow dirty. In the garden, she stares up at the trees, but now she touches her mouth, her cheeks, her lips, everywhere he touched her. I watch her shudder, and when we make love, I feel her shudder again. Carlie is excited and exhausted at the same time. She is thinking about him. But she can only show it at night when she has cover, when she can hide the reason for it. In bed she often makes the first move towards me.

But so long as she is awake, she is in possession of herself. She is trying to take control. I visit her computer and the modem has been disconnected.

I want to be relieved, but it means nothing. She can't keep him out like this. The computer was no more than his way in. He has Carlie's things. He knows where we live. And he knows what he wants. I saw him smile as he sat on the bench. The next step will be his. It is only a question of time. He will come for us, for what we have. He will come for Carlie.

In her dreams he has already arrived. I have begun to hate it when Carlie sleeps.

I talked to Carlie about Lydia and Saskia. I told her that Jonathan wants her to talk to Lydia. I watched her face, and...nothing. Carlie's face – that once upon a time betrayed every thought that scudded through her head – doesn't change.

'So...will you? Talk to Lydia, tell her not to meet up with this Sas?'

'Do you really think I should?'

'Don't you?'

'I don't think it would change anything – except how she feels about me. She'll think I'm against her too.'

'Jonathan isn't against Lydia. He's just desperate, frightened.'

'Why?' says Carlie. She sounds almost sullen 'Doesn't he trust his own wife?'

I look at her sharply, and this time Carlie blushes faintly. She looks away. 'I'm taking David over there tonight. I'll speak to Lydia then.'

I had forgotten. David is staying with Angus. Carlie is taking him round to Jonathan and Lydia's and then we are going for supper with Vanessa and Miles. Carlie was right. There was no getting out of it. Vanessa has us in her sights. She bundles David into the car together with all the paraphenalia of a boys' sleepover – skateboards, Warhammer pieces, CDs, sleeping bags. I watch them loading up the boot and am reminded of Carlie arriving at St Leonards . Half of David's room is going with him. Like mother, like son. Except he looks like me.

I pick up a pillow and an overnight bag and take them outside, add them to the pile.

'You look as if you're going away for a month,' I say. He smiles politely, something else that has returned to the way it was before. He *is* going away – further and further, unless I find a way to halt the journey. I remember Carlie and her father on the beach, stepping on each other's toes, and how *we* were on the beach in Dorset, before the dog. I think of our feet bunched under the covers.

On impulse I say, 'I wish none of us was going anywhere tonight. I wish we were all staying home, just the three of us, together.'

Something in my voice, unfamiliar to him, makes him look at me with interest. At the same time, my own words mock me. *Home*, in the house that we made, behind the trees Carlie planted. Safe. Except that Magnus has Carlie's things. He knows how to find us. Not safe any more.

Carlie is back sooner than I expected. She finds me in the bedroom where I am changing for dinner. I can see she is upset.

'I talked to Lydia. She didn't want to know.' She sits down at the dressing table and picks up a brush. 'God, I wish I hadn't opened my mouth. It was none of my business. I should have realised.' She sounds angry.

'What did you say to her?'

Carlie stares at her reflection. 'I told her not to meet her, this Saskia,' she says blankly. 'I said she might start something and not be able to stop. I said things might happen that no one...' She stops, turns from the mirror as if unable to hold her own gaze.

'What things, Carlie? What did you tell her?'

'Nothing. That's all. I just told her not to meet her. Now she thinks I'm interfering, accusing her of something that was never in her head. Just in mine.' Abruptly she puts down the brush, walks over to my side of the bed, tries to smooth out her features. Careful, she is putting the anger away where she thinks it can't be seen.

'Carlie...' I begin.

'Oh look!' she interrupts me, determined to change the subject. 'I remember this book.' She holds up my battered copy of Catullus. 'You used to carry it around all the time. *Flaming* Catullus – you said the Victorians called him. Remind me why it was, why they called him that.'

She is trying so hard, so flagrantly determined to distract me, that for a moment anger makes it difficult for me to speak. I have the sudden urge to slap her, the way you would slap a child who was lying to you. Except I have never hit any-one in my life. And certainly not a child. With an effort, I reach and take the book from her.

'He was a poet. He wrote about being in love with a woman he called Lesbia. But she was unfaithful. He'd keep finding out how she'd betrayed him. He tries to stop loving her but she's like a virus inside him, a disease. She turns everything upside down. He wants to live with her forever – next minute he just wants to see her dead. He watches her with her lover. He burns for her, yearns for her. And you know it will never stop, not till one or all of them is destroyed.'

There – I have answered my wife. In David's absence, a silence has settled over our house. Even the hamster is quiet on his wheel. For the first time in years, I find Carlie looking at me, uncertain about what she sees.

We arrive at Miles and Vanessa's for dinner. Immediately Vanessa drags Carlie into the kitchen, while Miles spills gin into a glass and tries to sell me a pension plan.

Miles is in financial services and, I assume, successful. There's £30,000 of landscape gardening going on in front of the house, and from the kitchen Vanessa's voice reaches us, talking about the brawny young men toiling on her drive, already shirtless in this mild March weather. If Miles can hear her, he makes no sign – unless it is to move the ice around more noisily in his glass.

'Here they come,' he says as Vanessa appears with Carlie, both laden with trays of canapés. 'The monstrous regiment of women.'

Vanessa puts down her tray in front of me. She is wearing another of those low tops, and her breasts tip forward as if about to pour themselves like cream over the filo pastries.

'Actually,' she says, staying bent, moving the pastries around, keeping her breasts where they can be seen. 'It's *regimen*. He wasn't talking about a monstrous army of females, but the reign of two – Elizabeth and Mary, Queens of England and Scotland. He didn't like women being charge.'

'Who?' says Miles. 'Who didn't like them?'

'John Knox.' Vanessa stands up, pops a pink shrimp between shrimp-coloured lips. 'That's right isn't it, Guy?'

Suddenly I see what Vanessa wants me to see. A quiet house with men outside, and Vanessa inside, scantily dressed, reading history.

'Monstrous army, monstrous reign,' grunts Miles. 'Same bloody thing.' He turns to me. 'Heard about Lydia and the dykey goings on with the email? It's just like I said, hot chums and all.'

'How did you hear about…?'

'Jonathan of course, drunk as skunk and going on about it all night at the golf club last Thursday. Don't blame him. Bloody lesbian feminists, bra burners, taking over the world. Sorely tried, he is, poor bastard.'

Carlie catches my eye, gives me the ghost of a smile. And for the first time in days, I feel at peace, close to her. In this at least, we understand each other.

'Of course, it's not just Lydia who's at it. Half of Patersfield is up to something.' Vanessa hands me a plate of raw, bloody steak tartare. We, her guests, have to hope that landscaped lawns and a designer kitchen are all it takes to keep salmonella, campylobacter and BSE at bay.

She picks up a fork, spears her first quivering lump of flesh. 'Although I have to say Lydia is the last one I would have thought of. Gallumphing Greta, that's our Lyd. I suppose it had to be a girl thing when you think about it.'

'Not so bad for Jonathan, though,' says Miles. 'Once he

gets used to the idea...'

'She has nice breasts though,' continues Vanessa, thought-fully. 'Not that you'd ever notice under those dreadful clothes she will insist on wearing. Did you ever notice, Guy?'

'Notice what?'

'That Lydia has nice breasts?'

'No, I can't say I did.' I cast a glance at Carlie, whose face remains expressionless.

'What's the betting Saskia is the mirror image of Lydia, right down to the incredible snorting? Do they breed them like that in the shires, Guy? Or is Lydia just a one off?'

'Vanessa,' Carlie's voice is soft. 'Don't.'

Vanessa's eyes flicker. 'Oh come on, Carlie darling, get down off your high horse. Good luck to her, I say. There's Lydia who hasn't seen a coat of paint for years and now every-one wants to bed her. Poor girl hasn't had that kind of atten-tion in her entire life – well, not since boarding school. Now here she is, suddenly part of the club.'

'What club?' says Carlie.

Instead of answering, Vanessa turns to me.

'Did you know Patersfield has its very own detective agency, Guy? No? Everyone else does – or if they don't, they find out eventually. Sooner or later, people simply have to know what's going on in their own bedrooms. They talk to nice Mr. Robinson, and voilà! – all questions answered. For a fee of course. *You* know all about Mr. Robinson, don't you Miles?' she snaps suddenly at her husband. 'Done a spot of business with him yourself, haven't you?'

Miles meets her stare. 'I might have sold him a unit bond or two.'

Foolishly, I ask a question. 'If everyone ends up going to him, why isn't half of Patersfield divorced?'

Vanessa looks at my dish, observes the steak only half eaten. 'Not much of a lawyer, are you Guy? You've left all the nice bloody bits on the side of your plate. But since you *are* a lawyer, you should know the reason for that. Look around you, look at what people have. They can't keep all that, not if they're going to get divorced. They'd have to start sharing out the assets, sell those nice big houses. God help them, they might even have to take their little darlings out of private schools and dump them in the nasty state system instead. Why put themselves through it? Especially when they realise that what's sauce for the goose can't be so bad for the gander.'

She turns suddenly back to Carlie and snaps, '*That's* what I mean by club, darling. Lydia and Jonathan will stagger on because, in the end, they'll find they can't face up to the alternative. They'll say they need to stay together for the sake of the boy – what *is* his name? – and call it being grown up. Jonathan will start giving young girls the glad eye, and Lydia will wish she had never switched on her computer. They'll have found out everything they need to know about each other and life will carry on in its usual way. I'm sure they'll both be very happy.'

There's a silence. Miles reaches across the table. 'More wine anyone?'

Carlie touches the tablecloth, her glass, and in a low voice says. 'What about love, Vanessa? Don't you think it's love sometimes that keeps people together? Don't you believe in it at all?'

Miles sloshes wine over the tablecloth. Vanessa seems not to notice. The wine seeps slowly into the damask staining it a dark indelible red and all while Vanessa observes my wife. Carlie, caught in the stare, colours faintly.

Finally Vanessa says, '*Love,* darling? Now you're talking about something completely different. *Love* covers a multitude of sins. Don't you think?' And Vanessa allows her lips to stretch, revealing a tiny piece of raw steak caught between her teeth.

We say our goodbyes, exhausted. Vanessa and Miles have

ground us down.

'Remind me,' I say to Carlie in the car, 'exactly why we came here to live.'

I mean it as a joke, but immediately the truth of it hits home. Houses slumber behind their trees. Well-fed, well-disciplined children lie dreaming in their beds; husbands and wives, faithful or otherwise, in theirs. A dormitory town, a town that sleeps at night. Where, according to Vanessa, people close their eyes to a multitude of sins just so everything can stay like this – asleep. We are a long, long way from the sea, winter skies and short summer nights swallowed up by the sun; and Carlie stretching at the end of my bed *I haven't slept the whole entire night.*

I glance at Carlie in the streetlight. There is a line I haven't seen before traced into the corner of her mouth. I take my hand off the wheel and touch the side of her face, and the line disappears. Carlie presses her cheek into the palm of my hand and leaves it there.

We pass David's school with its breeze block tower and graffiti painted gate. 'He's really happy there,' says Carlie as if out of the blue. But in fact she's giving me an alternative answer to the question, one reason to be here.

At home, there's still the peace between us as we undress. I feel close to Carlie, closer than I have since the rose garden, since I made her scald herself with coffee, since the need was born to fumble through Carlie's things.

Tonight, Miles and Vanessa have united us and we fall asleep straight away. Perhaps we have been soothed by the moment of understanding that we shared, and Carlie laying herself open with that one question: *don't you think it's love sometimes...?*

Later, though, I wake up; my arms are empty and Carlie is gone. There is no light in the bathroom, no light anywhere. I force myself to stay in bed and wait for her to come back. But

Carlie doesn't come. Somewhere in our house she is sitting in the dark. Alone.

A long time passes, and Carlie slips between the sheets. I stir as if I was just waking up.

'What's the matter, Carlie?'

A pause and then she answers me. 'It was David. He had a nightmare, that's all. He's gone straight back to sleep.'

She has forgotten that David is not here, he is staying the night with Angus.

Jonathan phones me in Chambers, pesters me to go for a drink with him in town. He doesn't understand I have to go home, watch for the signs in Carlie, find out what she has done with her day. But he won't take no for an answer and we make our way to a pub close to the inns of court, another wood panelled place where lawyers have drunk for the past two hundred years. My father came here when he was a young man. Only the Australian barman is new.

Why have we chosen here? This is not the place to try and work our way into the minds of our wives. But Jonathan is a creature of habit and it hasn't occurred to him to go anywhere different.

'She's done it, Guy. She's gone and met her, the bitch. They had lunch together last week.' Jonathan raises both hands with the fingers crook'd to denote quotation marks round the *lunch*. 'She didn't even try to hide it from me.'

'That's good, isn't it, that she's told you? It shows she's not trying to keep any secrets.'

'Shows she doesn't give a toss whether I know or not.'

He laughs bitterly. Jonathan is beginning to go heavy round the mouth, despondency is weighing down his face, making him look pouchier, older than before. The boyish look is deserting him finally. Much more of this and he will begin to look like Miles. Makes me wonder – is the same happening to me? I have more reason to age than he has; I have seen my wife dissolve under the kiss of another man. Fifteen years turned upside down. All Lydia has had is *lunch.*

Wearily I say, 'Carlie thinks you should trust Lydia. Trying to stop her...well, Carlie thinks it's counter productive. Makes Lydia think you're against her.'

'Against her? Of course I'm against her. I'm against Lydia for every second she thinks of carrying on with this...this bitch of a so called-friend. Against her? How would you feel?'

He dives into his pocket and takes out a packet of cigarettes. I'd forgotten Jonathan used to smoke, long ago and in the days when Lydia used to sing opera in the bath. Before children and miscarriages. Busy with the old paraphernalia of matches that won't seem to light, he doesn't notice that I have no answer.

How would I feel? I am different from him. I suspect my wife of standing on the edge of an affair, but I am not against her. I could never be against Carlie. It's what's inside her I'm against, occupying her dreams, making her shiver in her sleep. The sickness in Carlie, a case of kill or cure.

Is that how I see it, then, a sickness? Not her fault. What if there is no cure? If there is no curing Carlie, what else can be done with her?

Jonathan sighs, tosses aside the matches which still refuse to light. He probably fished him out of his gardening jacket, forgetting that it poured the last time he used them. These are matches for the garden, for bonfires, for standing in the rain, contentedly poking at damp decaying clutter while Lydia potters about inside – not for the nervous sparking of cigarettes in Lydia's absence. Those days are gone. Now he is looking at me, pleading, and I have to think of something to say. Something that would help him. Help us both.

'Maybe you just have to trust Lydia. What else can you do? You can't watch her every minute of every day.'

Jonathan frowns, then stops frowning and looks thought-ful, almost sly. 'You may be wrong about that. I can't watch her but I know a man who could. Vanessa was telling us just the other day about this agency in Patersfield, very discreet...'

I interrupt. 'Jonathan, what possible good would that do?'

He bristles. The tone of my voice has made him defensive. 'It would put my mind at rest for a start. *Trust her*, you say. Well, it will show if I can.'

'And if he sees something he shouldn't?'

Jonathan grips his glass. In a thick voice he says, 'Well we'll just have to see, won't we?'

Later he wants us to go home by the same train, but I tell him I have work to do. I can't talk to him any more, not tonight. Back in Chambers, Gary, who will be here later than anyone, calls to me from his office.

'Mrs. Latimer has just been on the phone. She wants to know what you've been doing all day.'

He has the deadpan face of all good barristers' clerks, does-n't raise an eyebrow when the message makes me laugh for no reason that he could see. Laugh? I sound like a man choking on stones. Carlie wants to know what *I've* been doing.

Carlie can make me account for every minute of the day if she wants to. Someone would be able to tell her where I am – or lie at least – and never bat an eyelid that she should ask. But how can I find out about Carlie? Who could I ask to tell me what Carlie does with her day?

Sitting in my room, I stop laughing. There *is* a man who could tell me exactly that. A man who could watch her, patiently dogging her footsteps, finding out what she does. Where she goes, who she meets. There's a man in Patersfield who could do all this, who could tell me what she does with her day. Is it a coincidence that two people have mentioned his name in as many days?

No.

No.

My mind says *no*, the way Carlie said *no*, jamming the word twice into her machine. Repeating the answer, once for him, and once for herself. *No.* And then what did she do?

Not me, though. I will not set someone to watch my own wife. That would be madness, a betrayal of everything we have. Faith and trust, this is how we have lived, Carlie and I all these years - our weapons and our reward.

David lets his knife and fork clatter against his plate. In a flat voice he says:

'Mr. Repton says to tell you there's good news.'

Carlie looks up slowly.

'Mr. Repton...?' She looks as bewildered as I am. For a moment neither of us is able to think who Mr. Repton is. We are preoccupied, the two of us, bound up in our own thoughts. Then she remembers. 'Your maths teacher. Of course. What sort of good news?'

'He says he's found a maths tutor to teach special needs. He wants me to have lessons, stay behind at school twice a week.' Our son's face crumples. 'What does he mean "special needs"? I'm *good* at maths.'

Carlie pulls herself out of her reverie. 'Oh David, love – of course you are. Special needs can be lots of things. What Mr. Repton means is that you're far too bright to be doing what everyone else is doing. You need that tutor, someone to give you the attention Mr. Repton thinks you deserve.'

David opens his mouth, then closes it again as he takes this in: he is brighter, cleverer than the rest. He deserves attention. Just like Carlie after all, the old Carlie who would have run across hot coals just to be noticed. The flat look is gone. Pleasure makes him squirm almost imperceptibly, in his chair, and Carlie and I are able to look at each other secretly, and smile. And remember.

'David...' I begin, and it occurs to me this is the first time in days that my voice has sounded normal.

The doorbell rings. Carlie is the first to get up, go to the door. David and I sit and look at each other in silence over our plates, trying to decipher the murmur of voices in the distance. The murmuring stops, but Carlie doesn't return. Presently I go out into the hall to see what has happened, and she is there, still next to the front door, holding something in her hand: long and slender, wrapped in a column of paper carrying the name of the florists in Patersfield..

'Carlie...?'

And Carlie jumps, almost clean out of her skin, stares at me blank eyed. 'It's a mistake!' The murmured words seem to have been torn out of her.

'What? What's a mistake, Carlie?'

But now I've seen what is in her hand, wrapped in the column of florists' paper. A single rose, the same shape and colour as the rose *he* gave her in the rose garden.

Carlie shudders then springs back to life. 'I told them it was the wrong address, to take it somewhere else. They said they weren't allowed. They had to give it to me.'

And before I can answer she strides past me towards the kitchen, wrenches open the bin and stuffs the rose right down inside, violently, breaking the stem, leaving the head to nestle, bruised, among the chicken bones. She slams down the lid and stands up straight, trying to look brisk, matter of fact. But she hasn't noticed that her hand is bleeding, caught by the thorns, snagged the way his hand was snagged. Oblivious the way he was oblivious. Drops of blood are falling on our kitchen floor.

Meanwhile David stares over her shoulder, down at the bin and its ruined flower, with a degree of awe. This was an act close to anyone's definition of vandalism. When Carlie turns her back to us, clattering pots and pans in the sink, he shoots a glance at me, but he gets nothing in reply. I meet the question in his eyes, deadpan, freezing him out.

Later, in bed, Carlie tries to stay awake. Fists clenched in the dark, fighting off sleep. I lie beside her, hearing her catch her breath as the thoughts drift through her head; wishing she could stave off sleep for ever. Stave him off.

But eventually, long before me, sleep takes her. Presently Carlie begins to shiver and I imagine there are roses now, roses in her dreams, roses everywhere, blooming out of season, weighed down by raindrops.

I tell myself that Carlie dreams, but I am not against her. I could never be against Carlie. I tell myself it's a sickness, not her fault. I tell myself to trust her, to keep the faith. But while Carlie shivers and moans *he* works away inside her, taking hold of her like a virus, like a disease. There is no trusting Carlie while she sleeps. In her dreams the sickness grows, something that wants to be choked out of her, destroyed. Broken like the stems of unwanted roses.

'*Wake up, Carlie.*'

I have to wake her. Have to. Immediately Carlie stops shivering and stirs.

'Guy?' She has whispered my name in the dark, as if unsure who is sleeping beside her, even now when she is awake. She reaches out and touches me, and it's all I can do not to recoil. She says, 'You're sweating. Is something the matter?'

'I was dreaming,' I say dully. 'Of roses.' And beside me in the bed, Carlie gasps.

Faith and trust. What are they after all, compared to dreams?

Robinson's Detective Agency is a single line in the Yellow Pages. No box, just that line of address that puts it right opposite the supermarket. I have walked, driven, even cycled past it every day since we came to Patersfield, and I never knew it was there. It was always the solicitors I noticed, next door, and the off licence on the other side...

...Suddenly I'm aware of a presence by my shoulder. Makes

me jump, making David jump in turn.

'Mum heard a noise in the study. She thought the cat had got in again, messing up your papers. She sent me in to get rid of it. We didn't know it was you. We didn't even know you were home.' He makes this last statement blank faced, as if reserving judgement.

And I stare at him. This is what I have done – walked through my front door, and carried on walking, straight upstairs to my study and the bookshelf to find this: the yellow pages and a line of address. I forgot to go to my family, to greet my child, to kiss Carlie on the cheek. I forgot everything that normally happens when I come home.

David waits a moment, his face oddly strained, expecting me to speak, and still I can only stare at him, speechless. Briefly I find myself wondering if there's not something else on his mind, beyond this – my surprise appearance at home. But before I can find the necessary words, he turns on his heel to go down stairs. I hear his footsteps in the hall, a muttered '*He's home.*'

Next moment Carlie is hurrying into the study.

'You *are* home,' she says faintly, as if not believing David until now. 'Why didn't you say?'

She stares at me a moment, her eyes searching my face, which tells her – nothing. Yet she knows something is up, something has gone wrong. Small rituals repeated every day – they come to have the force of nature. I have arrived home and not gone to find her, and she is mystified. When I don't answer she glances at the directory open in front of me. Instinctively I cover it with my hand, and force myself to smile. I force myself to smile at Carlie.

'Sorry. I must have had something on my mind. Is supper ready?' My voice is cool.

She blinks. Without an ounce of rudeness, courteous to a fault, I have rebuffed my wife. And it's the same as when I caused her to scald herself – there is a moment of a numbed satisfaction. A small measure of payback for not telling me what she does with her day.

Forcing me to find out in other ways.

Yet if she would only talk to me, tell me what she was thinking, I could close the directory with its address, its surprising proximity to everything familiar, and make myself forget about it. But Carlie doesn't talk to me. On the contrary, she takes a step back, away from me. I have managed to make Carlie shy, the way she would become shy every now and then, years ago when we were young, before she was sure of me.

She touches her arm instead, as if to steady herself. 'Supper's on the table. We were only waiting for you.' She turns, doesn't wait for me to follow her downstairs.

Chapter Twenty

Saturday morning. The men are abroad in the streets of Patersfield – and Robinson's Detective Agency is up a flight of stairs that lead from a narrow blue door slotted between the off licence and that firm of solicitors. There's a small brass plaque in the brickwork, something you'd only notice if you were looking for it.

I looked for it today, and before I quite knew what I was doing, stepped inside and climbed the stairs, followed a smell of disinfectant to the top floor and a neat white door.

And here I am. Mr. Robinson has just asked if I would like a coffee. He'll make it for me himself, he says. There's the Waitrose just across the street, so he can offer me fresh not powdered milk. Makes all the difference, don't I think? He'd like to proffer biscuits too, but Mrs. Robinson won't let him keep them in the office. He pats his large stomach by way of explanation and shakes his head.

'So, Mr....' he checks the note he made when I came in '...Latimer?'

He waits, makes no effort to hurry me. He reminds me of an old fashioned grocer behind his counter, with all his goods around him – which he might even have been once, before Waitrose and the Sainsbury's further up the road made grocers surplus to requirements. What he doesn't remind me of are any of the detectives I grew up with – Philip Marlowe or Peter Wimsey or Father Brown. But then, it's been a long time since I read a crime novel; maybe the literature has caught up, and between the pages the heroes wear cardigans and sit in offices smelling of cleaning fluids and egg sandwiches.

'You specialise in...' I say, and pause.

'...Writ serving and surveillance. That I do, Mr. Latimer. Although for the record, I should say I also track down relatives of individuals who have died intestate, not to mention my new line, genealogy. A nice little business actually – people's family trees, chasing up parish records, old census forms etcetera. Lots of book bashing. I'm thinking of including it next time I advertise…'

'But you *specialise* in…'

'…Writ serving and surveillance. Yes.' He looks at me. And waits.

I stare at my hands. Not so long ago, they would have been ink-stained, the ink never quite disappearing, proof of how I pass the day. Now I have computers – at home, at work. Carlie has one. David covets one he could call his own, as Angus does. We all have them. Mr. Robinson has one on his desk, an old one, which surprises me: probably it takes an age to boot up. Then again, Mr. Robinson's work isn't something that can all be done on a computer. It takes a man to sit in a car, patiently watching who goes up and down the garden paths. A man to work the camera that will record people opening their front doors, curtains pulled across bedroom windows in the middle of the day. A man to write down dates and times and names. Subject enters, subject departs. Mr. Robinson eats an egg sandwich made by Mrs. Robinson. Computers can only do so much. After that everything is human. Everything exchangeable.

I stare at my hands. Mr. Robinson waits.

'It's my wife,' I say at last.

'Ah yes.'

'I don't know what she does with her day.'

'I see. And you work…?'

'Long hours. Up in town.'

'Which is why you have no way of knowing what she does.'

I open my mouth – and close it again. He looks at me. Studies my face. After a moment he sighs.

'And do you think she might be doing something in particular – with her day? Something she would rather not let on to you?'

He wants to know about you, Carlie. He wants to know about you before he finds out about you. I steal a quick look at his face and see his expression is gentle.

Instead of answering the question, I say: 'You're next door to solicitors. That must be convenient. For both of you.'

'Oh very. I do all their writ-serving for them. They're proper gentlemen in that sense – old school, if you follow. So many of these firms will send their female clerks or secretaries to do the business – they reckon there's less chance of a girl getting a biff on the nose from someone who doesn't like what's coming. But old Mr. Fox, he doesn't hold with that. He pays a fair whack and gets me to do it instead.'

Again, I am hesitating before I speak. 'It's not just the writ serving though, is it? That's not the only business you end up sharing, you and the solicitors? There must be a lot of…family law.'

He nods. 'I get your drift, Mr. Latimer. Oh yes, there's quite a lot of business passes between us. I take the photographs, gather up the evidence. They handle the what-comes-after.'

'The divorce.'

'The divorce,' he agrees with me. 'Funny, people can suspect something's going on for years, but it's only once they see for themselves – photographic evidence and the like – that it changes everything. It's a good reason, when you think of it, for a client to ask himself: is proof really what he wants? Quite often folk come in here, demanding all sorts of evidence without knowing what they would do once they've got it. And having the lawyers next door – well it can be almost too handy.' He pauses, then gently asks the question. 'So, Mr. Latimer how much do you really want to know – about your wife?'

Stammering, I answer him. 'Nothing. Everything.' Then irrationally, my voice blurts out. 'I only want what she would tell me herself, if she could.'

There's a silence as Mr. Robinson watches me. I can hear the traffic passing below the window, people's voices in the street. Strangely I have no sense of belonging there, out where the people are, where Patersfield is.

Slowly Mr. Robinson says, 'So you think there is something your wife would like to tell you, but can't?'

I nod.

'And you want me to find out for you – what it is that she can't tell you. Not even you.'

Again I nod. Then shake my head. *No.*

No.

Abruptly, I stand up. 'I'm sorry, Mr. Robinson. I thought I could do this. I was wrong. I'm afraid I've been wasting your time.'

He shakes his own head. 'Not at all. Sometimes it's quite in order to have second thoughts, leave things alone. Better, even.'

He sees me look doubtful, uneasy at seeming like a man who would rather turn a blind eye.

'I mean it, Mr. Latimer! It's something that's been occupying my own mind these last weeks. Recently, right in the middle of watching somebody, I'll catch myself thinking how it's all down to me. Once I've seen what I've seen, got the proof, there's no going back, not for anyone. I do the observation. I record what I see – and I make it exist, whatever was happening, just by doing my job. Before me, everything would be up in the air; there could be an explanation for every little thing – if you're flexible. People can live with flexibility, you know – at least some people can. Then I go and get the proof, and it all falls into place. I've gone and changed everything.'

I remember Vanessa's observation. 'But it doesn't always have to end in divorce. People stay together despite everything.'

'True, but whether they can say things are the same after, well...' He sighs, and smiles at himself. 'But there you are. You've caught me in a funny frame of mind today. It happens. Wouldn't do for me to be like this all the time, would it – warning prospective clients against using my services. That's not the way to get rich, is it? And they wouldn't like it, all those lawyers next door. They'd end up not having half enough to do.'

Now he is standing up too. Despite Mrs. Robinson there are biscuit crumbs falling off the front of his trousers. He reaches out and shakes my hand. 'Good luck, Mr. Latimer. And if you want your family tree looking at, you come straight back. The past now, that's what I'd like to be interested in. That's something no amount of observation can change. Family trees and all – you can't hurt the dead by looking at them.'

I step out into the street, and the life in Patersfield picks up where briefly it seemed to leave off. I have only been inside for ten minutes, yet I feel as if I had been away, in a different world. The sad, observing world of Mr. Robinson who would prefer to specialise in family trees. But I should have taken more care, been more like the sign on the door – discreet, less noticeable. As I stand, gulping fresh air, a voice purrs in my ear.

'Why Guy, you've been to see the adorable Mr. Robinson! Such a funny little man, don't you think? Always has the strangest ideas if he can get you stop and listen to him. Very good at his job, though, or so they tell me. You'll have to let me know.'

Vanessa.

'Darling!' she exclaims, 'If looks could kill! Don't worry, pet, if you won't tell, I won't tell.'

'There's nothing to tell,' I say shortly.

She smiles, tucks a loose strand of yellow hair behind her

ear where it stays, trapped by a great chunk of twisted gold weighing down the lobe. 'Of course not. There never is.' She mocks me as she speaks. But only for a moment, before her eyes sweep past me. 'Oooh look, there's Tanya coming out of Waitrose. I'm going to have to grab her. I'm simply dying for a coffee.'

She leaves me, runs across the road, stopping traffic as she goes. She is surprisingly fast on her heels, a creature absolutely adapted to her environment. Lean, decorative, deadly. On the other pavement I see her tuck her arm through the arm of another woman, a smaller, grimmer, version of herself. Vanessa whispers something in her ear, and the woman glances over at me – and away again, quickly.

If I had the power to throttle the life out of someone now, I would. Slowly. Gladly.

Chapter Twenty-One

This evening, after work, I oiled the lock to the front door.

I had come home, put my key in the lock and heard it scrape. And so I reached into the cupboard under the stairs and oiled it. Only then did I walk on into the house to greet my family.

For fifteen years I have always loved coming home. The kitchen will be warm with the heat from the oven, untidy with school things and newspapers, the radio on low. I have always loved coming home; years ago it would be the moment when David would barrel towards me as I walked through the door, a toddler whose hands gripped the back of my calves. A human greave, warm against my legs.

I have always loved coming home, even in the last year, when I have known the conversation will stall as soon I enter; when Carlie will smile at me, and after a decent interval David will retreat to his room. Does he know he has a tendency to straighten his shoulders when I appear? On his guard, as if I were a teacher appearing on the scene, the way I used to be with my father. Yet I always thought it would be alright; somehow we would make good, grow out of it, both of us. Carlie would make it happen.

I have always loved coming home. But tonight, having oiled the lock to our front door, I would rather go straight to my study and close the door. I don't want to see the strain in Carlie's face, the reserve in David's. I fight the urge and make for the kitchen.

And the first thing I notice is that Carlie doesn't look so strained this evening. She has spent the last couple of hours with David. Perhaps she can forget the rest, remember only that she is a mother, immersed in his talk, the complexities of his life, so dependent on ours.

I walk through the door and Carlie smiles, and David

jumps off the table where he has been sitting till a moment ago.

I make a point of kissing Carlie. Small rituals with the force of nature. Smile at David.

'So – what did you do with your day?'

And straightaway Carlie answers me – but not on her own behalf. 'David started with his new maths tutor.' She smiles at our son. 'Tell him what you were telling me just now.'

David shrugs. He would rather not tell me anything now that he's said it all to Carlie.

'Well?' I try again, more warmly this time. 'Well?'

'He's good,' He says finally and pulls at his shirt which is grubby the way I remember my own shirts becoming grubby, long ago. Nowadays only a faint rime along the inside of a collar will show I have worn a shirt at all. Even the ironed creases remain intact.

'*Good?*' I repeat after him politely.

He shrugs. 'Like I said. *Good.*'

'So...' I cast around for a question *I asked Carlie what she did with her day. And she didn't answer* 'What's his name?'

'Who?'

'The tutor.'

And now he's scowling at me. I should have remembered – names are his weak point, the way they used to be for me, before I grew up and learned people require you to remember things like names. 'I dunno,' he says at last. 'Mr. Magnet or something.'

'He can't be called Mr. Magnet,' says Carlie amused. 'That's not a name.'

But having plumped for Magnet, David is sticking to it. 'No that's it.' His voice is firm. 'Mr Magnet. That's what he's called.'

'So,' I persist. 'What's so good about him, this Mr...Magnet?' But now it sounds as if I am mocking. David blushes, kicks the table, then remembers that I'm watching, and stops. *Kick the table leg, David. Don't stop because of me.*

He says, 'He's not like the other teachers. I mean he's like them in age, but he doesn't act like them. He's sort of strange, but interesting. Like in the things he says.' Unconsciously, he warms to his theme. 'Like he says Maths is good because it's...mind expanding. Like drugs. If you do enough of it, and know what you're doing, it'll change the way you see the world.'

Carlie glances at me half humorously. *'Doing maths, doing drugs.* I don't know if I like the way your Mr. Magnet puts that.'

David shakes his head, impatient. 'I probably didn't say it right. I'm just trying to tell you why he's good. He talks like he expects you to understand him, even when the things he says are odd. It's like he thinks I'm clever or something.'

I say, 'Don't the other teachers do that? They all tell *us* you're clever.'

And there it is, the dry note again, the one that impresses judges, reassures clients. The effect on my son is to make him retract into himself, unwilling to answer me. I have the feeling that he doesn't feel so clever, not when I'm around.

Carlie says softly, 'Are you trying to say he makes you feel special? Not like the other boys?'

He nods. And blushes again. Carlie's face is soft as she watches him. She understands why he likes this teacher. Shy Carlie, who used to struggle so hard to shine, she understands our son. She wants me to understand him too.

Making the effort, I say, 'Alright then, he sounds good, then, this Mr. Magnet. I look forward to meeting him.' I glance at Carlie. 'I'm going to get changed.'

It's my opportunity to leave the room before David feels he has to. The moment the door closes behind me I hear him talking to Carlie again, the way he was before I came in.

Letting her forget, keeping her occupied.

And while she is occupied, quietly I check her computer, already putting words into *his* mouth. *My lady of light, what did you think of my rose?* But the modem continues to be disconnected, and there are no more messages on her machine. He's not using the email any more.

In the middle of the night Carlie called my name. I was asleep but I heard her voice, anguished, reaching out to me.

I was dreaming when she called; dreaming of a tunnel, and the two of us heading for the light at the end of it. Carlie was behind me in the dark. I could hear her steps, feel the warmth of her breath on the back of my neck. *Follow me, Carlie.* The light is a small steady burst ahead of us – yet still so far away. Nevertheless, out of the light drift scents of a green, nearly forgotten world – of earth and grass and rain – mingling with the burnt sugar scent of Carlie at my shoulder. A reminder of what's there if only we could reach it.

We've come this far, Carlie.

Then something frightens her, and she calls my name. And, always alert, I turn.

Carlie-in-the-dream gasps. I see her shudder and stop dead, as if streams of air have turned to steel bands across her chest. She stretches out her hands to me, but it's no use, she is being drawn backwards, away from me, back down the tunnel, into the dark. And like the fool, always the fool in the meadow, I watch her vanish. Only her voice remains, there in my ear, calling for me.

I wake, and Carlie is still calling. Screaming. Her head twists and turns on the pillow, and her hands flail. I take her and hold her, and she struggles against me. She shouts for me to help her as she fights. She doesn't know I'm here, that I'm the one she's fighting.

Suddenly her eyes open and for a moment she stares. Then

she recognises me and her body collapses against mine.

'Carlie.' I feel her cheeks wet against my face, rock her in my arms.

Still she clings to me, as if to convince herself I'm real.

'Carlie,' I whisper. 'Talk to me. Tell me what you were dreaming about.'

Her body tenses again, then relaxes. A moment and then she whispers, so quietly I can hardly hear her: 'I thought you'd left me. You just gave up on me and turned away. I tried to come after you. I fought so hard but there was…' she pauses '…something stopping me.'

I hold her closer to me. 'Something stopping you, Carlie? *Or do you mean someone?*'

She catches her breath at the last part of the question. At the same time I feel her body lean into mine. And this time I know: finally Carlie is going to tell me; she is going to say who was in her dream, and how he came to be there. She is going to talk to me. In a heartbeat, in a spiral of time we will be back in the old days, when Carlie used to tell me everything. Carlie will take us back. And I am ready.

'Carlie,' I whisper again. 'Tell me what was in your dream.'

Faith and trust, Carlie. *We can fight him together.*

Then comes a faint sound in the dark. Our bedroom door has opened slightly, and a voice sounding younger than its years, high pitched with alarm:

'What's the matter? Why was Mum screaming?'

David. Carlie's body grows tense again. I say quickly, 'No reason. Mum was having a bad dream. But it's over. I'm with her.'

He observes us by the light of the landing, the two of us in bed, Carlie in my arms. I can see how it looks to him. When Carlie and I have nightmares we have each other. But who does he have? Now he stands at the end of our bed, trembling from the shock of being woken by the sounds of screams.

Probably he would like to climb into bed with us, like when he was small, inserting his soft body between us, keeping us apart, drawing us together. Or perhaps he's thinking of how it was in the cottage, the three of us, our feet bunched under the covers.

And I say to him, 'Go back to bed, David.'

Reluctantly he turns away, goes padding back to his own room, alone.

'*Go with him,*' Carlie whispers. And reluctantly I go. He lets me help him into bed, pull the covers over him, tucking them around his neck. On impulse, I kiss his forehead, and taste the sweat on his skin. Such a long time since I have kissed him. Our son has nightmares too. His eyes are begging me to stay, just a little while, just till he falls asleep.

Carlie, though. I have to get back to Carlie.

Yet when I lie down beside her, try to take her in my arms, she shakes her head, lays a finger on my lips.

'Go to sleep, Guy.'

With that she turns over on her side. She won't tell me now. She can't. Once she would have told me everything, but that was in the old days, when there were only the two of us – both of us children, when you think of it. Now there's a third child, who sleeps on his own, reminding us that everything has a consequence. He has only us. There is so much she can't tell me now. So much to lose.

Every year St Leonards sends us its university magazine. It arrives with the same thump of brown concealing manilla and tell-tale university crest. And every year one or other of us will throw it away, unopened.

This year, however, the magazine slithers through the letter box in a new format, wrapped up in see-through cellophane. So there it is on the mat, with the photograph on the cover catching me by surprise. This is the exact scene I used to see out of my window: the East sands – a long low line of dunes with the sea rising up behind. And, curved around the bay like a collapsed crescent moon, the old stone buildings of the university.

Instantly I'm hit by an unexpected blast of nostalgia. A yearning for mornings when the light hurt your eyes, and winds came sweeping straight out of the sun. And most of all for Carlie curling up on my bed – *I haven't slept the whole entire night…* We left footprints in the sand, the two of us, but nothing more than that. We abandoned the town, the university and the sands with indecent haste; and in its turn, the place would have forgotten us within minutes.

Or is that not quite true? As I flick through the pages, I see there are people who might remember us. Staring out of one page, there's a familiar face that turns out to belong to Walsh who has just been appointed Professor of Greek. Fifteen years on, he's grown fat, with fuzzy grey locks and a tweed jacket. But he's laughing into the camera. He looks *jolly.* Carlie comes into the kitchen to find me smiling over his photograph with a mix of amusement and regret. I hold it up and say, *remember him?* And with the smallest of shudders she retreats.

But here is another face, easier even to recognise than Walsh's. Senior lecturer Dr. Jennifer Saunders stands by her desk, her hair not in plaits now, but swept back from her face. She is slim to the point of thin, her fingers obviously ink stained, even in the photograph. She's still using pen and paper, then, still committing thoughts through the tips of her fingers. She looks calm, serious, and barely changed from when I saw her last. She teaches Lyric poetry. My subject. She looks happy.

In another world, it could have been me standing there. A specialist in poetry; in other words, a specialist in other people's jealousies, other people's loves. Two thousand year old passions and fears, so much easier to bear than one's own. Has she had a life outside the pages? As always with Jennifer, it's impossible to tell. I stare at the face in the photograph. Her gaze is so clear, observing rather than observed. I can almost believe she can see me. Grey eyes, just as I remember them.

What might have happened if life hadn't fallen into two paths, each making the other impossible? What if I had made another choice, years ago? What if I had been capable? Underneath the résumé of her university life and academic achievement Jennifer has attached a small but formal personal note: her email address, suggesting old pupils and friends get in touch with her.

And Carlie, where would she be now if we hadn't chosen? I put the magazine among my papers, ready to kiss her goodbye and drive to the station. On my way out of the door, I say to her, casually as I can. 'And what are you doing today, Carlie?'

This and that comes the reply, with a smile to make up for what she will not, cannot tell me.

So what does Carlie's day consist of? Supermarket, housework, baking, coffee with a friend – Lydia perhaps or someone else. Library, mending David's shirts. Hours brimming with this and that.

I remember a Carlie who used to be so busy, desperate to make her mark. What would she have said back then if she could see herself now, filling her hours with *this and that*, each activity leaving nothing more lasting than a wet footprint in the sand? Then again, where would she be if, like me, she had made another choice? Would she be anywhere at all? I always thought I saved her, stopped her from falling; picked her up and held her together like glue that takes an age to bind.

I thought that I saved her, yet I can't believe this is all she wants with her day. *This and that*. Not any more.

I walk onto the station platform, and there is Jonathan with his back to me, pretending to read his newspaper. He's muttering underneath his breath. I pretend I haven't seen him, creeping into the waiting room until the train comes. If I take my normal seat beside him, he'll want to talk about Lydia, how she and Saskia continue to email each other, how they have yet another meeting planned. He will tell me again how Lydia has positively blossomed, with roses in her cheeks, happier than she has been in years. As if we hadn't seen it for ourselves.

She doesn't even try to hide it, that's half his problem. We had them round for dinner the other night and Lydia's bloom is there to see. What's more, it seems to spread out all around her, something she is willing to share, so we all feel the warmth, whether we want to or not – even Jonathan. It filled our kitchen, Lydia's laughter, rich and spontaneous as when we first met her. At one point I saw Carlie staring at her, as if in fascination. Suddenly Lydia seems younger than us all. Especially Jonathan. While Lydia blooms, he wilts. You can actually see his shoulders wilting beneath his cashmere overcoat, his neck drooping inside the velvet collar.

I am sorry for him, afraid for him, even. But I am more afraid for myself. I avoid him because there's nothing I can say to him that would make him feel better. Nothing that I can believe when I hear myself say it. *Trust her.*

Who am I to advise anyone about trust?

On my work computer, I find myself tapping in Jennifer's address. For a moment, my fingers hover, on the brink of embarking on a long breezy message that would describe my work, my home, my marriage, David. Fifteen years arranged like a C.V.

Then, as if of their own accord, my fingers tap in just this. *I married Carlie.* And send it.

An hour later, a message arrives back for me. *I married Walsh.*

I am still laughing as I walk through the door.

Carlie takes one look at my face and the strained look vanishes. She laughs softly as I catch her by the waist and for a moment we stand, arms around each other, gripping each other tight, saying nothing. It feels as if one, or both of us, has been away. Now we are home again.

Eventually I say, 'Where's David?'

She steps out of my arms, but keeps hold of my hand. 'Still at school with that maths tutor. He says this evening they will mainly be solving problems.'

And now we've begun laughing all over again, because we both have the same picture in our minds. David – gravely solving problems. Nothing to do with maths though; we watch him working out the problems of famine, and poverty and the absence of world peace.

'He's so happy to go to this tutor,' says Carlie. 'Two whole weeks and I haven't heard him complain once.'

'Good,' I say. 'Like David says: *good.*' And I catch her in my arms again and squeeze her so hard she gasps. What has happened to me? What has changed? Just this: knowing that others can do the most unexpected things. Things you would tell them never to do. Jennifer married Walsh. She looks serious and happy. He is fuzzy in tweed, and has thrived under that grey Athene stare. People can live with being flexible. Walsh and Jennifer – things work. Love works.

'What is it?' Says Carlie. 'You're grinning all over your face. What's happened?'

'Nothing.' I tell her. Suddenly I want to keep touching Carlie, pull her closer even than this. Tickle her, perhaps. I nuzzle the top of her head and smell the burnt sugar scent of her, my own Carlie.

'It must be you telling me about this maths tutor.'

She doesn't believe me. But it hardly matters. She is in my arms, smiling at me. 'If you say so. Anyway, I'll be able to tell you soon if you're right to look so pleased. Tomorrow morning I get to meet him. David's come home with a message inviting me to come in and hear how he's getting on. He says Mr. Magnet wants to talk to me about the maths.'

'Good. I hope it's a…a mind expanding experience for you too.'

She smiles. Then, quite deliberately, she turns from the subject of David. 'You know you've been looking…' she pauses, choosing her words '…tired lately.'

'So have you,' I say. 'Too many nightmares.'

She takes my hand and lays it against her cheek. 'I know.'

I look into her eyes. 'Is it something you can talk about?

She blinks, but returns the stare. For a long moment we are caught by each other's eyes. Finally, Carlie says, 'I don't think there's any need.' She puts up her hand and touches me on the cheek. 'Just hold on to me, Guy, and I'll sleep tonight, all the way to morning.'

And I believe her. Suddenly I believe her. Things work. Love works. Walsh and Jennifer smile from the page. Carlie looks into my eyes and commands me to hold her. Why did I doubt her? For the first time I do what I haven't dared to do. Count up the days.

It's been a month. A month since the rose garden. And Carlie is here with me. Is it possible he might have blasted into her life, rocked her with a kiss, frightened her with a rose and then – nothing? Could it be that she has regained her composure, found her feet again? He has left his mark, that fine line beside her mouth is there, reappearing when she is tired. But maybe this will be all – a line in the skin, like a line drawn in the sand. A line Carlie herself has drawn. This far and no further.

'Carlie,' I whisper and she comes to me. I am holding her as the door opens and David rushes in, his face lit up.

'I've just had the best possible…'

He sees me kissing her and stops short, and looks away,

rolling his eyes.

Carlie laughs and steps away from me. But she is true to her word. Tonight, even as I take her in my arms, the tiredness comes over her. And this time she gives in without a murmur. Sighs into my shoulder, and falls asleep straight away. She smiles in her sleep, peaceful at last. Her dreams are her own again.

Tonight, it's only me that dreams.

We are back in that tunnel, Carlie and I. But the light is right ahead of us now, so close I feel like laughing. There are roots of things dangling through the ceiling, which isn't stone any more, but earth, brown and sweet smelling. A butterfly flickers past us out of the light, eager to join some invisible dance in the dark.

So close now. A sunbeam lands on my face, the first light of day. I have to tell her. I have to tell Carlie.

Carlie, look.

And see what I've done. I have turned around. Behind me, she stops and sadly shakes her head at me. The sunbeam falls short at her feet. Carlie is pulling away from me, sucked back into the dark, following the path of the butterfly and the downward dance.

I wake with a shout, sweat pouring down my face. And Carlie is there, staring down at me, her eyes shining in the dark.

'Guy? Sweetheart, darling, wake up.'

She touches me, and her fingers are warm on my cheek, reminding me that I am, that we still are, real. Carlie is here, with me. The dream retreats and I let her wrap her arms around me and soothe me, and carry me forward to the morning, to the light.

Things work. Love works. We are almost there.

Chapter Twenty-Two

'I'll phone you' she says. 'I'll tell you exactly what I think of him.'

'Who?'

Already I have forgotten. This morning I woke and Carlie was still holding me. She was smiling at me when I opened my eyes, as if she had never gone back to sleep. As if she had been watching over me.

'The tutor. I'll go and see what's so wonderful about him, then I'll tell you all about it.'

'I'll wait for your call.'

I am still smiling as I walk into Chambers an hour later. Gary glances approvingly round the door as I come in. He likes his barristers to be happy, we work better that way. Sometimes I think that all of us, from the head of Chambers down, are like a string of racehorses under his supervision. Gary coaxes the best out of us – ready and willing to put us down if we seize up. Unless we die first, like my father.

As if to put me through my paces, he comes through with a brief stacked high with papers. 'Ten years old this case. See what you think. Customs and Excise have a bee in their bonnet, and no one else is going to want to touch it, Mr. Latimer. Like I always say, it takes a special brain.'

In my room, the Graeco-Roman girl sucks her pen and sympathises, laughing at the seriousness of it all when life - real life - is somewhere else. And she's right. This morning, it's an effort just to undo the pink ribbon holding the papers together. I want to be home with Carlie who last night held me and watched me sleep, the way I have watched her sleep so many times…

Meanwhile, the phone rings repeatedly and Gary steps in and out wanting to talk about the pupillage scheme. I've had several pupils over the years, grave young men I have chosen often because they reminded me of David, grown up. Women seem not to apply to these Chambers. Lately I've been wondering if Gary doesn't have something to do with that, making choices for us, at a level we know nothing about.

Before lunch Jonathan sends an email suggesting we meet up for a drink at the end of the day. *Not tonight*, I reply. *Got to get home.* To Carlie. My father's clock ticks on the mantelpiece and the morning, the entire day, passes so quickly, so busily, sliding towards the evening and home that I hardly notice: Carlie hasn't called me.

And now something has happened.

I feel it the moment I open the front door. The house is too quiet. Even here in the hall where I would expect a kind of silence, it is too much – a perfect, intense quiet. You'd think there was no one at home, but there is life here, in my house. I can feel it. Except it's hiding, lying low.

I make my way to the kitchen, shivering. Still not quite April and it's cold. Carlie must have forgotten to put on the heating. Yet it's not just the cold that makes me shiver. Something has found its way into my home, its tendrils drifting in the air – another kind of life.

I open the kitchen door. She is sitting at the kitchen table staring in straight in front of her. 'Carlie,' I say in a low voice so as not to surprise her, but she does not hear me. Her hands are folded over something in her lap. She has no idea I am here. And there is no sign of David.

My throat contracts. For a moment I can think of only one reason for a cold kitchen, for the stillness, and Carlie staring blindly at the wall. For the change that has crept over our house. 'Carlie,' I say again. 'What's the matter. Where's David?'

At the sound of his name, her head moves. Dully she looks at me. 'What?'

'Has something happened to David? Where is he?'

Slowly she shakes her head, knitting her eyebrows, as if

trying to make a connection. Finally she says, 'Upstairs. He went upstairs.'

But I have to see for myself. I have a picture in my head, of David, not here. Because of the quiet, the stillness in the house, I am convinced he is gone, and this is the reason that Carlie is sitting in a state of shock. It's this picture – of David not here – that makes me shout out his name as I tear up the stairs.

And just as I reach the door, it opens, and David is standing there. 'What is it?'

I skid to a halt and stare at him, my own boy. And it's all I can do not to take him in my arms, touch him, smell him, so sure have I been that he wouldn't be here. But I cannot touch him, not like this. Already I have made him uneasy, shouting and now standing here, staring at him as if there's no convincing me he's real.

'What?' He says again. 'What's the matter?' When I fail to answer, unease gives way to concern. Tentatively, my boy reaches out, gently touches my wrist with his hand. I feel his fingers light as a caterpillar on my skin. 'Are you alright? *Dad*?'

Time to get a grip. I am alarming my son. I clear my throat. 'Of course I'm alright. Why on earth shouldn't I be?'

But see what I've done. Words, meant to reassure, have come out sounding dry and sarcastic as a judge. David shrinks. His hand falls away from my arm.

I try again. 'I've just seen your mother...' But it's no good. My father speaks through me to my son. Tries to make himself understood. And fails.

Suddenly David is sulky, a teenager with a sullen brow, older. 'So she's told you?'

'Told me what?'

'How she's not letting me go back to the tutor. She says she'll take me out of school if I go near him. She's says if I do, she's going take me out, put me in that poncey paying school with Angus. She's being...' He fights for words to express how he feels about Carlie. And he can't find them, because this has never happened before, this rift between them '...Unbelievable.' He finishes his sentence, and listens to himself almost in wonder.

I say, 'I don't know what you're talking about.' But yet again, words – meant as an appeal – sound like a dismissal, words to put him in his place. He bristles.

'She hardly spoke to him! She was only in the room with him five minutes. Then out she comes, and all she says is that I'm not to go near him. She says you wouldn't like it.'

'If that's what she said, then I'm sure...'

He takes a step back, looks at me, his eyes fierce. 'Oh I bet you're sure. You're sure of everything. I bet you told her not to let me go to him. I bet you *ordered* her to say that.'

'Why on earth?' Surely he can hear the bewilderment in my voice. 'Why should I do a thing like that?'

He stares at me, struggling with an anger blown in from nowhere. Then the words tumble out: 'Because he's different from you. He talks to me – all the time, not just about maths. Everything. He wants to know what it's like, being here, living with you. Living in Patersfield, going to the school. He asks me about you and Mum. Holidays. He wants to know what it's like being me, like he's interested. Like *I'm* interesting. And clever. He even tells me how things could be different...better. He tells me all sorts of things. He *talks* to me. I want to go back to him. I want him to teach me. And you're just jealous.'

He stops. The anger has drained from him as suddenly as it arrived, leaving him – leaving us both – shocked. He gazes at me, panting. Then he shakes his head at me, backs away from the door. And I, too, back away, down the stairs, to Carlie.

In the kitchen, Carlie is staring at something in her hand – a small silver backed mirror, the one I gave her for her last birthday. The one she left behind her in her purse, on the bench in the rose garden. She gazes into the small round shape as if she is searching for something that isn't there, her own reflection. Carlie looks and looks and can't see herself at all.

Mr. Magnet. I know who he is. And what he is doing here. He has found us. How could I have forgotten? Magnus was a mathematician. And he is the man teaching my son.

I leave Carlie and go to my study. There is no point in staying in the kitchen. She can't see me, hear me. Not at this time. She is in a state of shock. Later, in bed, I will hold her, make love to her even, if she wants me to. Try to impress myself on her, make my mark, remind her that we are, that we always have been, real. But already I know it will be in vain. I will hold Carlie and she will hold me, but we will be two creatures, struggling in the dark while his shadow leaps on the wall beside us. And on the other side of the wall, David will lie (listening?) hating me, wanting to be with him, Mr. Magnet, who makes him feel special.

Sure enough, in bed, Carlie sighs and reaches for me across the pillow, but her fingertips are icy. Shock continues to chill her to the bone. I can't make love to her after all. I cannot pretend I have a mark to make. We lie side by side, the backs of our hands touching, in silence, both pretending to be asleep. The walls of our house surround us, but they are flimsy as a pack of cards, likely to collapse around us.

He is back. He has found his way in.

In the morning, Carlie's face is pale, but strong and set as marble. She has passed the night preparing just for this, to face the day – to face me – with a mask that nothing can penetrate. Her movements in the kitchen are composed, contained. We go through the motions of normal life, washing, having breakfast. She removes a hair from my lapel, I pick up my loose change, patting pockets to test that everything is in place. Like the old joke – spectacles, testicles, wallet and watch. A lawyer's joke. It occurs to me that my face is as strong and set as Carlie's. This is a mask I have worn for years, preparing for a day just like this.

Only David betrays emotion, sitting with his arms crossed over his untouched cereal glowering at Carlie. Ignoring me, which is somehow worse. I notice that Carlie has written a note, addressed to Mr. Repton, which he tries to leave behind on the hall table on our way out of the house. It's me that hands it to him and without a word he takes it, hating me even more. I drop him off outside the school and he gets out without a backward glance. I watch him walk inside – and then allow my imagination to shoulder my way past him, pounding down corridors until I find my way to the staff room. And there, outside the door with its notices and graffiti, I stop. Is *he* in there, flirting with the French teacher, bringing a blush to the music teacher's cheek? Drinking coffee, holding his cup with those long fingers that flicked through the contents of our lives? Is he there?

I have an urge to jump out of the car, and find out for myself. Find him. Then I think what I would do if I did find him, and instead, I pull out into the Patersfield traffic, and carry on to the station.

In Chambers, the first thing I do is phone home. Carlie picks up immediately. Pauses before she answers. 'It's me,' I say and listen for the sound of air escaping from her lungs, then make some excuse to explain the call. An hour later, outside the courtroom, I phone her again while the client's solicitor stands impatiently by.

This time there is no answer.

In the afternoon, Jonathan phones me. 'Something wrong with your computer?' His voice sounds plaintive.

'What?'

'I've been mailing you all day, but you haven't been answering. Thought I'd better phone you. Need a word.'

'Oh?'

'I'm planning something. For Lydia.' I hear him swallow.

He can't even mention his wife's name nowadays without sounding nervous. 'It's her birthday coming up, big four O and all that. It's just hit me that I could do something special. Surprise her. Thought I'd arrange a party, in secret, make it a really good bash...' He stops, listens to the silence at my end. 'Guy, are you still there? Can you hear me?'

'I'm still here, Jonathan.'

Sounding only half-convinced he continues. 'Like I was saying – a really good bash, show the old girl she's appreciated....' he tails off, trying to keep the desperation out of his voice. 'Will you come? Bit short notice and all that, but the fact is, I don't know if I can do it, not unless you'll say you'll be there – you and Carlie. Lydia needs...she needs...' His voice trails away again. Jonathan has no idea what Lydia needs.

I speak up. 'Of course we'll come.'

'Good,' he says, relieved. 'Knew I could count on you two.'

And I can't say anything, because he can't count on us. We are unstable, Carlie and I, our lives suddenly as labile as oil floating on water. Anything could change us, set us alight, burning our way to nothing.

I put the phone down and continue to sit at my desk, staring straight at the wall ahead of me. Gradually I become aware of her, the tendrils of hair, the amused, questioning mouth. And most of all the eyes - eyes that tell you nothing except how things used to be, ten, a thousand, two thousand years ago. Finished now. I get up and tear her off the wall, the Graeco-Roman girl. Take her and tear her into little bits. The bin is full of her - eyes, hair and hands, all in pieces.

Nothing there now, where she used to be, just a blank mark on the wall.

Driving home from the station, it occurs to me: Jonathan is lucky. He doesn't have *this* against him. Proximity.

By which I mean Saskia lives far away, down in the west

country where – he says – she does pottery, or weaving or *something*. It's hard for him to keep the contempt out of his voice when he mentions this. It's all of a piece to him. The four children from her marriage, divorce, same sex love. *Pottery.*

But Saskia is far away, turning clay on a wheel, dreaming of Lydia. Magnus is here, where we are, in Patersfield. He has followed us here. He is moving closer. He has engineered a meeting, and this time I wasn't there to see it. What did they do in the room together when she walked in and found it was him? He would have locked the door. What did they always do when they were alone? I remember what Carlie used to tell me and my hands shake on the wheel.

He is here. I can feel him as I drive down the high street, the closeness of him. He'll not just be working here, he'll have moved right in – found another rented room, in yet another person's house. Maybe he's behind one of those lighted windows above the shoe shop. Somebody's lodger, more exotic than usual, giving a landlady something to be excited about. I crane my neck, scanning the pavements as I drive home. This is Patersfield, this used to be safe.

Now he's here, and nothing looks the same. I put my foot on the brake, watching the shop doors, the people walking from the station. The pavements are filled with brief cases, handbags and countless pairs of shiny shoes, all with people attached. I see how we look from the outside – sleek, affluent. Every night we look the same, half asleep in our clothes. Easy pickings. Look at it his way – we deserve to lose what we have. He chose the right place. Patersfield belongs to him now, simply because he is here.

And Carlie, what is it doing to her, knowing he is close, so close now? Last night, and nearly a week since the mirror reappeared, Carlie woke with a gasp. Instantly I was awake too.

'Carlie?'

But she didn't answer, not in words. It was other sounds

that told me: the old story of air trapped and useless in her lungs, suffocating her by degrees. Something that hasn't happened in so long it takes a moment to recognise, like an enemy you'd managed to forget. I snapped on the light and sure enough, here she was again, the old Carlie. Writhing, eyes closed, teeth bared as she fought to breathe.

And somehow all I seemed to want to do was watch her.

So I did. I watched Carlie writhe on the bed like something possessed, watched her and did nothing. Fascinated, because isn't this exactly the way I see her now? A creature possessed, fighting the demon inside. And wasn't this all I ever wanted her to do? Fight it, wrestle with it. Get rid of it. Get rid of him. Even if it kills her. I watched for those few moments, and it was back: the feeling of numbed satisfaction.

Did she struggle like this in the room, in the school, with the locked door? How hard did she fight the demon then? *Did you writhe like something possessed, Carlie - or did you not fight at all?*

Then Carlie opened her eyes, wide against the ceiling, and I saw; Carlie was fighting air, not demons. And I was doing nothing. Watching her die, my own Carlie.

I sprang to my knees and seized her hands and held them, hard. 'Carlie. I'm here. I'm here, Carlie. Look at me.'

Slowly her eyes find mine and stare. It's as if she can't quite remember who I am. And then she does remember. We both remember – exactly how it used to be, and what we used to do. *Look at me. Count with me, Carlie.* And we count as I hold Carlie with my hands and with my eyes, until little by little she begins to breathe again. Some things stay the same. I can still hold her, like a girl dangling on a cliff edge. I am still the one who can bring her back.

But other things have changed. Afterwards she sighed, and let her head fall on my shoulder - only to feel me stiffen. Without a word, she took her head away and let it sink into her own pillow.

This is what's happening to Carlie. This is what is happening to us. This is the aftermath. This is what happens when Magnus is so close he taints the air we breathe, choking her.

And every night now as I drive home, my hands shake on the wheel. It takes a full five minutes after I arrive to make them stop, so that I can walk through the front door giving nothing away. So that I can smile at Carlie, pretend everything is normal – and ask her what she does with her day, now that he is here.

If I am pretending, though, Carlie is pretending even harder. It frightens me how well she pretends: the composed sway of her hips, the warmth, back now in her fingertips, reminding me – of what? Some days I hardly dare to remember. She can pretend in front of me, but she can't pretend in front of him. I have been there in the garden. I watched her search for her reflection in the mirror. I've seen her try to pretend – and fail.

I've asked David if he's seeing his tutor, and he shifts his eyes away from me.

'You told me not to, remember?'

Not a lie, then, just a reply that is also an accusation – repeating my own words back to me. Sometimes, out of the three of us, I believe he is the one most aware of what is going on. He watches us, almost fearfully, knowing something has changed, unable to say what. We have to be careful, Carlie and I, what we do to our son. He walks into school on legs that seem too spindly to take him far. Fragile. I imagine him going to *his* door, and hovering, lying in wait for the man who makes him feel special, who wants to know what life is like at home. Our home. And David desperate to tell him.

Fragile is what *he* looks for. Magnus homes in on *fragile*, feeds off it. He recognises fragile when he sees it, like a wolf marking out the youngest of its prey. He'll be making sure he's there now, closing on our son, closing in on Carlie.

And Carlie and I just keep walking towards the danger, pretending to smile, giving nothing away.

Chapter Twenty-Three

'Mr. Latimer.'

Gary has appeared in my door. He surveys the empty wall in front of my desk, and observes. 'Not replaced her then, your ancient bit? Maybe put a nice photo of your wife up instead?'

'Anything I can help you with, Gary?'

'Thought we could have a chat, Mr. Latimer.' He eases himself into the room, and rests his thin haunches against my desk, rotates a shoulder inside the tight pin stripe jacket. 'Seeing as you're not busy.' There's a hint of irony in his voice as he speaks these last words. 'So...everything all right with you?'

'Of course.'

'That's good.' There's not the slightest sign that he believes me. He glances round the room. 'You know what's different about you from the other gentlemen, and I've only just noticed it?'

'What?'

'You don't have no photos up. Not of your wife or nothing. How is she by the way? Nice lady, Mrs. Latimer.'

'She's well.'

'But like I say, no photos of her. Even I've got photos, Mr. Latimer, pinned up in the clerks' room. Right above the diary. Got my Sharon beaming down at me with little baby Gray.'

'I thought you and your wife were divorced, Gary.' And have been these ten years.

'Oh sure. But I keep the photo. Reminds me what I got out of. Always helpful, that. Case I get tempted to dip the old toe again. But you, Mr. Latimer - looking round this room, people would think you were a bachelor boy. Even your dad had photos.'

'Did he?' It seems I have forgotten. 'Of what?'

'Why you, Mr. Latimer. Right through from when you were a babe in arms. Very fond of you, he was.'

There's a silence. 'What did you want to chat about, Gary?'

'You know everyone's expecting you to take silk next year, Mr. Latimer.'

I don't answer this.

'Looking forward to it, I am. These Chambers could do with another QC. Don't know what stopped you applying years ago myself. Specially as you've always worked so hard. Always so reliable. Mr. Results, you've always been to me, Mr. Latimer. Never let me down. That's why I wanted to know.'

'Know what?'

'Like I said, if everything was all right. Because these last few weeks...' He pauses.

'These last weeks...?' I prompt him. Although we both know what he's saying.

Gary examines his nails. 'These last few weeks I've been having to turn work away on your behalf. Haven't been around much, have you Mr. Latimer?'

'I've been working at home.'

He bares his teeth at this. 'But we like to see you, Mr. Latimer, me and the boys in the clerks' office. I'd venture to say it's not the same when you're not around. Specially when I'm needing to explain to clients why I'm turning away work. It's not like you, Mr. Latimer, not showing your face. Going home all the time...'

Going home. That's what I've been doing. This is what Gary is getting at. Going home all the time, at odd hours. When no one would expect me. Least of all Carlie.

Which reminds me. 'Nice of you to say so, Gary. And now if you'll excuse me...' I stand up and gather my papers together. Gary's face hardens.

'It's half-past one, Mr. Latimer. Can't we tempt you to stay?'

I smile politely over his shoulder, at the blank space on my wall.

Half past two o' clock in the afternoon, I let myself into

the house, easing the door shut. And Carlie is definitely not expecting me.

She looks up, startled, as I stroll into the kitchen – and before she can stop herself, glances at the piece of paper in her hand.

'Guy,' she says softly. 'What are you doing here?'

'Thought I'd work in my study. You don't mind, do you?'

'Of course not, it's nice to see you.'

'And it's nice to see you.' I lean forward and kiss her lightly on the cheek. Small rituals with the force of nature. Then I catch hold of her hand, the one holding the piece of paper. 'But what's this, Carlie? A letter?'

Carlie's hand freezes in mine. 'It's a note from Mr. Repton, that's all. He…he wants to know why David isn't staying to be tutored any more.'

'And?'

'And…what?'

'Well, actually I'd like to know myself. Why *did* you stop him seeing the tutor? You never did tell me what happened when you went to see him that day.'

Now there's a silence. 'Oh I'm sure I did,' she says finally.

'No, Carlie,' I say gently. 'You didn't.'

Colour is flooding into her cheeks. 'There didn't seem much to say, I suppose. I just met him…and realised he shouldn't be teaching David. Or anyone for that matter.'

'And you told Mr. Repton that? You made a formal complaint?'

Carlie hesitates, then shakes her head.

I smile into her eyes. 'So what *was* it, Carlie? What didn't you like about this man? You're being awfully vague.' I let go her hand and catch hold of her wrist, so she can feel my fingers, warm against her skin. And so that I can feel the beat of her pulse, picking up speed. Beginning to race.

She tries so hard to keep her voice smooth. 'Honestly, I don't know what to say. He…he's a chancer – who just happens to be good at teaching. Attractive...'

'...Attractive?' I interrupt.

Carlie flinches, shakes her head. 'I mean *influential*. He has a kind of...draw. I was afraid he'd use it on David, in a bad way. Remember how he compared maths to a drug? Didn't you think that sounded odd?'

'Maybe I should meet him,' I say. 'Find out for myself.'

And I watch the colour drain from her face.

She takes her wrist from under my fingers. Carlie can't pretend any more, not today. But I have one more question before she goes, eluding me, slipping out of my hands. 'Is he just passing through, this Mr. Magnet – or do you think he means to stay, here in Patersfield?'

She stops and stares at me. Without knowing it she is biting her lip. Then quickly, sharply, she nods.

And it's good that she leaves the room then, because with that small nod, suddenly I understand what I never did before. Magnus is here to stay – for good. He is not just revisiting his past, reviving his sense of himself. This is about creating his future. Security. He's tired after all these years. He lives in rented rooms, his clothes are old. Carlie never had anything to offer him before. These days she has everything. So now he wants Carlie. He wants what Carlie has, and what she can give him. A future.

Our future.

Five minutes later, mask intact, I go to find Carlie in the hall. She is putting on her coat.

'Where are you going, Carlie?'

'Shopping – for Lydia's surprise party. Jonathan has given me a list as long as my arm.' Her fingers are trembling on the buttons of her coat. Is it because of the conversation we just had – or in anticipation of something else? Is Carlie really going shopping?

'Poor you,' I say. 'Both of us having to work.' I point up the stairs towards my study, making it clear where I will be.

She nods, can't hide her relief. It's becoming easier for Carlie to be away from me than with me.

I wait till the sound of her car has died away – then jump into my own to follow her. She says she is going shopping. What else can I do?

And yet she really is going shopping. She goes to the florists, the candle shop, the printers. Then the wine merchants and the specialist cake shop. As she goes, she consults a list she is holding in her hand, and walks with a purpose, with an energy and a spring in her step that in a strange way brings me hope. Makes me believe that shopping really is all that's on her mind. That is until, in the middle of it all, she stops, abruptly, right there on the pavement, in front of a large plate glass window, as if snagged by her own reflection, while people have to walk around her.

Carlie is standing, staring at nothing.

Suddenly, interrupting the stillness, a hand appears on her shoulder, makes Carlie jerk, then freeze. I'm not the only one to have been watching her. Somebody else has been observing, calculating, choosing their moment – and then closing in. With an effort, Carlie forces herself to turn and face the owner of the hand. And breathes again. It's Vanessa, smiling at her, pleased with what she caught, a fox with a soft spot for its prey.

I watch as Carlie is dragged off, back towards the cake shop which is also a café. And in a way, it's a release. Vanessa has got her captive. She'll be going nowhere else today, nowhere she shouldn't. I can go home, be at my desk, busy with my papers when she gets back.

Carlie will come home and I will be careful to smile, and she'll tell herself everything is normal. As normal as it could be with him so close, so close now.

At home, it hits me, what I'm doing to Carlie. I am stalking her, stalking my own wife.

For a moment the idea horrifies. Distaste floods over me.
That I could do this.

The next moment, the distaste vanishes, for something else
to take its place. Because with the realisation comes the fear.
If I am stalking her, then am I stalking her well enough?

Half a day snatched here and there. Where does that leave
me? With a wife who has the other half of the day to do exactly what she likes. Go where she likes. See who she likes.

So how much do I really want to know?

Carlie is not home yet. She is still in the coffee shop, under
the playful, predatory gaze of Vanessa. I climb into the car
again, and go back to the blue door between the off licence
and the solicitors.

Today I don't even have to knock. The door at the top of the
stairs is standing open. But there is no Mr. Robinson. Instead
a young woman, plump, is kneeling on the floor, almost hidden by a small mountain of box files.

'Oh,' she says, unsmiling. 'I thought I'd locked that door.'

'I'm looking for Mr. Robinson,' I say. 'Is he…?'

'…No he's not. He's gone. If it's a job you want him for,
you'll have to try someone else.'

'I don't think I can. You see, Mr. Robinson…'

'I told you,' she snaps. 'He's gone.' She has round cheeks,
and intelligent eyes, that for some reason are lit up by anger.
Eyes that strike me as familiar.

'I know who you must be,' I say slowly. 'You must be Mr.
Robinson's daughter.'

She throws back her head. 'So?'

'Has something happened – is he alright? I hope so. He
seemed a nice man. I liked him.'

These last words seem to have an effect. For a moment I see
her struggle with herself. Then something gives way inside her.
'*Nice?* He's a fat bastard, that's what he is. And I'll tell you why.

Last week that *nice* Mr. Robinson went and ran off with another woman. *Nice?* You should see what it's done to my mum, the state of her. They had to take her into hospital a couple of nights ago, for observation. Even the doctor thought the shock had done for her. Now tell me again if you think he's *nice.*'

'Oh.' There's nothing I can think to say to this. 'I'm sorry.'

She whacks a box file in anger. 'And you know the best of it? It's only a bloody subject he's gone off with. He was meant to be doing his job. He was there to observe, to watch her, this…this bitch. He *told* me about her. Night after night he watched her. Saw them coming and going, all her fancy men. He saw the kind of woman she was, what she was up to. Then what does he do? He goes and…'

…Falls in love with her. The girl's shoulders droop. She looks tired.

'It's so…unprofessional,' she adds suddenly. 'He always taught me to be detached. Just get the facts and stay out of it, that's what he told me. What was he thinking of?' She lifts her head and looks straight at me, and repeats the question, slowly and soberly, reminding me again of her father. '*What was he thinking of?*'

'I'm so sorry,' I say. 'I really don't know. I only talked to him the once. Maybe he just couldn't stay detached, not any more. He told me it changes things, watching people. Nothing's the same after.'

She rolls her eyes as if this is no sort of answer.

I leave her to get back to sorting out the box files with their twenty years of watching what goes on in Patersfield.

And no Mr. Robinson. No one to do the job properly. Unless…

Gary comes into my room to have a document signed. As he turns to go, I say, 'Wait a moment.'

He waits. I have a feeling he knows what I have to say.

'Gary, I'm taking time off. I can't keep working, not well, not at the moment.'

He looks at me squarely. 'This isn't temporary is it, Mr. Latimer?'

'What? My being sick?'

He lifts his shoulders, shakes his head. 'I don't think you're sick, Mr. Latimer, not physically. You've lost your concentration, and now you just want to take off. So what will people say? Let's see if I can put this politely...people are going to be pissed right off - clients, solicitors, all of them. They're going to wonder what happened to Hugh Latimer's son.'

'And...?'

'...And I think you should think about it. Decide which way you want to go. Onward and upward. Or right off your fucking head. You choose. Only do it soon. I'm already palming your work off right left and centre.'

He pauses to watch me, expressionless, waiting for me to make up my mind, as if it really is all a question of choice.

I put the lid back on my fountain pen, my old Mont Blanc. I've been using it more and more recently, writing opinions in long hand, making the solicitors, who are used to printed matter, look at me oddly. Quietly I say, 'Perhaps you'd better keep doing just that.'

He gives a short sigh of annoyance, and turns to go. But at the door, he stops. 'I'll tell you what I'll do, Mr. Latimer. I'll cover for you for a month, make up some story about a sabbatical, some rubbish like that. You pull yourself together in that time and we'll pretend this never happened. Like we did with your dad.'

'My father? What do you mean?'

He shakes his head. 'You don't remember? I suppose you were only a kid. What would you have been - six? Seven? I was only junior myself. He was going to pack it all in, go and live on a hillside in Greece and dig up bones. Right off his trolley he was, had a crying fit in front of the Divisional Court and all. Your ma had to pack him off to hospital for three months. Mind you - that was only after he'd half throttled her with a dog lead. Nearly bloody killed her. Thought she was having an affair with the handyman or something daft like that. You *sure* you don't remember?

Slowly I say. 'I went away to school when I was six.'

'Well there you go. Got you out of the picture, didn't they. Good for them. Point is, Mr. Latimer. We held on and he came back. Right as rain he was after that, mind. Just a bit quieter. Well - a lot quieter actually. But reliable. No one to touch him after that for reliability. I reckon you'll be the same. Just don't throttle anyone while you're at it.'

He nods and makes to leave the room.

'Wait!'

Smirking, he stops. 'What is it Mr. Latimer? Come as a bit of a shock has it, hearing about your dad? Sorry about that.'

'What you said about my mother. Just tell me this. What stopped him? You said he half throttled her. What stopped him going all the way?

The smirk disappears. 'Why ask me? I don't know. Maybe he just realised it wasn't worth it, all the stuff that would come after. None of it is, if you think about. *Women!* Maybe he had that much sense.'

I let him go then. There's nothing more he could possibly tell me. And it's time for me to go home. Like my father before me. I thought I never knew him. Now it seems I know him better than I ever dreamed possible.

He never did go to his Greek hillside. He went home. And three months later he came back.

And does Carlie notice, when I walk through our front door, that for the first time in weeks I have not asked what she does with her day?

I don't ask because I know – more or less. I know that

today she left the car at home and walked everywhere; into Patersfield, around the shops, to the dry cleaners. To the hairdressers where she sat in a chair close to the window, and where a man in black, young, good-looking, chatted with his mouth close to her ear as he fingered her hair. Once or twice he made her smile, but most of the time, she let him chat while she stared at…what? Nothing. Carlie stared without seeing. He talked until he realised she wasn't listening, and then he shut up. But in the mirror he watched her, while he cut the curl out of her hair.

Later she stepped out into the street – only to step smartly sideways into yet another door. Vanessa was crossing the road. And it takes my breath away, the way Carlie hides without missing a beat, without breaking her stride. As if she was used to hiding. Which, of course, she is.

And since I am in the business of watching, I observe Vanessa too, just because she's there. I watch her stride into the same hairdressers and stand, tapping her scarlet nails on the desk, until the man in black notices her, which is almost immediately. I watch the way they step neatly into the shadows of the shop where they could only be seen by a careful watcher. By me.

Minutes later Vanessa steps outside again. Her lips are bright red, and moist, as if she has just given herself a new coat of lipstick - or else she has been lapping blood from a saucer. The man in black goes back to what he is doing. He's putting money into his back pocket. And it's only now I notice how very young he is. Scarcely more than a boy.

What a lot there is to see when you decide to do nothing but watch. Carlie is watching too. Have I mentioned that? Her eyes are everywhere as she walks, sliding this way and that despite herself. She is wearing herself out by watching. She's like me, looking for *him*, expecting him to appear, waiting for it to happen.

The only place she doesn't look for him is near David's school. She walks past it with a quickened step, eyes cast sideways as if she doesn't want to see, as if this way she can't be seen. But why walk this way at all, Carlie, if there's nothing you want to see?

Chapter Twenty-Four

So today, there is no need to ask what Carlie has done with her day. Instead I ask what is in the parcel, the one sitting on the kitchen table, wrapped up with a silver bow.

'Lydia's present,' says Carlie. 'Tonight's the party, remember. I got her a pottery vase. Sorry, I didn't show it to you, did I?'

But of course she didn't have to. I've already seen it. I watched Carlie buy it today, an earthenware pot covered with swirls and whirls. Something to put flowers in - or more likely in Lydia's case, old hairclips and articles cut out of *Horse and Hound*. 'Pottery?' I say mildly. 'What do you suppose that will remind Jonathan of?'

And Carlie's hand flies up to her mouth in horror.

Is it my imagination or does Carlie dress with extra care this evening? She examines a black frock with sequins, then puts it back in the wardrobe, takes out a brown dress I have seen once and forgotten, lays it on the bed. From behind my book, I watch her making up her face. It takes her a long time. Painstakingly, she sweeps her eyes with silvers and greys, brushes colour along her cheekbones, scarlet on her lips – what Vanessa would call proper war paint. An art in itself. Finally, though, her hands fall into her lap. For a moment Carlie stares at the finished result. In the glass a siren, lit up with glittering, black ringed eyes stares back at her.

Then her hands become busy again as, from behind my book, I watch her set the whole process in reverse, rubbing and stroking until all that is left is a faint patina of cosmetic dust, barely visible to the naked eye. After that, she gets up and shrugs the brown dress over her shoulders where it settles, the sort of frock you'd look at once and then forget.

Carlie, I know what you are doing. You're trying to make yourself unnoticeable with your nondescript frock and almost naked face. Trying to escape attention.

But you've got it all wrong. You've dressed so no one would ever notice what you were wearing, thinking this was the way to become invisible. And the result is this: a woman who will stand in the centre of a room, drawing the eye of every person present, without the distractions of sequins or mascara. People will notice you, Carlie, not your clothes; you might just as well go and stand there naked.

She catches me staring. Awkwardly she touches her dress. 'I didn't feel like dressing up to the nines,' she says, as if she needed to explain. 'I saw Vanessa earlier, and she said she was going to wear something simple...'

'You spent time with Vanessa today?' I ask the question, alert. Because I know she didn't. Carlie hid when she saw her coming. I watched her.

'She collared me in the street, dragged me off into Yentls for coffee. She made me buy her a cream horn which she then insisted on feeding to the poodle of the owner. You know, the way she always does. She told me then she wasn't going to dress up, because this is Lydia's night, and I agreed...'

She stops, smoothes the dress which is already smooth, skimming her breasts and her hips. She has just lied to me, elaborated a tale with dogs and cream horns, and everything. But why? She should know it wasn't necessary. She didn't meet anyone today, she has nothing to cover up – except the simple matter of a dress, and the reason for it.

That must be it. She thinks even a dress could give her away, her state of mind.

She turns back to the glass and continues to brush her hair. Carlie who used to tell me everything is telling me nothing. I am the one she is hiding from.

Suddenly I need her to look at me. Pay attention to me.

'I found out something strange today, Carlie.' I hear myself say. My voice sounds odd - too loud for a bedroom. 'Gary told me. He said my father had some sort of breakdown years ago.

He said he attacked my mother, nearly strangled the life out of her. He thought she was having an affair. She was lucky to escape with her life. What do you think of that? Do you think I should believe him?'

Carlie's mouth opens slightly. Slowly she puts down the brush and stares at me. 'Guy...' she begins.

But downstairs the doorbell rings and David calls up to the bedroom. The babysitter has arrived, and it's too late to hear what Carlie has to say.

Jonathan is pacing the floor between his guests, gulping on his cigarette.

He hurries towards us through the crowd, flushed as if he's had a fair amount to drink already. 'Lyd's going to be here in about ten minutes. Vanessa's taking care of that end of things. She's been keeping her busy over at her house, locked her in with a bunch of – what do you call 'em? – beauty consultants who try to sell you stuff. Clever touch, that. Lydia will get her face done up thinking it's part of the fun. Then, when she walks in, she'll be all nicely powdered and painted. We'll sing happy birthday, and she can canter on upstairs to find the brand new frock that's waiting for her on the bed.'

'A frock?' says Carlie raising an eyebrow. '*You* chose a dress for Lydia?'

'Actually, Vanessa helped pick it out. Designer something or other. Said it would knock the pants off everyone here. Lydia can say what she likes about her, but Vanessa has been a complete boon lately. Couldn't have done any of this without her – or you, of course, Carlie,' he adds hurriedly. He looks round. 'Do you think it will pass?'

Gently Carlie says, 'It's good, Jonathan. You've thought of everything. And I think the room looks lovely.'

The room looks different, certainly. Carlie has been hard at work here. The chaos of Lydia's domestic reign has disappeared, cleared to make way for the candles that are burning every-where; and flowers, lots of flowers. Carlie's touch is everywhere.

It makes me remember another evening, years ago. A different house, a different time. No flowers then – unless you counted the garland in Walsh's curls. But there were candles burning everywhere – lighting up Carlie's face turned to mine. Rounder, softer than it is now. Nothing closed or shuttered about her then. Nothing quiet or composed. That night Carlie's lips had parted to say something to me. A night of true colours. If I had only stopped, if I had only stayed to hear what she had to say...

'...Then there's the big birthday surprise,' Jonathan is saying. 'The *pièce de résistance*.'

'You mean the dress?' Says Carlie.

'No no, even better. Something else. You don't know about it, Carlie. Vanessa dreamed it up, said it was right up Lydia's street, insisted I got it sorted...you've got to come and see. It's in the other room.'

He's pulling at our sleeves, anxious that we follow him. Whatever this surprise is, he wants us to see it first, before Lydia; as if deep down he suspects it may not be quite so much what Lydia would love after all. Carlie glances at me, and suddenly there it is, still alive – the flash between us that shows we have been thinking exactly the same thing.

'Show us, Jonathan,' she says, with just the smallest hint of urgency in her voice. And we can all relax; if it's wrong, Carlie will put it right.

His face brightens and he begins to usher us forward. But then comes a commotion from the window. Someone has seen a car pull up in the drive, is calling out: 'She's here.'

Jonathan looks at us, panic in his eyes. 'They're early.' Carlie touches his arm, steadies him, and in silence we turn to watch the door.

A moment later Lydia stands on the mat, her mouth open,

speechless to find her house full of people and flowers and light. The hush deepens as we wait for her reaction – a move, a word, anything. Jonathan takes an awkward step forward but he seems to be having as much difficulty speaking as Lydia. It takes Vanessa, standing behind her to say, a touch dryly. 'So…happy birthday, Lydia.'

A champagne cork pops, and everyone begins to cheer and sing happy birthday. Like a heart that missed its beat, the party picks up again around her. Lydia is smiling, laughing at the people crowding round. She turns to Jonathan with a hug – impetuous, almost girlish, then drags him with her through the crowd as she finds her way to us.

'Happy birthday,' I say again, adding. 'You look…different.' And she does, scarcely like the Lydia we know, whose only brush with make up tends to be a hasty collision with a lipstick. Thanks to Vanessa she is wearing what Carlie wore briefly – before she rubbed it away. On Lydia the effect is startling. She has eyes and cheekbones, suddenly noticeable, as is the wide, well shaped mouth.

She touches her face crossly. 'Actually, I was thinking I couldn't wait to scrape all this muck off. I wanted to give my face a good scrubbing at Vanessa's but she wouldn't let me. And look what they did with my hair…' She points to her head where the hair seems to have been respun and remoulded to her scalp.

'Feel that,' she says earnestly. 'It's like bloody concrete, they put so much hairspray on me. And they took out all the grey. There was no stopping them.'

'You look lovely, though, Lyd,' offers Jonathan almost fearfully. Lydia looks disbelieving.

Carlie says quietly. 'You do, Lydia. Leave it on, just for tonight. Pretend it's fancy dress.'

And Lydia hesitates, then nods, as if this was what it took, a word from Carlie. Something in her relaxes, and she turns to

Jonathan. He makes a small helpless gesture. 'Actually, Lyd, you do look most awfully fancy.' Then his own face breaks into a smile, adoring her. The smile spreads between them and for a moment we stand, watching them, briefly alone in the crowd.

Then Vanessa sweeps down and the moment is gone. She seizes Lydia. 'Come with me, madam. I haven't finished with you yet. Upstairs.'

Lydia hesitates. 'Carlie?'

Carlie stirs. 'I'll come with you.' She steps firmly beside Lydia, protective. Vanessa looks from one woman to the other, then deliberately catches my eye, lets me see she is mocking them both.

Jonathan watches them go and drains his glass with a flourish. 'There you are – sorted,' he says triumphantly. 'Vanessa's got it all under control.'

We part company, for Jonathan to head back to the drinks table and me to plunge into a sea of faces, so familiar it's like stepping into a warm bath; the water washes against your skin not hot, not cold, so it's almost like bathing in your own fluids. Not uncomfortable. A woman I can't remember, dressed in frills, talks to me about fundraising for a second swimming pool for the school, forgetting that David goes to the establishment with the graffiti and no swimming pool at all. Her husband asks me a question about inheritance tax. I answer, smile and move on. Repeat the process over. Answer, smile, move on. Someone mentions a website that brings old friends back together. Someone else says they've been on it non-stop. Say nothing, smile, move on. A waiter fills my glass, and within a few minutes is coming round to fill it again. And again.

Apart from the waiter, there is not a strange face here. With only the smallest effort, I could put a name to every person present. These are the people we bump into every day of the week, the folk we run across in all the expected places. No getting away from them, even if we wanted to.

Yet how well do we really know each other? Who in this room remembers the Lydia who used to sing opera in the bath? Carlie and I do – just – and Saskia does, of course, but she's not here. And who remembers a Carlie who ran through life in a fur coat and button up boots? Who needs to? This must be what Jonathan wanted, the reason for the party. He wants Lydia to see: this is her life, her present. She doesn't need a past. She doesn't need Sas.

Listen, smile, move on. The temperature remains the same.

My glass will soon be empty for a third time. I need to talk to the waiter. I need to talk to Jonathan, congratulate him on a job well done. The wine is plentiful, the catering – though I haven't sampled it – is probably excellent, because it always is in Patersfield. There's no room here for female potters and lone wolves looking for a place at the table. Both would stand out a mile. A sudden rise in temperature, and this crowd would drive them out with axes and bells. At the thought of it, at the thought of Magnus fleeing a mob brought together by school fees and taxes, I feel my face glaze over with a smile. Maybe Jonathan has the right idea after all. Here we are safe. Carlie is safe. This is the place to be.

So why are so many people looking back, searching the websites, trawling for the people who genuinely used to know them? Carlie, maybe you don't want to be safe any more.

Suddenly the champagne takes on a mineral taste in my mouth, like aluminium. The smile is wiped off my face.

'Guy, my darling boy – what ever is the matter? You've got a face on you to curdle milk.' Vanessa is there, observing me, scarlet lips drawn back over bleached, brilliant teeth. She has changed her outfit too, sheathed in a clinging slick of sequins that look like the scales of a snake. Something that coils towards you in the water, making ripples. Adding heat.

'So what's wrong? Is it the champagne, not quite to your liking?'

I look past her. 'Where's Carlie?'

She reaches for the glass in my hand, puts it to her lips. 'You may well ask. She and Lydia have closeted themselves in the bedroom. Call me sensitive, but they seemed not to want me with them.' Vanessa's eyes sparkle wickedly over the edge of my champagne. 'Maybe you should go up there. If Lydia has discovered a liking for the ladies, maybe no one is safe. And she's so very fond of Carlie...'

'Be quiet, Vanessa...'

But Vanessa only laughs, eyes gleaming brighter than ever.

'Poor Guy. You're not in the least bit interested in Lydia, are you? Old Lyd, who doesn't know what's hit her, what with Jonathan *and* some burly lesbian both fighting to get into her knickers. That girl could be having a whale of a time if she only got the chance, but of course, there's *Jonno*, simply refusing to see the funny side. He should be careful, though, don't you think? He could turn it all into something *soo* much more serious. It's not even as if she's asking for much – a bit of fun, jolly old hockey sticks and all, a bit of *talk*. Jonathan should be able to do that for her, for goodness sake. He's known her long enough, he must remember the sort of thing that used to make her smile. If he can't see it for himself then he deserves what's coming.'

She pauses. I am aware of her closing in, focusing the attack.

'Aren't you going to ask me what's coming, Guy?' She watches me. 'No,' she says, more softly. 'You've got other things on your mind. I looked at you just now and thought *there's a man who hasn't slept in a month.*'

'Vanessa, I...'

'Oh, don't scowl at me, darling! Did you know you can look *so* forbidding at times, a kind of upmarket Heathcliffe. We all love it, you know, we girls – that frowning look of yours. Tanya can sound almost unhinged, talking about you.

She swears she's going to commit a murder, just to have you there for her, all dressed up in your wig.'

'Vanessa, I think you're going to have to excuse me...'

'Don't run off, my pet! All I'm saying is, I notice these things. I should be doing Mr. Robinson's job really. Seriously, I'd be a wonderful detective. I could tell you odds and sods about people here Mr. Robinson would never find out in a hundred years.'

'Oh?' I hear myself say dully. 'What people?'

Vanessa's lip curls upwards. 'Gosh, where would I start? How about...let's be naughty...Carlie?'

And she has me. I force myself to breathe. 'Yes? And what about Carlie?' There is a mirror behind her in which I catch a glimpse of myself. My face shows nothing beyond amused enquiry.

But Vanessa knows. She takes another sip of my wine, makes a face and hands it back to me. 'You're right,' she says. 'There is something wrong with the champagne. Tinny.' She observes me a moment, then slips her hand through my arm. 'Darling, come with me. Somewhere quiet.'

She leads me through the party, through the kitchen, where we overhear more people talking about the website. No getting away from it. Vanessa gives me a mischievous, meaningful look, then opens the back door, and pulls me outside. Now we are alone, as she intended, surrounded by Lydia's garden, carefully tended lawns gleaming with a spring frost. Cold air rushes over me, makes me shiver, reminds me I have drunk too much, too quickly.

'Chilly, Guy?' Murmurs Vanessa. Then she laughs. 'Actually, chilly is the one thing you're not, is it? Not chilly at all, not on the inside. It's just the way you like to be seen – all frosty, and cold, and distant. But it's skin-deep, all that – the perfect mask. To be honest it's what I like about you, darling – the contrast. Cool on the outside – and all that heat burning away on the inside. It's very sexy. Does Carlie know what she's got, I wonder.'

I say nothing. But the mention of Carlie has made me more alert than ever. Vanessa senses it and smiles at me. 'Do you know – silly girl – I'm beginning to think she doesn't. Sometimes it strikes me that her husband is the last thing on her mind.'

'What makes you say that?'

She gives a me long considering look, then as if on impulse, moves closer to me, places her hand on the flat of my chest. For a moment neither of us moves.

'Well?'

And for the first time Vanessa looks slightly thrown. She is staring at her hand, almost with astonishment. Perhaps that movement really had been impulse. Now she expects me to step away, stopping something before it begins. Instead I am perfectly still, watching her.

'Well,' I say again. 'What makes you say Carlie has something on her mind?'

Vanessa is still looking at her hand.

In a low voice, I tell her, 'Don't start what you can't finish, Vanessa.'

A tremor runs across her features, which she tries to twist into another smile. 'It's probably nothing, Guy. I...I see a lot of Carlie, that's all. And I've known her – how long? – ten, twelve years. You can read anything into anything.'

'Are you sure you know what are you trying to say, Vanessa?'

Vanessa is on the retreat. 'No, of course I'm not sure. Better not to talk about it...' She starts to remove her hand, but my own hand flies up and keeps it there, stops her from moving. She draws a quick breath, then gives up.

'Alright,' she says. She makes herself relax, allows her fingers to spread across my chest. 'If you want to know – she's looking fragile, Guy. Strung out, stretched, the way she might look if she were on the edge of something, and didn't know what she should do about it. Paralysed is perhaps a better word – like a rabbit caught in the headlights,' She pauses, and her voice drops slightly. 'Hypnotised.'

'Hypnotised by what?'

She shrugs. 'By the attraction of it, I suppose – the chance to throw it all away.'

'What do you mean, Vanessa. Throw what away?'

She stirs. 'Oh...*this.*' She lifts a hand towards the lawns, the trees, the lighted house, the people we have left inside. By which she means everything..

I take a step closer. 'Why would she do that? What would anyone throw everything away for? An idea?...a *person?*'

Now, now we have arrived. Vanessa looks at me. Softly she says, 'Oh Guy, there's always a person.'

She speaks, and whatever held my heart in place drops away, for it to fall right through the centre of me. Nothing there to catch it. As if I am hollow, empty inside. Flatly I say, 'Has she said anything to you? About anyone?'

She looks at her hand on my chest.

'Has she said anything to you?' I say again. My hand tightens round hers.

A shiver ripples across the bare skin of her shoulders. She sighs. 'Darling, she doesn't *have* to say anything. You know me – I'm an expert. I know about these things.' Vanessa allows herself a wry smile. 'I'm tempted to say it's all I know, nowadays. And I just thought – maybe you should know too. *If you don't know already.*'

Her eyes have begun to glitter again. Her dress shimmers as she leans forward in the moonlight, puts her mouth to my ear. 'She's a fool, Guy. I wouldn't let my attention wander from you, not for a moment. Not with all the heat inside you. So locked up.' As she speaks, she takes my hand and places it against her own body, holds it there to her breast. And watches my face.

'You shouldn't take it so hard, though, if Carlie wants to be...foolish. We are all free if we choose to be – Carlie, you, me. Free to do what we like. All we have to do is keep within the rules, and that way nothing has to change, not so anyone would notice. People don't even have to get hurt. Do you see what I'm saying, Guy? Do you understand what I'm offering?'

Slowly she takes away her hand. And my own hand stays, clasping her breast. She sighs and throws back her head, gives herself up to the contact; all the same, from under her eyelids she is watching me, proving that Vanessa – the hunter – is not sure of me, has never been sure of me.

Something makes me whisper: 'Close your eyes, Vanessa.'

Her eyelids flutter, uncertain – and then they close. And I study the effect – of Vanessa with her eyes closed, her neck exposed. She has made herself defenceless, easy to strike down. Vanessa as I have never seen her. She looks younger, softer, expecting everything – and nothing. I see her and something in the space where my heart used to be comes alive, begins to pulse with a rhythm of its own. Allows me to see what the heart had obscured. I gaze at Vanessa and – as if by magic, by the cooler revelation of the moon – it's Carlie I see. My Carlie – hot and cold in the dark, in the cover of the night.

Carlie, her eyes closed, lips trembling, giving herself away. Not to me, though.

Not to me.

Slowly my hand leaves her breast and travels to her throat – Carlie's throat. Carlie quivers to the touch. I feel her pulse begin to race. And what sweeps over me is stronger than anger, profounder than grief. My other hand drifts up, fingers clasping – a circle for Carlie's neck.

Keep her or kill her. Those words again. Spoken in my ear. Another turning point. Another night of true colours. The fire inside dies away, and something is released, like a sigh escaping. I feel cool, perfectly calm, knowing what has to be done. I close my eyes.

My hands press, gently at first, coaxing the flesh under my fingers. Then harder, feeling the veins beneath constricting and filling up, hearing the soft gasp from somewhere in the air beside me. But I have to keep pressing – hard, harder still. Wringing the flesh until he's gone from her, and all that's left is Carlie. My Carlie. Stop her giving herself away. The only way to keep her.

A bird cries in the dark. I open my eyes. And it's Vanessa's eyes that meet mine. Vanessa's eyes, not Carlie's. Eyes pale with terror, a whole life suddenly concentrated in a gaze. The wrong life. Not Carlie's.

I let go my grip, but my hands stay where they are, locked about her neck. But the impulse to squeeze is gone. Vanessa-not-Carlie continues to stare at me. *Why hasn't she run away?* Incredibly the fear is already vanishing from her face. Vanessa gazes at me, her expression rapt as if she is seeing a vision; as if she is the one who is hypnotised. Slowly she reaches up and touches the hands braceleting her throat.

Then she moves, pushes her body, hard, against mine. 'Do it, Guy. Do anything. Now.'

The savagery in her voice breaks the spell. I pull my hands away, so quickly she almost falls, reminding me of Carlie in the park, when *he* kissed her, then let her drop. She stands, as Carlie stood, swaying slightly, watching me. Then slowly she begins to straighten up and, little by little, to retreat behind the hard walls of herself. Already Vanessa is pulling herself in, putting up defences. Not like Carlie. Wilder than Carlie, she has a certain dignity, is a creature to be respected. A she-fox trapped in the town, forced to hunt between dustbins.

Makes me see: at least when Vanessa goes hunting, it is for what the present has to offer. She doesn't scour through the past. Nor does she allow herself to be sniffed around by old dog-foxes. Vanessa belongs to the here and now. If Magnus were to come after her, years after he had used, abused and all but destroyed her, she wouldn't stand and let it happen. She'd take a knife and carve him right out of her own heart. Then, bleeding, she would make him bleed. She would make him pay, and pay again.

This is what Vanessa would do. Why can't Carlie do the same?

Vanessa smoothes a lock of hair behind her ear, then lifts up her head and gives me a smile brilliant as lime. 'Ah well,' her voice is calm. 'Maybe it's me I'm talking about, not Carlie. Maybe I'm the one who's caught.'

I say nothing. She allows her arm to brush against mine as she stalks back into the house.

I follow her inside. Vanessa disappears and from the kitchen tap I draw a glass of water that has the same metallic taste as the champagne. My entire mouth tastes of metal. In the hall, more people try to talk to me and this time I can't think of anything to say to anybody. I am waiting, but for what? For Carlie of course, to see she if she can displace the image in the garden: the image I have now, indelible: of Carlie giving herself away.

Presently she is there, appearing with Lydia at the top of the stairs. Lydia has put on the frock Vanessa chose. Was this a deliberate mistake? Concentric circles of print cling to every bulge in her body, as if put there to highlight the existence of each and every one. Lydia is suffering in lycra. She knows what she looks like. A woman leans to the left of me, to whisper in the ear of the woman next to her. 'Versace.' There's an answering murmur of approval, which then flits around the room like a ripple of applause. So Vanessa knew what she was doing after all. Things could still turn out alright.

But I have reckoned without Jonathan, who has spent too

long in a corner closeted with Miles next to the drinks table. He has not used the time well. Now he's too drunk to know when to leave well alone. He lurches forward and grabs Lydia by the hand.

'Surprise time, Lyd. Can't wait any longer. Got to see your face. Been telling Miles all about it. Come on everyone. Time for Lydia's big surprise.'

Carlie tries to catch my eye, to signal something. She wants me to stop Jonathan, but I can't do anything. Because this is what happened, and this the result: I have seen her – Carlie in the garden – and now it's all I can see. I follow, numb, good for nothing, as Jonathan starts dragging Lydia through the crowd. 'To the study,' he calls out. 'Everyone's got to see this.'

Outside the study door, Lydia halts, refusing to be dragged any further. It is as if she has a premonition of something on the other side. Jonathan would do well to stop and look at her, listen to his wife.

But he doesn't. He reaches past her and flings open the door to reveal Lydia's birthday surprise – which turns out to be a man, all dressed up as Tarzan, muscles shining with bronzing oil. He stands, huge and incongruous beside Jonathan's desk and Jonathan's golf prints, a triumph of steroidal science. Despite the body mass and the muscles, however, his face betrays his youth. I look again, and this time I recognise him. It's the hairdresser from the salon, got up in a blonde wig.

He stares at us, panic in his eyes. For coiled around his body, one hand thrust deep and searching under the leopard skin loincloth, is Vanessa. She has her back to us, her face pressed against his well-oiled nipples. But hearing the commotion and then the silence, she pauses and the hand in the loin cloth freezes. Slowly she turns from her task, looks round at the watching crowd.

'Oh,' she says calmly. 'You're early. Jonathan, I thought you were keeping the strip-o-gram till last.'

Jonathan's mouth opens and closes, soft as a jellyfish. Speechless, he turns to Lydia but her face has hardened. Without a word, she leaves the room to go back upstairs, passing Miles who is slowly putting a glass to his lips, smiling like a man subjected to the same joke over and over. Only a certain moistness about the eyes gives him away.

Carlie and I walk home, side by side, but not touching.

'He was only doing his best,' I say. I am talking about Jonathan trying to show Lydia what they had, trying to paint the present brighter than it actually was.

'And all he's done is show Lydia how he knows absolutely nothing about her. That dress. And the strip-o-gram. What was he thinking of?'

'That was Vanessa's doing. She persuaded him.'

'Vanessa.' Carlie's voice is scornful.

We walk on in silence. There's a distance between us, spreading like a crack in the ground. Carlie is angry with me. Why? Because I am such a staunch defender of the present? Because I still want her to think that the present – any present – is better than the past?

But her anger is nothing compared with mine.

Because I don't trust Carlie. Not now. There is no part of her remaining that I trust. We walk home under a chill moon, not speaking. I see Carlie's face as it was in the moonlight, her lips swelling. I see Carlie's breasts filling and longing to be touched. I see Carlie and Carlie and Carlie. Giving herself away.

And *him*. I see him. Old and sly, and down on his luck. A thief who dyes his hair. She meets him in her dreams, just as she met me tonight in Lydia's garden. This is the past that is worming its way, deep into the present. This is the hold he has on her.

This has been a night of true colours. I saw Carlie in the moonlight. I saw what happens in her dreams. Lydia's party has changed everything.

We lie in bed, still not touching. The time for talking is gone. Anything we say now would betray the secrets we have been keeping from each other. Carlie doesn't even pretend to sleep. The moon shines through the window, touches eyes that are staring, sightless, at the ceiling.

What if I killed her in my sleep? I am so angry with Carlie. I am so in love with Carlie.

I touch the space beside me in the bed. We are lying so far apart the sheet between us is cold.

Then I feel Carlie's hand move into the same empty space. Our fingers lock and twine, and the distance closes by this much: the span of a hand.

Chapter Twenty-Five

But in the morning it is back. The ache is back. I saw Carlie in the moonlight.

And now, for some reason, David has dragged a rucksack out onto the landing. He is kneeling on the floor, filling it up with clothes and books, CD player and gameboy – everything he owns, it seems to me.

'Packing?' I say politely. 'Are you going somewhere?'

He ignores me. He hasn't spoken to me for a fortnight, since Carlie stopped him seeing Mr. Magnet. It's still only me he blames, although he speaks to her.

And of course he speaks to *him*. I know this. Even if he's not allowed lessons with him, I imagine my son seeks him out. And if he doesn't, then Magnus will find him. This is what he's here in Patersfield to do. To work his way inside. A new and terrible thought occurs to me: is David carrying messages between them?

Panic takes hold of me. 'I think your mother is right about influences. Bad influences. We should do something about finding you a better school, a proper one.'

His mouth drops. I avert my eyes, address the wall.

'I'd been away for years by the time I was twelve. You could go to my old school...'

'...You hated that school, you hated boarding. You said you'd never send me away.'

'Nonsense. It did me good. It made me...strong.' My voice quails with this last word. I drop to my haunches, and blurt out, 'Are you seeing him still...Mr. Magnet? Are you talking to him?' And when he doesn't answer I grab him by the shoulders, so slight and skinny I can feel the bone between my fingers. And I shake him. 'Are you still seeing him?'

My son's eyes on my face, my son seeing me as he never has.

Instantly my hands fall away from his shoulders. But it's too late. He watches me a moment, then stands up. He picks up his rucksack and retreats into his room, closing the door after him.

In the kitchen I say to Carlie. 'David is upstairs, packing.'

She sighs, comes out of her thoughts. 'Already?'

'What do you mean *already*?' All at once I'm shouting. 'Where does he think he's going?'

She blinks. Is this the way to shake her out of the reverie, the contemplation of other things, other people: by shouting at her?'

'Cornwall, remember?' She speaks to me gently. 'With the school. You signed the cheque.'

'When?'

'I don't know – back in November. Months ago.'

I search through the contents of my mind. And still I can't find the memory of a trip. Everything is in disorder, like a room that has been rifled, objects flung in all directions. A room I'm not even sure I recognise.

'It's not for another week,' says Carlie. 'But he does this, don't you remember? When he went on the French trip, he was packed and ready a whole fortnight before. It's excitement, that's all.'

I stare at her, helpless. It strikes me I can't remember anything from before three months ago. Before that first email. *Hey you!*

Carlie steps close and puts her fingers to my cheek. They are warm, a reminder that she is, that we still are...

And I pull my cheek away, making her blink. As well she might. Because I've seen her haven't I? I see her all the time now. Sudden images of Carlie painted over my eyes, images of Carlie I don't want to see. Carlie's eyes closing, Carlie's lips parting, her breasts swelling. Carlie hot and cold in the moonlight. My hands at her neck.

I have seen too much.

Carlie goes and stands on the other side of the kitchen. 'What is the matter, Guy?' Her voice is breaking. 'What's happening to you? Ever since the party...' She lifts her hand and lets it fall.

I have to stifle the desire to laugh. Carlie's eyes glisten in the moonlight, her skin shimmers to the touch. I have seen Carlie as she gives herself away – and she asks what the matter is with me. It strikes me it's lucky that she is standing on the far side of the kitchen or else the urge to stretch out my hands would be too great, too strong to resist.

But come the night, in our bed, she is so close, only a touch away. And for a moment I remember that she is mine, as I am hers. I reach and take her in my arms, rest my lips against her neck.

'What do you want, Carlie? Tell me what you want. Help me, Carlie, so I can help you.'

I whisper the words - and Carlie doesn't answer. She lies on her side, breathing noisily into her pillow, not knowing even that I have her in my arms. And not dreaming. Her head and body are loose and heavy, sunk into the bed like someone who has drowned. Carlie is sleeping without hearing or dreaming

How has she done this?

Instinctively, I reach past her, open the drawer of her bedside table. No reason to be discreet. Carlie is sleeping so hard she could never hear me. And there, on top of the letters, and the old birthday cards, and handkerchiefs, is a small bottle of pills.

This is Carlie's answer to the dreams. She has shut him out as best she can. He can't touch her while she sleeps.

And neither can I. Carlie has locked herself away from both of us until the morning. So what does she want? Carlie won't tell me. Can't tell me. Either I go back to work. Or I find out.

Carlie lies without dreaming and I am alone. So I think about my father. What stopped him in the end? What stopped him killing my mother even when he was mad? Was it really because she wasn't worth it? Because he didn't love her enough?

Questions without answers. But I can't live without answers. Any more than I can live without Carlie.

Over supper the next night I say to them: 'I have to go away for work. There's a case in the high court in Nottingham. It's just for a night, two at most.'

'When?' says Carlie.

I concentrate on making an efficient cut into my steak. Red meat, its insides quivering, the way Vanessa would eat it. I had a sudden hankering. I went to the butcher's and gave it to Carlie to cook. I notice, though, that she has grilled some salmon for herself. David's is lying almost untouched.

'Eat up,' I say to him automatically. 'It's the best you'll get for a while. It will be all school food next week, down in Cornwall.'

'When?' asks Carlie again. 'When are you going away?'

'Next week. Same day that David goes.' I smile fiercely at him, and say to Carlie, 'Will you be alright on your own?'

'Of course. Why shouldn't I?' She takes a sip of water. Carlie is not eating her salmon.

I wave my fork in the air. 'Think of it. An empty house. Things happen. David won't be here, remember. Do you really want to be alone?'

She puts down her glass, says quietly, 'I didn't say I *wanted* to be alone, Guy...'

Suddenly David speaks. 'I could stay if you wanted me to. I don't need to go...'

Carlie touches his hand briefly. 'Thank you, darling. But

that won't be necessary.'

'I expect you'll enjoy it,' I say smoothly. 'No one else around. Just for once, you'll be able to do anything you like.'

She looks up from her plate, tries to smile. But she's finding it hard, since the party. She is tired. *He* tires her out; inside, outside her head – wherever he is, whatever he's doing, he's tiring her out. Carlie can barely summon a smile nowadays, whereas I seem to have found the knack of smiling more and more as the days go by. Her mask is crumbling. Mine just keeps getting stronger.

We drive David to the school at some unearthly hour in the morning. The sun hasn't even come up yet. He sits jammed against the corner of the car, his rucksack taking up more space than he does. He has the peaked look of a child who has been hauled out of bed long before he's had enough sleep.

'You can have a doze on the coach,' I say. He nods, doesn't look at me.

'It's such a long way to Cornwall,' says Carlie in a small voice, half to herself.

I steal a glance at her, sitting beside me. We are up so early, have wasted so little time in getting David to his coach. Perhaps the pills meant her to sleep longer than this. Her cheeks are still pink from being buried in her pillow, her hair is tousled, the way it used to be all those years ago. She looks like the young Carlie, the Carlie who would stretch out on my bed and sleep, the warmth stealing into her cheeks as she dreamed. Did she know I used to watch her, counting every breath she took? Guarding her until she woke up, and in waking became lost to me. Yes, she did. I'm sure she did. Isn't that why Carlie came to me, and kept on coming? Does she remember?

Carlie turns her head and catches me looking. And smiles, because she does remember. And my heart twists, because she doesn't know what I have in mind; how close we are, how close to everything coming to an end. I am going to find out what Carlie wants.

We get out of the car. I hand David his rucksack. In the shadow of the coach, other boys are standing around with their parents, awkward on the edge of goodbye. You can see it's a relief for most of them when the pneumatic doors open with a hiss and they can climb aboard. Only David lingers, keeping close to us both.

It's as if he knows, is trying to make the moment last. By the time he arrives home again, everything could be different.

Carlie presses her cheek against his, then steps back. He turns to me – and without warning darts forward and kisses me, his lips brushing the side of my face. Then just as quickly he darts away and leaps onto the bus. I can still feel the warmth on my cheek as we look for his face in the window. And there it is, a white smudge through the smeared glass, his eyes fixed on us. Pleading with us to be there when we come back.

The bus disappears and Carlie forces a laugh. 'He was very serious, wasn't he? Do you think he's going to miss us?'

Without waiting for an answer, she slips her hand into mine and, treacherously, I squeeze it with my own.

'Let's go home,' I say. 'I need to throw some things in a bag and get going myself.'

As I park the car back in the drive I say to her, 'Got any plans?'

'Plans?' She echoes the word. Her hand hovers on the car door.

'For tonight. Have you arranged to see a film or anything like that – with Lydia perhaps?'

'No,' her voice is dreamy. 'No plans.' Then she says, 'You know, Nottingham's really not that far. You could come home. Make another early start tomorrow.'

I shake my head firmly. 'I promised to have dinner with the solicitor who's briefing me. He thinks we need to talk about the case. There's absolutely no sense in my coming home.'

She nods. But now Carlie knows for a certainty: I am not coming home. The house will be empty. She can do whatever she wants.

That is what I have made her believe.

Carlie showers while I pack an overnight bag. When I'm ready she wraps a robe around herself and sees me to the car. 'Phone me,' she says bending to speak to me through the window. She is still wet from the shower, tiny drops water clinging to her neck and arms. She looks clean and well washed. An innocent Carlie.

'I'll be home tomorrow.'

'Phone me anyway.'

She studies my eyes, the first time we have looked directly at one another since the party. 'Guy,' she begins – and stops. She puts her hand on the window frame. Carlie is trying to reach me, but she's going about it all the wrong way. She tells me nothing. Secrets have toppled over into lies.

'What is it?'

She tries to laugh, doesn't quite manage it. 'It's silly, I know. But I was thinking – I could come with you. David's away, there's nothing to stop me.' She turns and points at our front door. 'Look. It's an empty house. You said I could do anything I like. Well, I'd like to jump in the car and come with you. I'll find something to do while you're in court. You can have that dinner with the solicitor and I'll wait for you in the hotel, be there when you come back.' Her eyes are steady, fixed on mine. For a moment I would swear that Carlie guards no more secrets than David.

My mask. Where is my mask? I glance at the hand resting on the window frame, and feel the hot flood flushing through the veins of my throat, and up. A dark, ugly, male blush. For the first time in days, I don't know what to say to my wife. I don't know what I can say. There is no court. No hotel. No trip to Nottingham.

A moment passes. Her eyes fall from my face, her hand drops from the window. 'Well,' she says softly. 'Never mind. It was just a thought.'

She straightens up and turns, walks back into the house.

I drive through Patersfield, past the detective agency with its discreet plaque, past the station. I spot Jonathan trudging along the pavement, his eyes glued to the ground. He used to stride with a spring in his step, with the walk of a man who never realised his luck. Well fed, well looked after, well loved. The strange part is that he is all those things now. I do believe Lydia loves him still. So what has gone wrong?

The past, that's what's gone wrong for him, crashing through the fabric of the present. Not even a bad past, by the sound of it. It's just that it was Lydia's past – and only Lydia's – with its friendships and its loves and its reminders of Lydia as she used to be. But looking at Jonathan now, you can see how well the present had suited him, how it kept the spring in his step. It was only Lydia who slightly lost her sheen, who forgot that once she used to sing in the bath. Jonathan could have gone on for ever with Lydia's past safely in the past. But Lydia? What does Lydia want?

And Carlie? *Why did Carlie want to come to Nottingham with me?*

Because she loves me and wants to be with me. Only me.

Why did Carlie say she wanted to come to Nottingham with me?

Because she needed me to think she loves me and wants to be with me. Only me.

Leaving the roundabout, I speed up to join the slip road on to the M40, insert myself in amongst the queue of traffic heading into London.

I park the car in Lincoln's Inn Fields and walk to the British Museum. I'd been thinking what to do with my day, and this was all I could come up with. Old familiar stones, the comfort of marble. I trail in the wake of the schools' parties winding between the statues in the Greek and Roman rooms. Next to the Elgin Marbles, a young teacher is talking to her class, nine and ten year olds.

'Who can tell me why we study the past anyway?'

She asks the question, looks round, eager for the answer. But doesn't she realise these are children she is talking to and children live only in the present? The reply doesn't occur to them. I doubt if they even heard her ask.

So she is forced to answer her own question. 'We study the past because the past is what made us. Think of it – before there was you, there were your parents. You wouldn't be here if weren't for them. If you want to know why you have brown hair and blue eyes, look at your parents. If you want to know why we speak English not French, look at History. The past helped to make you. There simply can't be a present without the past. If you want to know why your world, your *lives*, are as they are today, you have to look back, take a *good* look back, at the past…'

But she has a battle on her hands. Some of the little girls are listening, taking it all in. But behind them, the little boys are sniggering and swapping pokemon cards, not lending even half an ear.

Halfway through the morning, I step outside the Museum to phone home. When there is no answer I go back in and sit with the statues a while longer, then come out and try again. And again. I want so much to speak to Carlie. I want to hear her voice, one last time before I come home, before things change for ever. I phone and I phone until a tannoyed voice fills the spaces between the statues: the museum will close in fifteen minutes. What has Carlie been doing with her day?

What will she do with her night?

I am going to find out.

I am next to the Rosetta Stone, reading the laundry lists written down in Greek, ordinary words about ordinary things that helped crack the code for a civilisation. Nobody seems to spend much time looking at it. Who reads Greek any more? People pass it on their way out and down the steps, heading for home. Not me. I leave with the rest of them, but there's still time to kill – past, present and future. I have to wait for the night. Steal home with the darkness, steal the secrets from my wife.

And after that? When I know Carlie's secrets, when I have found out what Carlie wants, what happens then?

I drive from Lincoln's Inn long after dusk has fallen. The headlights glare on the M40. My hands shake on the wheel.

I stop at a pub just outside Patersfield, checking first there's no one here who knows me. There is a crowd of boys, vaguely familiar, sixth-formers, probably, from David's school; but none of them even glances in my direction. They are playing snooker, talking about girls. Tall and skinny, their Adam's apples bob as they down their pints of beer. They are living in one long continuous present. The past has no more interest for them than for those smaller boys swapping their pokemon cards at the museum.

I was barely older than them when I met Carlie. She is my past and my present. I always thought she would be my future.

I drink one whisky, and immediately want another. But if I keep drinking here, I will be driving with the heat of it in my brain. Round Patersfield the police know to look for men who are coming out of pubs in the evening, delaying their arrival home, for all the different reasons. Imagine if I was stopped and charged, what it would mean: a night in the cells, a cuckold who drives drunk. And Carlie's secrets left intact.

I leave the pub and the forgetful boys, and continue all the way into the centre of Patersfield to park behind the super-market. Next to the off licence, Mr. Robinson's plaque winks at me. Inside, the shopkeeper has already closed up his till – it's a minute past his licence – but he lets me have a bottle of single malt because the price of it makes it worth the risk. But to the person I hear enter the shop behind me, he says, 'Sorry, I'm closed.'

'Hey friend, give me a break. Look, just let me have one of those.'

Out of the corner of my eye I see a hand point to the shelf behind the counter, holding up the shop's most expensive wines. The shopkeeper hesitates, then turns to bring down a bottle. He puts it on the counter and waits for his money – a lot of it – and then sees me, still standing, not moving.

'Something else I can get for you?'

I shake my head. To appear normal, I need to turn on my heel, leave the shop. And I can't move.

'Sir?' he says again, cautiously this time. And watches me, still rooted to the spot.

I need to move. I put my hand out for the whisky, steel myself to turn and face the man beside me, who has just bought the most expensive wine in the shop.

Magnus.

At this moment he's flicking through his wallet with the same careless care he flicked through Carlie's purse. He extracts three twenties and places them on the counter. But the licensee is watching me, puzzled because I am not moving. Seeing his money has remained on the counter, Magnus glances first at the shopkeeper and then at me.

And he doesn't recognise me.

Fifteen years of course – but even that has nothing to do with it. Magnus never did recognise me, not in all the years I knew him. I wasn't important enough, not to him. If he noticed me at all, it was as an adjunct to Carlie, something she carried round with her – and dropped the moment I seemed to get in the way. Even that last time he saw me, at the hospital, he had had to take a second look, struggling to work out if I was connected with her.

But he notices me now, if only because I am staring at him, without the power to stop myself, taking in the changes in him. Magnus looks better than he did in the park. With a shock I can see what he has done: he has adapted himself for Patersfield. He is better dressed, better shorn, with even the ludicrous black dye removed to let the grey show through. A distinguished look that will go down well with parents and teachers alike. He has changed in the way of a man who knows when his luck has changed. A wolf who makes his own luck.

He sees the involuntary nature of my stare and raises his eyebrows enquiringly, waits for me to speak. But I cannot trust myself. So Magnus, in control of everything, says: 'Hey, have we met?' He is relaxed, but attentive. If I were a woman I would be flattered by the singleness of his gaze.

To my amazement, I find my voice – and it sounds cool, devoid of anything to cause alarm. 'I was just wondering if I had seen you before...' I pause, pretending to think. 'At the school? Don't you teach there? My son...' I swallow. 'I think my son has pointed you out.'

'Your son? And he is...?' He has the bottle tucked under his arm, ready to go, but he is still looking at me, curiosity aroused. Something about me – it must be the stare – has interested him.

The air in the shop seems to have become rarefied, thinned of oxygen. I have to force myself to breathe – and yet still my voice sounds easy. 'Peter.' I have said the first name that enters my head, find myself cannibalising the roll call of old friends. 'He's Peter. You're new, aren't you – perhaps you don't remember him.'

'Peter? Oh yeah – of course I know Peter.' He smiles slow-ly as he lies. 'Bright kid…Peter.'

The shopkeeper signs that he wants to lock up his shop. We walk out together, Magnus and I. Our shoulders touch and suddenly I can smell him, the acrid, half-rank tang of something wild. I have known this scent of old, had forgotten how I used to catch the vestiges of it on her, every time she had been with him; how it would cling, mingling with the burnt sugar smell that was Carlie's own. Catching it again now, I have to swallow a sour rush of nausea rising in my throat; makes me stumble and sway, like a drunk.

Magnus sees the unsteadiness, smirks, then glances at his watch. 'Look, do me a favour. I'm early for something, and I don't know this end of town. You got a pub nearby?' He has noted the bottle of whisky in my hand, smelt the whisky on my breath; he knows he is asking the right person. I see him taking a further note of my shoes, the cut of my suit.

Magnus decides it's all to his advantage, and nods when I say: 'I'm early too. I'll buy you a drink.'

I indicate a direction, and he falls into step beside me. It comes as a jolt to realise we are the same height, he and I. When we walk we match each other stride for stride. Somehow, all through these years, I have thought he was taller than me.

Out of the blue Magnus says, 'Are you sure it's just the school – where we've seen each other?'

I stop and look at him. In so far as it is possible to read the eyes of a wolf, he seems to have asked the question without any hint of guile. And guileless, I say, 'Pretty sure. I think it's the school. Just the school.'

In the pub I buy two large whiskies, and we take them through to the snug. Magnus sits and stretches out his legs, takes possession of another slice of Patersfield. Already he looks as if he's been here longer than I have.

'Fucking far out!' He's laughing at the horse brasses, the beams, the fire in the hearth. 'Merrie England, home sweet home – all that shit. Come here a lot, do you?'

I let the question slide, as if the answer were self-evident. For no sooner have we sat than I have gulped down half my glass, confirming that I am what he takes me to be – a middle class drunk who still remembers to shine his shoes. So eager not to drink alone he'll even accost the teachers from his son's school.

Magnus, who is sober, stretches his legs still further and waits to see what else the evening will have to offer.

'My son – Peter – he tells me you're teaching part time.'

'Actually they want to make me a member of the department. Contract, pension, the whole fucking shebang. Not enough numbers of teachers, you see, not here, not anywhere. Turns out we're right up there, all us math-heads. Suddenly everyone wants us.'

'You speak as if it's come as a surprise.'

'I had no fucking idea, man. Too busy wandering the groves of academe. Never could bring myself to leave the hallowed stones of university. The maths is more interesting and as for the kids – well let's just say there's a world of difference between fifteen and twenty. I've always liked my students to be mature.'

Mature? Isn't legal what he means? A question of who he can and can't screw. You can do what you like with a twenty-year-old. And he did. Aloud I say, 'So why didn't you stay in…in academe?'

'Ah fuck it, universities don't want you once you've passed thirty. They have to think about tenure then, pay you more.' He sounds almost peevish as he talks, surprised, as if thirty came and went a moment ago. *Just how old are you, Magnus. Fifty, fifty-five?* Something Carlie always kept quiet about, exactly how much older you were than us all.

I say, 'But now you know, and you could teach anywhere –
in schools at least – why come here? Why Patersfield?'

He looks amused. 'Why not Patersfield? Shit, don't *you*
dig it?'

As he speaks he watches a pair of girls walk to the bar, his
eyes lingering on the bare stretch of belly between their jeans
and their tops. Aware of his gaze, the girls nudge each other,
preening. An old man watches them and they are flattered,
twisting and sucking in their navels. It makes you realise what
can happen when you have no use for rules, when you make it
obvious what you want, the things that come to you. When
you don't even care that some words flew out the window
before half the world was born. *Dig it.*

Nevertheless I mumble into the air between us: 'Personally
I know people who would find it...limiting, living in
Patersfield.'

'So, more fool them. Maybe they just haven't lived enough
to earn a bit of peace and quiet. How about you? Do you find
it...*limiting*?' Again the mockery is there.

I don't answer this. I need to stand up, turn my back on
him while I get another whisky. Magnus watches me return
from the bar, wonders idly how much I've had already, how far
he can take this. It seems he's in search of entertainment, a
way to pass the time.

Or maybe he genuinely has something to tell me – about
Patersfield. Already knowing things I don't. He seems willing,
eager to communicate with me, waits till I'm seated, makes
sure I'm listening. Overlaying the rank smell, there is the
scent of something else, citrusy and male. Magnus has anoint-
ed himself with something more expensive, as if in readiness –
for what? I catch the traces of it as he leans towards me.

'OK, you think Patersfield is *limiting*. Let me tell you, so
do half the kids I teach. They say to me it's dead, too fucking
middle class to breathe. And you know what I say to them?'

'What do you say to them?'

'I tell them it's their problem. Because they're babies, too young to know what's there, underneath the skin. They come to school like they're shell shocked with the tedium, worn out by wanking. I tell them to look around them, get a life.'

'There is no life here,' I say blankly. 'Not in Patersfield.' Why? Is this what I believe? What I want him to believe? Nothing here for him. No reason to stay.

But Magnus is shaking his head. Mocking me again. 'You think there's no life here? Man, you want to be a teacher. You should see the mothers when they come into school. Most of them too fucking numbed to remember their own names! You can spot them the moment they walk through the door, dead from the neck down. I reckon they must be peeing Prozac here. But then...' Magnus is watching me. '...*then* comes the occasional one, like a rocket ready to go off. No life in Patersfield? Forget it. Women like that, they're what gives the place the edge.'

'Why?' My voice is thick, whisky clogged. 'What do they do? Exactly?'

And Magnus smiles because I've had to ask. He leans back and closes his eyes as if enjoying a private memory. Lewd, his mouth twitches. Suddenly heat seems to be pouring out of him. *Or is it me?* I imagine if I were Miles I would be panting in my chair to hear more. What makes Magnus think I'm like Miles? What makes Magnus think it's safe to talk to me like this?

Almost panicked, I blurt out: 'So why are you telling me? I'm a parent – you're teaching my child – he could be one of the boys you're talking about. Aren't you worried I'm going to remember all this?'

He opens his eyes, breathes in the whisky scented air, flicks a glance at the whisky bottle on the floor – and at the sweat that's broken out on my brow. 'Oh, I dunno,' he says lazily.

'You just look like a guy who knows the way the world whirls.'
There's a pause, then Magnus adds slowly, by way of a question: 'Have I met your wife?'

Smirking, he watches my shoulders as they sag.

Now he is on the offensive, coming after me with details. 'So you want to know why I'm in Patersfield? I'll tell you. I'm in Patersfield because I'm the man, fuck it. The school, the kids, my landlady, everyone seems to want me suddenly. Not to mention the mothers. I'm in demand. And what the fuck, maybe it was all meant to be. I grew up in the 'burbs, place just like this one. Spent all my life running away from it. Maybe the truth is I was just ready to come back, settle down amongst the old tribe. See what they have to offer.'

'You're not here, then,' my words are sounding slurred, 'because of anyone...in particular?'

And there it is, the slow lizard blink of satisfaction. 'Oh. Didn't I tell you? Naturally there's someone in particular. She's the whole fucking reason, Our Lady of inspiration. She's the one who told me, going on like it was her life's work to get me down here. So – here I am. Everyone's number one man. Here to stay.'

And I have to look away. He's telling me that Carlie brought him here. Brought him home.

But then, *I* know *him*. I know this man. Magnus is here to take what he can get. And with the knowledge a wild notion fires up inside: I could offer him money. Here, now, we could make a contract between the two of us, with Carlie knowing nothing about it. I could offer him money to go away. I could buy her back from him.

Slowly I get out my wallet and place it on the table in front of us. There is something elaborate about the gesture, a warning of a larger transaction to come. Without a word we stare at it, and for the first time, I am aware that Magnus has become tense, waiting for me to speak.

How much would it take to buy my wife? I try to gauge the needs and wants of the man sitting opposite me. How much can I give him? How much can I afford to give him? *How much is she worth?*

At which the sob of nausea, there all the time, rises so high I can taste it on the back of my tongue. *What am I doing?* How can I buy Carlie?

My hands have started to shake again. He must be able to see them. I pick up my wallet. For the first time my voice lets me down. Hoarsely I say, 'I'm going to get another drink. What will you have?'

Is it my imagination, or does he look disappointed? He waits to see if I am about to change my mind then shakes his head. 'No, another time.' He flicks a glance at his watch. 'Look,' he says. 'Nearly fucking eleven. Gotta get going. That certain someone is watching out for me. My lady in waiting. Can't let her down, now, can I?'

He smiles as he speaks – and then he yawns. Lips drawn back over his teeth, tongue quivering and wet. And now you see it. Stretch back the skin and the essence of Magnus is betrayed. His gums are bad. His breath is spicy with poor food and now alcohol. He is old and hungry and tired. He needs a future. He needs Carlie. And now he's come to get her. Perhaps she's got her already.

He stands up and something forces me to cry out, 'It's early still. Stay a while.'

He looks down at me, amused by my eagerness to make him stay. He lingers, taking a moment to calculate my future value to him – a drunk who will buy him drinks, and not remember anything he says. He could tell me that he slept with my wife, even, and know that I'd listen and forget. Anything for company.

'Another night, man. Watch out for me, I'll be around.'

Of course. Because that is the plan. Already, Magnus' eyes

are sliding past me towards the door and a future suddenly much improved. Now is the time to jump to my feet, tell him who I am, revealing how I have tricked him into telling me his intentions. As if I didn't already know.

And I don't do any such thing. It's not the drink that stops me, keeps me sitting where I am; or the shame of thinking that I could buy back my wife. It's not even the fear that if I try to get in his way he will laugh in my face.

I stay in my seat because I know exactly where he is going from here. I know everything about him. It's my wife I don't know. I want to know what Carlie wants. Who Carlie loves.

Hours have passed since then. A hiatus, a pause in time.

I have sat in this car with the bottle between my knees, still unopened. I lost the taste for whisky when I drank it with Magnus, convincing him that I am already what I might yet be. Another Miles, another disappointed man. Too late, too old to change anything. Worse than Miles, even – someone who can't go home any more.

But that's the future. Here, now, still in the car, I still have a home and a wife. It's observation that changes the event, makes what happens, happen. Makes it real.

Presently I will lock the car and go home, just I have done countless times, strolling away from an evening with Jonathan and Lydia, or any of those other people familiar over the last fifteen years. But didn't I always have Carlie beside me when I walked? Her head leaning against my shoulder, her hand warm in mine, reminding me that she was, that we still were, real.

Now I am about to walk home alone, listening to the sound of my steps as each one brings me closer to Carlie, and the end of the present. These days are ending. I will open my own front door, and see who is in my house. It will be the future.

And then what?

Who knows? We know the past. We think we know everything about the present. Put them together and we have every-thing we need to know the future, but still we are helpless. We know nothing. We have to see for ourselves. Seeing changes everything.

Not alone after all. I am going home as my father went home. He walks beside me as we go in search of our wives.

Chapter Twenty-Six

The garden whispers to me.

Wind in the trees, rustling in the bushes. The crunch of gravel under my feet. Noises only I can hear. For fifteen years we never paid them any heed, Carlie and I, when we were together, inside our house. They were the sounds of safety. In the dark, David's old swing stands sentry, its seat creaking in the breeze, and it too kept us safe.

A flash of sunshine – a five-year-old David laughing as the swing climbs higher, small plump legs outstretched. Higher. Higher.

It is three o' clock in the morning. If David is not lying awake thinking of home, wondering if it will be there when he comes back, he will be asleep. And Carlie? She's awake, of course. There's a light on downstairs, and another in the bedroom. What is Carlie doing? I walk up to my front door to find out. The swing creaks, the garden whispers, unaware that I am the intruder now.

I put my key in the lock. It turns without a sound, unable to warn anyone. A reminder that it was me who kept it oiled, the way my father always kept our old locks oiled. How could I have known it was for this, for silent, unforced entry into my own house?

The hall is dark, but light is escaping from the living room. I make my way towards it, expecting my tread to betray me, but there is no sound. I seem to have a talent for silence, for not giving anything away. I touch the door and, finely balanced on its hinges, it swings softly open. The curtains are drawn, and there are the remains of a fire in the hearth; red embers the only light apart from a single lamp on the table beside the sofa. Next to the lamp are two empty glasses, red beads of wine clinging to the sides.

Fire and lamp, together they cast a glow on the figure lying on the sofa. Magnus is stretched out, head thrown back on the cushions, one arm trailing contentedly to the floor, his fingers grazing the rug. His eyes are closed and he is smiling. He looks like what he is – a man at rest, finally safe, finally with everything he ever wanted. Magnus smiles in his sleep, back where he belongs. His future is assured.

All these years of wondering what Carlie wanted, what she really wanted. And the answer is here, stretched out on my sofa. Smiling. It was all so simple. And she never even lied to me. Not once has Carlie lied. I am the one. I lied when I flushed away Magnus's letter all those years ago. I lied to Carlie and I lied to myself. It seems I have been lying for years.

And Magnus sleeps. Never stirs as I step closer to observe him in the firelight – the man who took her, and shook her and laid his stamp on her, who never let her go. He sleeps. He sleeps even as my hands reach out and close around his neck, and squeeze. Gripping his throat harder than I ever gripped anything, squeezing with a force that drives out life. This is what I wanted to do to Carlie. Only it was never her I was trying to drive out of existence, it was him, forcing him out of her like a devil, because she wouldn't, *couldn't*, drive him out herself.

And Magnus sleeps.

He has not moved, not once, not even to open his eyes. My hands are bone hard about his neck and still he sleeps and smiles.

And slowly, slowly, my hands lose their grip. I can't kill a man who is asleep. Any more than I could kill Carlie. Any more than my father could kill my mother. I cannot even kill Magnus, not if he is sleeping.

I take my hands away, and Magnus's head lolls sideways on the cushion. And now I see it, the tiny gash beside his eye, the line of blood threaded discreetly into the shaggy hair. And finally I begin to understand. A noise alerts me and I look up. Carlie is standing in the door.

'He's dead,' she says. She points under the sofa, to the bottle I had seen him buy earlier in the evening, empty now. There is a tiny snail trail of blood running down the label.

I close my eyes. But I can't see it. I can't see the bottle crashing down, the moment of stun, the slow fall. Magnus is lying as if he were asleep, smiling, as if at any moment he could wake up.

Slowly I say to Carlie: 'What happened? Did he attack you? Did he hurt you?'

'Hurt me…?' She repeats the words softly as if in wonder. She walks across the room and picks up the bottle. Puts it on the table beside the lamp.

'Carlie,' I whisper. 'Are you going to tell me what happened?'

She stands very still and looks at me. She looks tired. 'How much do you want to know?'

I open my mouth, then close it again. Carlie's eyes are telling me to stop and think before I answer. I pause and look at my wife. Magnus lies between us, smiling still.

'Everything.' I nod as I say the word. 'Everything, Carlie.'

She hesitates then sits down next to the fire, laces her fingers together. And finally, Carlie speaks to me, tells me everything. Just like she used to.

'He arrived late this evening. I opened the door and there he was, just as I expected. Do you remember how he used to come for me all those years ago? Leaning against the bell until someone answered. That's what he did tonight.

'I knew he would come. I knew he was in Patersfield, that he had come after me. I had given myself away, you see. On that website. That was how he found me.

'He got in touch, months ago, and I never told you. I thought if I saw him – without you knowing – it would be alright, a way to get free. All these years he's been planted inside me, where nothing could touch him, still doing damage. I told myself I could change it if I could only see him *old*, turned over by time. I could get rid of him for good.

'But really, I was lying to myself. I must have wanted him to be the same, and that was the reason I didn't tell you. And when I did see him, when I saw it had gone, all that...that...holy draw, I was disappointed. Angry. I hated him, Guy, not for what he did to me, but for growing old. I'd wanted to see the man who ruined everything. Now I looked at him and I couldn't remember why it happened, any of it.

'A moment later, though, the anger vanished. I suddenly realised I'd got what I came for. There was no hold any more. At last I was free, rid of him. At long last I had grown up.

'After that I talked to him, like I would talk to anyone, and all the time I was marvelling at myself, at what it felt like to be free. I could see the effect I was having and I was laughing inside. Then I left him to come home to you and David, and I swear I could have flown. I honestly thought that would be the last I ever saw of him.

'And then we went away, remember? And it was like heaven, the three of us. The way it should have been all these years. When we were together, keeping warm by the sea, I realised, we've been in the wrong place all this time. We thought we were safe here, in Patersfield...instead the place was like amber keeping him intact. But I thought it didn't matter any more because I was free. And anyway, it turned out to be dangerous by the sea; there was the dog ruining everything, making Patersfield seem safe all over again.

'But then we came back and he contacted me again, and...and I went to him. I was stupid, Guy. Something to do with the dog, I can't explain. I'd killed the dog, Guy. Now all I wanted to do was *flaunt* myself, make him see. All those years of carrying him around like a virus, like some kind of disease, still waking up with the memory of him inside me. Now it was all gone...now I could show him what he could have had, what he threw away. I wanted to show him what *you* had in me. How strong I was.

'The second time was even better than the first. I talked about you and David, our lives, and I could see it was destroying him, hammering home the difference between my life and his. I even started to feel ashamed about what I was doing, and in the end I stood up to go, just put him out of his misery. Then something made me stop and look at him, one last time. And that's what I did wrong. I was looking *for* him. Searching for something to remind me of why I had been so...mad, so easy to impress. I think I was looking for an excuse for it all, a reason to feel better about myself. Vanity.

'And that was his way in, that was the moment he came back. He'd been there all the time, the old Magnus, powerful as ever. He saw me looking for him and he leapt up and...'

Carlie stops. 'He kissed me, Guy. That's all he did. He kissed me and everything changed.

'Maybe it was because he smelt. Rank. The old smell of him, still there, but ripened, gone sour. Yet it did something, the smell of him, the closeness of him. That kiss, his smell, it wakened that thing I had carried around all this time, brought it back to life. How do I explain? Suddenly *he* was alive again, like a poison, like cells injected into my body. I could feel him inside me, in my blood. Like a disease, nothing to do with me. At least, that's what I wanted to believe: that it had nothing to do with me.

'I came away. And I saw you – remember? – at the station. That was just the beginning. For weeks I walked around with this *sickness* inside me, and I couldn't tell you. How could I? I felt as if I was sinking, slowly being sucked into the dark. Every night I dreamed of him, but often I dreamt of you, standing and watching as I sank. I dreamed you couldn't bear me any more because of him, because he had touched me. And how could I blame you, when it was all my fault? Somehow I'd let him come alive again.

'Then more weeks went by. And nothing seemed to happen, not after the rose – remember the rose? I didn't hear from him. I began to think it was over. I even began to wonder if it had all been in my head, if I hadn't simply created the danger myself, the sickness. And that made me feel ashamed too, because then there really would only be me to blame. It even began to feel as if he had rejected me a second time. Worthless all over again.

'But you were there, Guy. The way you've always been. Little by little I began to feel the ground beneath my feet again, and all because of you. The truth was he could only harm us if we...if I...let him. It was simple. All I had to do was close the door in my mind, like I've done before. Seal him off so there was nothing to keep him alive. And that's what I was doing – with your help. Things were becoming normal again. Remember that day, how you came home laughing?

'But it's hard sealing away the past. Look at Lydia and Jonathan. All the time I was feeling sick, Lydia was battling with Jonathan over Sas – and I could see why. I could see why Lydia couldn't turn her back on her, why Saskia was so important. I'd tell Lydia to shut her out, but I never really meant it. You get rid of the past, and you get rid of a part of yourself. I would do it with him, with Magnus; but how could I tell Lydia to get rid of something that was part of her, that was never anything but lovely?

'Selfish, though – I never could worry too much about Lydia. I was just so thankful to be safe again, steady again. Things were getting better. I could control my thoughts, keep the past locked up. I could stamp the sickness out.

'Then it happened. David started with the tutor, the one he likes so much – the one who made him feel...special. Mr.

Magnet, stupid name. Stupid of *me* because I should have guessed. I went to the school, when he called me in, and it was him, it was Magnus. He'd followed me down here. And he knew everything about us – more than I had ever told him. He'd been using David to get to us, and now he was in. I stepped into that room, and he was there.'

For the first time since she started talking, Carlie stops and looks at me. She wants me to ask her. For weeks I have imagined what happened in that room. Alone. No one to see them. If I ask, Carlie will tell me, she will tell me what happened.

Finally, I feel my lips move. 'Did he touch you?'

Carlie shakes her head. 'No,' she hesitates, and suddenly my wife looks haggard, older than her years. And younger. 'He didn't have to. I stood in the room, and I was the one longing for him. I *wanted* him to touch me, anywhere – my breasts, my mouth, my cunt. He made me sick for the touch of him, the way people are sick for heroin or death. And he knew it. He knew he didn't have to touch me. He had more power that way. I told him to leave Patersfield and he just laughed, said he was here to stay. He said we were meant to be together, and sooner or later I'd see it.

'I came away then. Halfway home, I had to get out of the car to be sick. Did David tell you that? I pushed my fingers down my throat to make myself vomit, to try and get rid of Magnus that way. I wanted to vomit him out onto the ground beside the car and leave him there. I tried and I tried, and he was still there, like a worm inside me.

'And after that, *you* changed, almost as if you knew. I saw it after Lydia's party. It was as if you knew I was contaminated. You saw right through me and were disgusted. That's what I thought, and I didn't blame you. And when you changed, everything seemed to change. All the certainties disappeared, all the polarities switched. I felt you were beating me away, at the same time he was pulling me nearer. Everything began to feel inevitable, as if I had no choice, as if there had never been a choice because I should never have thought I could escape from him.

'And then tonight...'

Carlie stops, and closes her eyes. Opens them again.

'Tonight he arrived at our door, leaning on the bell, and I was expecting him. I'd never told him you were going away, but still I expected him. There was David, telling him everything he needed to know. So he came, knowing I was alone, and there was no question that I wouldn't let him in. He had wine with him, a vintage bottle, told me he'd spent every penny he had on it. He even showed me his wallet and it was empty. He didn't have a job any more, not after today. He'd been given the sack, and that was because of me. This morning I went and told Mr. Repton what I knew about Magnus's past, the drugs, the effect he would have on our son and anyone else he taught. And he believed me.

'Magnus came and laid all that at my door. He said I was to blame. I had taken away his living, now I had to make it up to him. I had to give him a future, the one we were meant to have. That's what the wine was for – to drink to just that – our future. He had it all planned, so sure of me he'd even quit the room he'd rented. His stuff is all there in our kitchen. He'd come to stay. He just lay down on the sofa and smiled at me. And drank his wine.

'And still he didn't touch me. He just talked. He told me how he'd been going to marry me, but then I'd disappeared. He told me how he'd never stopped loving me, how I was in his blood, in his dreams, how he couldn't live without me, not now he'd found me again. All the things I used to want to hear, he said them to me now. He might have been reading a script that was years old and I had written every word of it.

'But *then* he said other things. He told me I had ruined his life; but worse, he said had ruined yours. He said you were cold, a…a man of ice who couldn't care for anything. And when I asked him how he knew, he said David told him. And that was when I began to believe him.

'You see, I always knew what I had done to you. You should never have become a lawyer. You should have stayed in St Leonards and been what you were meant to be. You would have ended up with Jennifer – I've never forgotten her, how alike you both were. You could have done all the things you wanted to do, and you would have been happy. No one could ever have said you were cold. No one.

'All the same, I told him he was lying, and David would never have talked about you like that. But he just laughed and told me about a man he'd met in the off licence, who went with him to the pub. And it was you. He'd recognised you, Guy, he knew who you were straight away. And what's more, he knew that you recognised him. He said you sat and listened to him talk, and there was nothing in your eyes, no emotion, nothing. He said he lied, telling you he'd be a permanent fixture now, at the school, just to see what you'd say. But it didn't seem to affect you. Guy, he said that when he left, you knew exactly where he was going. And you did nothing to stop him. Because you didn't care.

'And that's when I knew. He was right. You didn't love me, not any more. Why should you love me? You worked so hard to save me. But I stopped you being happy. I ruined you, the only man I ever loved. I ruined you because I loved you, because I have always loved you – and I should have let you be. I should never have let you stay with me, not after him.

'He was lying on the sofa as he talked about how you let him come here, telling me you didn't care. He was so sure of himself. He thought it was all mapped out. He thought I had no choices, because that's what I'd always believed myself. And as I watched him smiling, it all just vanished. The sickness went away – it just went. All that was left was anger, terrible anger for *you*, for what I'd done to you, for what he was saying about you. I picked up the bottle and brought it down on the side of his head. He never saw it coming. He never even stopped smiling.

'I killed him because I hated him. I chose to do it and I'm glad I did it, just like I was glad when I killed that dog. Now it's over and you know everything. It was you I wanted, Guy, never anyone but you.'

Carlie stands up and walks slowly over to the door. For the first time I notice she has an overnight bag, packed and ready.

'I don't know if I can drive,' she says quietly. 'I've been drinking his wine. And my hands won't stop shaking. Will you take me to the station?'

'The station?' I repeat after her. Then stupidly, 'There'll be no trains, not yet.'

Carlie almost smiles. 'The *police* station. I killed a man. Where else is there to go?'

I walk over to the door. Carlie watches me, then bends to pick up her bag. 'Will you look after David? Somehow, make it right for him.'

'Carlie,' I say quietly. 'How can I do that?'

She sways. Then takes a hold of herself. 'I have to go the police, Guy. I did what I did.'

I look at her. Carlie stands. Her eyes are clear. She has made her choice and she knows what the future holds. And me? I know nothing about the future, but I know what Carlie wants. She wants me. Only me.

Outside the window a bird sings out from one of the trees, the first note before the dawn. In half an hour it will be light. The night will be over, and Carlie will be telling her story to a heavy eyed policeman who will be unable to believe a word she says. So she will have to tell the story again, slowly, in simple terms he will understand. And at the end of it, he'll know nothing about a girl who caught a sickness, or a woman who lived with it. Or a man who took her and shook her and stamped himself on her.

Most of all, he'll know nothing about a boy who looked at a girl and hesitated before he had the courage to tell her that he loved her and, in hesitating, lost her.

Not this time. Not again.

'No, Carlie. No.' And I take her bag away from her, and take her in my arms.

Carlie, my Carlie.

The trees that screen our house and tried to keep us safe screen us from the road. No one sees me carry Magnus to Carlie's car. He is a dead weight on my shoulder, a burden, a millstone. Something to be got rid of. Have we left it too late, though? Soon Patersfield will be waking up, executives hauling themselves, weary, out of bed to beat the morning rush to their desks.

'Perhaps we should keep him until tonight...' I suggest to Carlie, but she shudders. Not because he is a corpse, but because he is still here, still with us. Magnus just keeps on smiling, even in the back seat of the car. Carlie shudders because he still looks as if he could wake; and if he woke she would have to kill him all over again.

So we put a blanket over Magnus and the smile, pulling out of the drive as the first streaks of light are appearing in the sky. Already there are other cars on the road. We are visible to everyone. 'Carlie...' I say again. But she shakes her head.

We drive down the high street, over the railway bridge, where a train is pulling out. Past Waitrose where a container lorry is dropping off a load. On the other side of the town we get caught behind a milk float that sails out from a side road in front of us.

Where can we go? My mind tracks a route in front of us. I'm thinking of Scotland, of remote cliffs, and lonely moors. We have overtaken the milk cart and come to the outskirts of

Patersfield. Suddenly it seems all of the world is laid out – and it is still too small for what we have to hide.

'Stop,' Carlie calls out in a low voice, warning me. I have been thinking so hard, I was about to drive out onto the roundabout, into the path of a coach of sleepy eyed children, bound, like David, for some school trip to the West Country or the Lake District. I wait for it to pass, then pull out. When the bus is gone, the roundabout is empty.

'Stop!' Carlie says again. We are already on the roundabout, but I slow the car and look at her.

'I can't do this,' she says quietly. 'It's wrong. I don't want to go looking for a place to hide him. I don't want to bury him. I just want to get rid of him. I don't want to tell lies and I don't want to escape. I killed him. I made my choice. I just want to...' She glances out of the window. 'There. We can put him there. He'll be out of the way.'

She is pointing to the roundabout itself, with its broad rising curve of long grass and bramble and bushes.

'Carlie...' I begin, but she looks at me, and I know what her alternative will be. To carry on, right around the curve, and back into Patersfield, to the police station. Carlie has made a choice and she demands to live with it. I stop the car, right there on the inside lane of the roundabout. Carlie gets out on her side. Together, we haul Magnus from the back seat and onto the kerb of the roundabout. Then we pull him through the undergrowth towards the centre.

And it has to be done slowly, for Carlie's sake. I know what she is doing. She is daring Fate to intervene – with other cars that any moment could barrel round the curve of the roundabout, witnesses in broad daylight to us, disposing of a corpse in the undergrowth. Nor do we need a spade. Carlie frowns at me when I begin pulling at brambles – until, seeing that they scarcely do a thing to cover him, she relents. Magnus is there, underneath his blanket, visible to anyone who can be bothered to use his eyes. Finally we walk the few yards back to the kerb and climb into the car, still parked in the inside lane.

But even now, she lays a hand lightly on mine, making me wait before I put the car into gear. We are sitting with daylight streaming all around us now. Traffic is humming on the motorway less than three hundred yards away. Yet here, on the roundabout, everything is still. For a moment we sit, listening to the birdsong.

'All right,' she says at last. I start up the car and we drive off. In the undergrowth, Magnus smiles beneath his blanket, his future assured. And just as we take the turn into Patersfield, a line of traffic – slowed down by the milk float at its head – streams impatiently on to the roundabout. Suddenly it becomes busy again, thronging with cars. Carlie watches them, then reaches across and takes my hand again.

Nearly home, and we are passing Vanessa's house. The landscaping is almost finished, with all the old trees cut down to allow a clear view of gleaming stone terraces and low exotic shrubs bristling in their tubs. It used to be that you couldn't even see the front of their house from the road. Now, treeless, it stands with its brand new frontage exposed, complete with pediment and pillars. It looks like a film set, a front for something completely different behind it. Like so many houses here.

'Look,' says Carlie. 'What on earth is he doing here?'

Jonathan is coming out of Vanessa's front door, his velvet collar up around his neck. He has a guilty, half terrified look on his face, but there's an undeniable spring in his step. He walks down the bald landscaped drive, and gets into his car.

Across the road, a figure in another car watches him go. I touch Carlie on the cheek, and pull up beside it, and get out. Someone winds down the window as I step close.

'Mr. Robinson,' I say. 'You're back in business.'

Mr. Robinson brushes the crumbs off the front of his shirt

so that they fall, sprinkling the long lens of the camera sitting on his lap. He sighs. 'Sadly, yes.'

Together we watch the back end of Jonathan's car. I say to him: 'It's Miles – the lady's husband – I suppose. He hired you for this.'

Mr. Robinson shakes his head. 'No, Mr. Latimer, you're all out there. In this particular case it's the Missus.'

'Lydia – she's paying you?' My heart sinks for them, Jonathan and Lydia both. Observation changes everything.

'No, *this* Missus. Her inside.' He nods up to the house, where presumably Vanessa is roaming, bored with her landscaping, bored with everything. 'I said it was funny to her face. *She* wants me to take photos of *her* having an affair with that gentleman who left just now.'

'What's she going to do with them?' I say, bewildered.

'Ethically, I shouldn't tell you that, but I reckon I will anyway. She didn't seem to mind me knowing. She tells me she's saving a marriage.'

'She thinks this is the way to save her marriage?' I look at the house in disbelief, at the curtains and bald terraces.

'Not her marriage,' says Mr. Robinson comfortably. 'She says there's nothing that can touch that. They're in for the long haul, she and her hubby. No, she means *his* – the marriage of the one who's just left…She says that particular gentleman isn't playing fair with his wife. Something to do with trying to have everything his own way. She says these photos will keep him from doing something everyone will regret.'

'Blackmail,' I say.

'That's exactly how she describes it,' says Mr. Robinson promptly. 'She claims it's going to work a treat. She says if he's done something he shouldn't, how can he pile the blame on someone who's not done anything wrong at all? She says it'll get everything all nicely back into balance. I have to tell you, Mr. Latimer – she's quite something. Tells me she knows the folk here better than anyone, sees the messes they keep getting themselves into. She says it's a rare old treat watching them all, but at the end of the day someone's got to keep the nice ones from hurting themselves. And *this*, apparently, is the way to go about it.'

I glance up at the house. In a downstairs window a curtain twitches.

'Well, who knows,' I say. 'She might very well be right.'

I wave towards the window, and walk back to the car. And Carlie who is waiting for me.

Later in the day, we build a bonfire at the bottom of the garden, piling up the debris of winter. Then we watch it burn - all the dead wood and rotting things of the past few months; and in the middle of it, a battered suitcase full of other debris.

Now we wait – Magnus in his bracken bed, and Carlie and I here, in our house behind the trees, to see what the future holds.

Three months later, on the very morning of our move, Carlie hands me the *Patersfield Advertiser*.

The police have found a body on the M40 roundabout. Headless, unidentifiable, they still have to find out what sex it is. The way the paper describes it, you'd think it was a very bad case of littering, thankfully out of sight. A tramp probably, and too late to lock him up or fine him. The foxes have dealt with him instead, the wild urban foxes of Patersfield. It seems unlikely the case will be taken any further.

'No hiding. No burying,' I say. 'Good enough for you?'

She reads it all again carefully, then nods. Carlie is free. But then Carlie has been free for months. And now we're about to find out what we can do with our freedom.

Before we can say any more, David bursts into the kitchen.

'The removal men want to know if they can pack my lap top! I said I want to take it with me in the car.'

'The car will be full,' I said. 'Are you sure you need it?'

'Yes,' he says, scandalised I even have to ask. 'I won't see it for a week. What do you expect me to do without it?'

'Whatever you did before you got it off your mother.' I say. 'Walk, run, talk, read. You could even go fishing in the harbour. We'll be in the right place for all of that.'

His lip curls. 'Oh yeah?' He is mutinous again, the way he's been for weeks, rebelling against a move that's taking him away from his school, his friends, everything he knows.

'There'll be the sea, and the two beaches. West Sand, East Sands. We could hire a boat. We might even buy one, a small one – a rowing boat, if you promise not to drown. And you'll be able to cycle everywhere. St Leonards is that sort of town. You won't need a computer.'

'Yeah,' he says again, dismissive. 'Like I can just do all that by myself. Fishing and stuff.'

'You won't be by yourself,' I say. 'School will be starting next week. You'll make friends.'

My son looks more scathing than ever. 'That's what you say. Like anyone would want to be friends with someone whose own dad's going to be teaching in the same school. How sad is that? I thought you were supposed to be a lawyer. A proper job.'

'I was never supposed to be a lawyer. It was all a mistake. And teaching is a proper job – the only job some people might say. Anyway, it's a big school. You won't see me. No one need know I'm there – not unless you tell them. You're not touching Latin and Greek. Our paths need never cross. In the meantime, if you can't find any friends, then all those things – fishing, cycling, exploring – you can do them with me.'

He stands by my chair, frowning at the prospect. He is thirteen and has grown a whole four inches taller in the last three months; but he is still skinny, still my son. And he still looks at me with Carlie's eyes, anxious and excited at the same time, drawn to the past – *his* past – worried about the future. In a smaller voice he says, 'I just think I should keep the computer for emergencies. In case Angus wants to email me.'

'You can talk to him on the phone, all night, every night if you want to. We won't mind.'

And still he frowns, touches the back of my chair. 'And you won't let on at school that you're my dad – unless I say so?'

I shake my head.

'And those things, like going in the boat and fishing – if no one else wants to, you'll do them with me?'

'I'll do them with you anyway if you let me.'

And still he looks doubtful, on the verge of miserable.

I say, 'I want to do them, David. I want to even if you have more friends than you can count and we have to do them in the middle of the night so no one knows we're related. All those things – I want them. Am I making myself clear?'

There's a silence in our kitchen, punctuated only by the sound of a removal man dropping something that sounds like porcelain. No one moves. Carlie's lips are curved into a smile, watching us. Suddenly David's face clears. My son is grinning at me. 'OK,' he says simply. 'They can take the computer. But I still need my skateboard in the car.' And he goes away to bother the removal men some more.

Carlie drops the newspaper and touches one of the books by my elbow. 'I notice you're not letting them pack *that* away. Flaming Catullus. You're keeping that close by you.'

'Ah well, I have to. I'm going to be teaching it in less than a week. I've got to know my brief.'

I pick up the book, open it at the poem I will be reading with a class of boys and girls, sixth-formers who no doubt will yawn and scratch and day dream their way through it. Because they live in a continuous present and have no idea of what the future holds; and haven't learned that two thousand years can seem like yesterday with messages for tomorrow.

Perhaps one or two will find out, maybe find their way into a lecture room with others like them, complete with tweed jackets and bobbly jumpers, and just possibly, be happy that they did.

Out loud, to Carlie, I read the poem that, conceivably, might just make the difference to someone.

Live with me, and love with me
And we'll ignore what
The old folk say.
The sun will rise and
The sun will fall
And light will die, but
We will sleep together.
Forever.
So kiss me now one thousand times
And then a hundred more,
And...

And Carlie's lips are warm, smothering the two thousand year old words, a reminder that we are, that we always have been, real.

* * *

Kisses me until tearing my mouth away I say to her, 'And Carlie what will you be doing with *your* day?'

And Carlie draws a breath, deep and long enough to tell me all the things she has in mind, something that might take all day and all night. Carlie has so many plans. Some of them may well be bound up with this book – the other book I am keeping close – still in manuscript, lying on the kitchen table between us.

This book that she has just finished writing, and I have just finished reading.

This very book.

Carlie has been busy.

LIMERICK
COUNTY LIBRARY